b

She shouldn't have said yes...

Great, Melanie thought. It was raining, she was locked out of her own car, miles from home, and stuck in a tiny space with the last man on earth she wanted to spend time with. Sam was too sexy, too appealing—and too much like the kind of guy she'd always fallen for before she wised up.

I don't have to talk to him, she thought, scrunching into the passenger door in an effort to put as much space between them as possible. She closed her eyes tightly, but opened them quickly when she had a rushing memory of Sam's hands keeping her from tumbling backward when they collided in the lobby. Talk about the old Melanie. One touch and her whole being had jumped to attention, ready to run headlong into disaster. *Stupid, stupid, stupid.*

Even as she told herself not to talk, she said, "It's a terrible night, isn't it? I wonder if it's going to keep raining." She knew she sounded inane, but couldn't stop. "I love the rain, when you're inside, dry and comfortable." The next thing she knew, she'd be talking about the barometric pressure. But then Sam spoke.

He glanced at her—she could feel his eyes on her—then he said, "If you're in bed, making love, rain makes great atmosphere."

Dear Reader,

Spunky guardian angel Angelina thought she'd been given the ultimate challenge last year when she'd introduced Reggie Clark, confirmed career woman, to Dr. Ben Grant, sexy single daddy. But her struggles there, told in Mary Anne Wilson's earlier American Romance novel *Mismatched Mommy?*, are nothing compared to the difficulties she faces getting Reggie's sister, Melanie, together with her perfect man. After all, Angelina's got Melanie convinced that she wants to marry Mr. Perfect…. And Sam? He's sexy, irresistible…Mr. Wrong.

Join Harlequin American Romance and talented Mary Anne Wilson as she brings you the latest installment in Angelina's adventures.

And just in case you missed *Mismatched Mommy?*, you can find it—and all of Mary Anne Wilson's other American Romance novels—by writing us at:
Harlequin Reader Service:
U.S.: 3010 Walden Av., P.O. Box 1325, Buffalo, NY 14269.
Canada: P.O. Box 609, Fort Erie, Ontario, L2A 5X3.

Happy Reading!

Debra Matteucci
Senior Editor & Editorial Coordinator
Harlequin
300 East 42nd Street
New York, NY 10017

Mary Anne Wilson

MR. WRONG!

Harlequin Books

TORONTO • NEW YORK • LONDON
AMSTERDAM • PARIS • SYDNEY • HAMBURG
STOCKHOLM • ATHENS • TOKYO • MILAN
MADRID • WARSAW • BUDAPEST • AUCKLAND

For all the special people at
MICHELLE'S BOOKS
in Calimesa, CA.
Thanks for everything.

ISBN 0-373-16700-8

MR. WRONG!

Copyright © 1997 by Mary Anne Wilson.

Printed in U.S.A.

Chapter One

A kiss, they said, was just a kiss. It shouldn't have been this much work…or taken this long to happen.

It had taken six months and enough hard work to exhaust an army for Melanie Clark and Dennis Benning to finally kiss. When it happened, Angelina felt such a rush of pride at her success that it stunned her. She'd never before experienced that as a fairy godmother, but at that moment she could have danced a jig and laughed out loud.

It wasn't as if Dennis or Melanie could have seen or heard her anyway while she was in the hovering mode. She was so close she could hear Melanie sigh softly, and she wasn't about to look away from the intimate moment. Angelina wanted to savor every element of her victory.

She watched as Melanie twined her arms around Dennis's neck, sinking fingers into sandy-blond hair, a tad longer than he'd once worn it. One of many changes in the man, along with his clothes—the perfectly tailored three-piece suit and leather loafers now abandoned in favor of casual slacks, a natural wool sweater and leather boots.

The man was loosening up, and Angelina didn't hesitate to take credit for his new look and new attitude. She'd been the one to nudge him, to get him to think about being so uptight, so frozen in the Benning mold. She was the one who had planted the seed of an idea in him to start his own practice in tax law, to get away from his father's influence, and go in a direction where his new life could intersect with Melanie's new life.

But if she was pleased by Dennis, Angelina almost gloated at the changes she'd wrought in Melanie. The woman had stopped being so wild and impulsive, was consciously trying to calm down, grow up and settle into adulthood with a sense of decorum and control. A distinct change from someone who had held seven jobs in one year and had once lived in a tent for six months in her parents' backyard to have "breathing space." A person who had plunged into relationships heart-first and always lived to regret it.

Even the clothes had changed, from oversize tops, leggings and combat boots, to tailored slacks, simple blouses and stylish shoes. It had been hard work getting Melanie and Dennis to intersect on such a personal level, but well worth it. They were made for each other...now.

"Nice, very nice." Angelina heard the combined thoughts of Dennis and Melanie, a mingling of murmurs and reactions to the kiss. Oh, there were no real fireworks, no earth shaking explosions, but "nice" was just fine for now. Sometimes "nice" grew into a great deal more than that. Especially since the Council set up this match, she knew that "nice" would definitely flourish into deep, abiding love. If—and this was always a big "if"—the humans cooperated and didn't do something totally foolish to mess it up.

Angelina barely had time to frown at the thought of

how many ways humans could ruin the most promising relationships before she was abruptly jerked into a place she didn't recognize. In surprise, still tingling with pleasure at her success with Melanie and Dennis, she looked around her. There were no walls, crystal or otherwise; no sense of restriction to the space. True blue was overhead, a field of delicate flowers underfoot, and a shimmering brightness all around.

She swallowed hard. The Council. The seven who instructed the others in their assignments through Miss Victoria. This had to be their place, a place she'd only heard of in whispered stories about those of her kind who had come here and never returned to duty. But weren't they just stories? Maybe fables, fairy tales of sorts?

She turned full circle, not seeing anything or anyone, then suddenly came face-to-face with her superior, Miss Victoria. The tiny woman in her long blue gown and dust cap over gray curls had come from nowhere. She hardly ever materialized like that, which unnerved Angelina even more.

Pale blue eyes behind rimless spectacles flicked over the loose shirt and jeans Angelina favored when she worked with humans. Comfortable clothes. The gaze hesitated slightly and Angelina knew that the outfit wasn't quite in accord with Miss Victoria's tastes. But it was infinitely better than the shorts and halter top she'd been wearing when she'd been zapped to Miss Victoria two months ago to be told she was taking much too long with the matchup of Dennis and Melanie.

"Angelina," Miss Victoria said softly as she adjusted her spectacles with the tip of one finger. "We are sorry for the abrupt summons, but this could not wait."

Angelina glanced around. "We? Is the Council—"

"The royal 'We,' Angelina," Miss Victoria said with a touch of exasperation.

"Yes, ma'am."

"They are much too busy at the moment to take part in this…situation, a situation that must be facilitated as quickly as possible."

Angelina wanted to say she wasn't used to any assignment being this difficult and complicated. It had been a real challenge to her skills to help two people change from what they had been into something that made it possible for them to intersect in life. But they had finally kissed. That was a definite accomplishment.

Melanie had been so disillusioned by that Robert Something-or-other—the weasel, being married and not telling her until she'd caught him in a lie! And Dennis… Poor Dennis had been fighting the suffocating control of the Bennings. He was doing so well. Things were very good indeed, if one considered the bigger picture.

"Is this summons about the Benning/Clark assignment?" she asked as calmly as she could.

"Yes," Miss Victoria said.

Melanie spoke quickly. "Well, ma'am, they're closer, much closer than when we had our talk about them earlier. They actually kissed tonight. A mutual decision that went rather well, even if I do say so myself."

"Kissed?" Miss Victoria asked, her eyes widening behind the rimless glasses.

Angelina didn't understand any of this, and she spoke in a rush. "Yes, ma'am. Oh, it wasn't an explosion on either side, but it was…nice. Melanie liked it, and Dennis liked it. They aren't like Reggie and Ben were at the first. You know, her older sister and the doctor? Now those two created fireworks. They're still explosive together, even though Reggie is eight months pregnant—''

Miss Victoria abruptly cut her off with an uncharacteristic wave of her hand. "Enough. Enough," she murmured. "This is not what we wish to hear."

"Oh, ma'am, I'm sorry. I thought you knew that Regina Clark was expecting a child, and that—"

"Please, that is not what we are here to discuss. We must concentrate on the problem at hand."

Angelina knew where this was going. She'd failed to meet their timetable and they were going to send her back for a refresher course. She cringed at the thought of the classes, the therapy sessions, and those horrible virtual reality machines.

"Ma'am..." She barely controlled a shiver of distaste as she took a breath and tried to talk her way out of that terrible experience. "Let me assure you and the Council that I've been very successful nudging at Dennis and Melanie.... With tonight's kiss, I promise all of you that they're on the right track."

Despite her reassurance, Angelina could see that Miss Victoria only looked more distressed. The tiny woman shook her head, making her curls dance around the cherubic face shadowed by a frown. "Oh, my, how can we say what we must?"

"Ma'am, we... I..." Angelina spread her hands, suddenly as uncertain as a novice. "Trust me, if I were human, I'd want this slow, steady growth that turns into love instead of the fireworks and earthquakes that humans seem to favor."

"Humans? Oh, my dear, thank all that's good that we are not of that species." Miss Victoria seemed to stand straighter. "To put this clearly and simply, there has been a grievous error in judgment."

Angelina stared at Miss Victoria. What was she talking about? She'd been so careful, so steady in this mating. Not like that fiasco in Monaco with the princess and the commoner. That stripper had come out of nowhere, something she could never have foreseen. "An error? What error?"

Miss Victoria waved her right hand, and a crystal chair materialized. Slowly the lady sank down upon it, then looked up at Angelina. "Oh, my, but there are so many Clarks," she said, pressing a hand to her ample bosom. "All three remaining sisters are in line for our services. And with Mr. Benning's brother, and all… Francine Clark was suppose to be the one, then Mr. Benning's brother, and all…" She shook her head. "It is an error that is vastly understandable, yet nonetheless, totally inexcusable."

Angelina was confused. Francine and Dennis Benning were meant for each other and Dennis Benning's brother… No, this was all wrong.

"Ma'am? I don't understand. Francine Clark and Dennis Benning…and a brother? With all due respect, ma'am, Francine is doing just fine, buried in her studies right now. And as to Dennis Benning's brother, there isn't one. Dennis Benning is an only child."

Her superior sighed softly. "We see we must start at the beginning to explain this clearly." She waved her right hand again, and the air began to shimmer with pixels.

Angelina couldn't believe it. She was in Paris! And so was Miss Victoria.

"What is this, ma'am?" Angelina breathed.

"A new tool for our business," Miss Victoria said in calm acceptance of the Eiffel Tower in the distance and the sounds of busy Paris streets. Even the air that surrounded them held the fragrance of freshly baked goods as it mingled with the exhaust fumes of the cars clogging the avenues.

At the front, nearest Angelina—so close she felt all she had to do was to reach out and tap his shoulder—a man stood beside a table at a sidewalk café. Dennis Benning? The sandy-blond hair, the wide shoulders, the set of the jaw. But in Paris?

As the pixels settled, Angelina watched as the man turned to a lady standing at the table, and knew just how wrong she'd been. It couldn't be Dennis. Dennis was with Melanie. In Santa Barbara. Outside the small cottage behind the boutique that she was in the process of buying. This man in Paris wasn't Dennis at all.

He wasn't quite as handsome by human standards, she didn't imagine. Oh, the coloring was the same, and the general build in jeans and a band-collared white shirt was as broad-shouldered and strong-looking. But this man was a bit larger, his hair a bit longer, carelessly swept back from a vaguely harsh version of Dennis Benning's face.

"Mr. Samuel Harrison," she heard Miss Victoria murmur. "The illegitimate son of Dennis Benning Senior."

Illegitimate son? "No way," Angelina whispered. Dennis Benning Senior was the quintessential perfect human. He never erred in any phase of his life, never veered from his flawless reputation and esteemed position in Santa Barbara society.

The man in the scene was talking to the woman at the table. She was very slender, with hair so blond it was almost white. A beautiful woman, probably, but a woman who looked very upset right now. No, Angelina amended. The woman looked mad, with angry tears making her eyes overly bright.

"Of course I did not expect you to stay here and settle down," the woman was saying in rapid French. "But I also did not expect you to just leave like this. To just smile and say it is time to go."

The man raked his fingers through his hair, spiking it vaguely around his face. He spoke calmly in French touched with a decidedly American accent. "I told you the job is finished. You knew it was for four months. I never lied to you."

"Maybe you should have," she whispered softly as she got closer to him. "Just a bit."

"Veronique, honey, it's tempting. Hell, you're tempting, but…"

The woman looked up at him from under veiled lashes, her full bottom lip jutting out in a provocative pout. "Not enough? Sam, trust me, I could give you reasons," she murmured as she touched his chest and slowly started to brush her palms up over his shirt toward his neck.

His hands caught hers, then gently held them away from him. "No," he said, but a smile took the edge off the abrupt rejection. "I already have another job offer. One I did not expect, and my agent told me I have to be back in Los Angeles right away. Unless you want to pull up stakes and come on back to the U.S. with me…"

"How could I?"

"Exactly. So it's time to part. It's been fun."

"We can have more fun, much more fun."

"I bet we could, but not now. I'm sorry." He didn't sound sorry.

"Sorry?" She all but stomped her foot. "You are *horrible*."

He actually smiled at that, then chucked her chin with his forefinger. "Hey, I told you right up front that I'm not good at this. I don't like being pressured, and I certainly never intended to stay here longer than I had to."

She pulled back, the anger fresh in her eyes, but she kept her voice down. "Do you ever stay anywhere long enough to connect with anyone?"

That did touch him, but not, Angelina suspected, the way the woman wanted it to. He stepped away from Veronique and reached for the bag at his feet. As he straightened, he looked right at her, his smile a bit forced. "I stay until I leave," he muttered. "And that's what I'm doing now. My flight leaves in an hour."

"I can't believe that that man is the illegitimate son of Dennis Benning's father," Angelina murmured to Miss Victoria.

As the man turned and held up a hand to flag down a taxi, Angelina heard Miss Victoria say, "Believe it, Angelina. Sam Harrison is indeed the product of the only impulsive thing the elder Benning has ever done in his life. He met a girl in college and the pregnancy was not on his agenda as a Benning. He had his life mapped out for him. But he took care of her and the child. Support checks and such for eighteen years.

"We might add to this scenario that his marriage to Emily Sinclair, the daughter of another socially prominent family in Santa Barbara, took place despite our persuasive efforts to refocus the man's life. That marriage produced the perfect, acceptable heir. Dennis Benning."

Angelina watched as Sam tossed some francs onto

the table, then with a few murmured words to Veronique, headed for the taxi that had come to a screeching halt by the curb. "He's the one you—the Council—means for Melanie to connect with?" she asked.

"Yes. We saw the name Benning, not knowing that it was his birth father, whose name he never took, and we assumed..." Miss Victoria sighed. "A grievous error that caused this mix-up. If it had said Samuel Harrison right up front...but it did not. Thankfully the mistake was found in time, and it is not uncorrectable. Since there has only been a kiss..."

Only a kiss? A major commitment on the part of both parties. "But he's going to Los Angeles, ma'am. And Melanie won't just take off for Los Angeles." The old Melanie would have gone anywhere on a whim, but not the new version. "She's so busy now with her new business, what with the holidays and all. Besides, she's so...so...sensible now."

"Never fear. We have already helped with that problem. Mr. Harrison will be in Santa Barbara tomorrow afternoon. The rest is up to you. But there is no time to waste."

As Miss Victoria spoke, Angelina noted that she was getting what humans called a "headache." Throbbing behind her eyes and tension in her neck and shoulders. "Samuel Harrison *is* the correct choice for Melanie, isn't he, ma'am?"

"He is definitely the right choice. He has never been married, is a loner, but at a point in his life when he will either become attached to someone or stay single."

Miss Victoria held out her hand and a silver folder appeared in it. "His file. It has all the information you shall need to do this assignment."

Angelina glanced to her left to see Sam getting into the taxi. "Does he know about his half brother?"

"Neither one knows about the other. Family secrets, and such. The wishes of his father and the demand of his mother."

Sam slammed the door, the taxi took off, and Angelina reached for the folder. She opened it, scanning it quickly. *An only child...impetuous...a free thinker... Likes living on the edge, loves traveling and being on the move. No connections. Profession: stunt coordinator in the motion picture industry.*

The headache was starting to make Angelina feel sick. She was about to ask Miss Victoria why she should suddenly be afflicted with one, but realized she knew the answer. If she hadn't been so successful in changing Melanie's outlook on life, Sam Harrison would have been perfect for her. An easy match by anyone's standards. A man who was like the old Melanie. A man who seemed appealing, although not quite as appealing as Dennis Benning could be.

She frowned. What a mess. Dennis had to be rerouted to Francine, and a half brother he never knew existed had to be introduced into his world. *Complicated* hardly described what this assignment would be. But, if it was meant to be, it was meant to be. "Mr. Benning—"

"Angelina, concentrate on Mr. Harrison and Miss Clark. Rest assured that Mr. Benning will be taken care of later. We have plans for him. But first this present situation must be resolved as quickly as possible."

"Yes, ma'am," Angelina said as she closed the folder.

"And, Angelina?"

She looked up at Miss Victoria as the three-dimensional Paris dissolved and the pixels shifted to reveal Melanie Clark standing alone in the darkness of her cottage. She was leaning back against the closed front door, her arms hugging her middle.

Her dark brown hair, cut in a modified wedge, framed her delicate freckle-dusted face. A slightly bemused smile played at the corners of her mouth. "Well, old girl," Angelina heard her murmur to herself. "You're doing the right thing. Finally, you've figured out what life is supposed to be all about." She touched her lips and looked just a bit confused, then shook her head sharply. "The right thing. Absolutely the right thing."

Her slight hesitation gave Angelina a glimmer of hope. Her transformation wasn't as solid as she'd thought it had been. Now, instead of being disappointed, she was relieved. There was hope, a light at the end of this tunnel.

Suddenly Melanie was gone and Dennis was there, driving along the coast in the black Jeep he'd just recently purchased, whistling softly to himself. He reached for the mobile phone on the console, entered a number as he slowed for traffic, then spoke quickly. "Mother?" He listened, then said, "I just wanted to let you know that I'll be coming by tomorrow evening, and I'll be bringing someone with me."

He smiled, a slow, easy grin as he listened to the woman on the other end. "No. It's my surprise." He listened for a moment, his smile slipping more and more. "Yes, I'm still moving. No, Mother, not to Eagle Point. Actually, I'm looking at a place tomorrow afternoon. I'll tell you all about it when I see you and Father tomorrow evening. See you then," he said quickly, then hung up.

"Angelina?" Miss Victoria prompted as Angelina stared at Dennis and the way he took several deep breaths to ease the tension she could see tightening his jaw and his grip on the steering wheel. This hadn't been easy on him, getting out from under the Benning name and finding himself. She admired his strength.

Miss Victoria caught her attention as the pixels began to dissolve into the blueness of the skies again. "My dear, all you have to do is find the connection, a place for the intersection where all three of these people can come together."

"Yes, of course," she murmured. "The intersection."

"We might offer a suggestion, if you wished for one?"

"Yes, ma'am." She'd take any help at all.

"Mr. Harrison loves open, unlimited views, horizons he can see without buildings blocking the view. An ocean house might be just the ticket for him while he's in Santa Barbara. And Mr. Benning is looking for a new residence. Perhaps that could be a starting place of sorts for you?"

The ocean. Huge, mysterious. It drew people. Sam. Dennis. She understood. "Thank you, ma'am," Angelina murmured, suddenly ready to get started. Actually, a bit excited by the new challenge. "If that's all?"

"Yes, for now. But we need to be kept informed."

"Yes, ma'am," Angelina said, and turned to leave, even though she didn't have a clue where the exit was in this place.

"Over there, Angelina," Miss Victoria said with a motion of her tiny hand. "The way out. It's always there when we look for it."

She turned and, in the distance, across the field of flowers, she saw the vague suggestion of an archway. "Yes, ma'am," she said, and headed for it.

"Angelina, we regret this inconvenience."

"Yes, ma'am," she responded, thinking that "inconvenience" hardly described what Dennis Benning would go through.

"Focus on the intersection," Miss Victoria called from a distance.

"Yes, ma'am," she said without looking back and deciding right then and there that this would be her last assignment involving the Clarks. For the first time in her career, she knew she ran the very real risk of becoming too involved with her subjects. And that wasn't good. Not good at all.

Chapter Two

Sam liked being alone. The idea of a family didn't appeal to him. But the idea of taking one look at a father he'd never known existed until six months ago pricked at something in him. Curiosity? Morbid fascination? Whatever it was, when he'd got word of the job in Los Angeles and the fact that the production company wanted him on their payroll for a year, he'd made his decision with surprising ease.

Sometime while he was in the same city as the man who had fathered him, he'd find him. He'd come face-to-face with him, look him in the eye and walk away without ever saying who he was. Just one look, one moment to see the man who had walked out on him and his mother, and that would be enough. He'd figure the logistics out later, but he knew that however he did it, it would be on his terms. Neat and simple. The way he liked his life. That was the way Sam wanted it, and that was the way it would be.

As he drove along Coastal Highway north of the city, with the Pacific on his left and the rolling hills of Santa Barbara, a city built on the hills, to his right, he pushed the idea of finding the man who fathered him into the back of his mind. He'd told the production company that he'd get settled in and be ready to work in four days. The day after Christmas he'd be in their offices to start work on the movie.

Actually, things had fit into place with remarkable ease, he thought as he drove the rental car, a very lethargic sedan, through the failing light of the December afternoon. Find a place to stay for six months, a private place with space all around. A place he and the crew could make as much noise as they had to, where they could work out the logistics of the stunts, then he'd worry about Dennis Benning, C.E.O. of Flushing International.

Sam could feel his hands tighten on the steering wheel and he forced them to relax. There was no room for regret or even anger. None at all. Life was too short. And Dennis Benning was nothing to him beyond the half of the contributors to his genetic code. Nothing at all.

He spotted the road the Realtor had given him for the turn. He made a right onto a narrow road that switched back along the top of a steep bluff just below the main highway. On his left, the fallaway view was stunning. The Pacific, bathed in the glow of the setting sun, was almost ethereal in a light mist that had just started to fall from a darkening sky.

At the same time that he saw the road was about to end, he spotted the house. A taxi sat out in front of it, right by double gates set in a six-foot-high stone wall that blocked the view of most of the house, except for the soaring red tiled roofline. As he got closer, Sam felt something in his chest begin to ease. The location was perfect. The house was the only residence on the street, and the beach stretched out below the bluffs. Unlimited space and view.

He pulled over onto a graveled area that ran alongside the stone wall, and stopped next to the taxi. As he stepped out of the car into the damp chill of the early evening, the only sounds were that of the ocean and the faint hum of traffic in the distance. Yes, he could work here. He could breathe here, he thought as he went around the taxi to the gates.

Aged to a dull green that exposed the lines of surreal waves etched into the metal, they looked as if they had been formed out of whole sheets of heavy copper.

He glanced at the taxi driver, who never looked up from a clipboard he was writing on, then pushed open the gates.

He went through them and, across a small expanse of ivy and low hedges that framed a stone walkway, got a clear view of the house. It was a single story that stretched out onto the edge of the bluff in both directions. Its bare wooden siding was darkened by moisture and dulled by salt air, and it looked as if it fit in its setting. Yes, perfect.

He followed the path to the entry door whose design echoed that of the gates. The barrier was partially ajar and as he stepped inside it occurred to him that the house fit him just as well as the location. He couldn't believe that it had all been so simple. A call to The Connection Realty, a single conversation with their agent, Angela, and she'd found him just what he'd been looking for. This was where he'd live, do his work, make his plans and, when he was ready, look up Dennis Benning.

MELANIE DROVE SLOWLY through the late-afternoon traffic and the persistent mists, wishing that Dennis hadn't been held up at the office. Since setting up his own law offices, he was busy so much. But after last night she wanted to see him. She wanted to look at him, to match her feelings about the kiss to her feelings about the man. Confusion wasn't something she endured with any grace, and right now she felt very confused.

She was doing the right thing. She knew that. She had to settle down. She had to grow up. She had to start doing things in the sane, mature way. God knew, Reggie had told her that often enough. Her older sister, the one who had gone through life with such precision. Melanie smiled a bit. Until Reggie had met her match in Doctor Ben Grant and his tiny son, Mikey.

Reggie, the one who liked kids as long as they were someone else's, was now a mother to Mikey, and was going to be a mother by birth just after New Year's. "Talk about change," Melanie muttered to herself as she slowed to try to spot the side street Dennis had told her to look for.

Dennis. The man Reggie had met and thought she loved. The man that Melanie was now dating. The man she'd kissed last night. That thought stopped her. She's always been one to jump into relationships, get in too deep before she knew what she was doing, and the one who invariably got hurt when she found out she'd found Mr. Wrong…again.

Now she was being rational and sane. Dennis was the perfect man to be rational and sane with. Definitely not Mr. Wrong. And he'd made changes, too, setting up his own law firm, and now a house by the beach. Change was in the air, she thought as she pulled up in front of the only house on the street. She stopped on crushed gravel and parked beside a dark sedan—probably the real estate agent's car, she assumed—and got out.

She loved the scents at the ocean, all mingled with

the fragrance of wood smoke in the air. Quiet and seclusion, only the distant hum of civilization to let you know there were others in this world. Not like the gated community where Dennis lived. None of the obvious trappings of wealth, although she was certain this place would cost a fortune to buy. It just wasn't in the "acceptable" area where a Benning would live.

She passed the sedan, went through the open gates and crossed the stones to the entry. She quietly eased back the partially open door and the moment she stepped inside, she knew why Dennis wanted to lease it.

She was in a space that seemed to take up the whole center of the house, with soaring ceilings, white walls, hardwood floors and furniture shrouded in dustcovers. The only light was from the flickering fire in a massive stone hearth to the left. The back wall consisted of multiple French doors. The view through the doors all but took her breath away.

In the distance, the ocean was dark and mysterious, the night almost here, with a light mist skimming over the surface, blurring and haloing lights farther down the coast. Then she saw Dennis outside by the railing of a deck that swept in either direction.

She felt her breath catch slightly in her chest at the sight of the man. It had never happened before with Dennis, the way her heart sped up a bit, a touch of warmth under her skin. She crossed the room and as she neared the doors she noted the width of his shoulders in that denim jacket, and the way those worn Levi's hugged his lean hips and strong legs. Boots she'd never seen before added an inch or two to his height, and his hair was ruffled by a light breeze off the water.

She slipped out the open door into the chilly evening,

but the coolness didn't do a thing to diminish the heat that this man was producing in her. It both shocked and pleased her. The kiss had been nice, comfortable, but seeing Dennis now was anything but comfortable. You never knew, she thought as she took in the way his shoulders strained the denim as he leaned forward, as if looking down the bluff at the beach below.

When he straightened and uttered a rough sigh, the sound ran riot over her already very alive nerves and she lowered her purse to the deck by the doors and went to him. With the first impulsive action she'd ever taken with Dennis, she came up behind him and circled his waist with her arms as she murmured, "If you don't take this house, I will."

Whatever reaction she'd felt at the sight of Dennis, it was nothing compared to the response that shot through her as she felt his heat and strength and the way his breath caught sharply when she touched him. It was almost violent, jarring her to the core, breeding a hunger in her that both shocked and seared her. As he slowly turned, she gave in to the sensations, closing her eyes so she could absorb them.

Then his arms were around her, closing her in a circle that felt as complete as anything she'd ever experienced in her life. A need shot through her, a need that she'd only experienced in a paler form until now. Offering her lips to him came with a low moan, and when his lips found hers, she could have sworn that the earth shook beneath her feet.

Every atom of her being responded in almost pagan-like fervor, holding to him, pressing to him, wishing she could melt right into him until she was part of his soul. His kiss ravaged hers, and she gave as good as she got. She welcomed the invasion, relishing the burning connection that she'd never guessed would be possible with him. A man she'd always seen as more of a friend than a lover, as stable and sure, a man she'd kissed the night before and been pleasantly surprised that the contact was "nice," was exploding her world.

God, it could work with him. She'd been right all along. Knowing someone, liking them, taking your time to build a relationship could lead to something as all-encompassing as this. It was working, and working better than she'd ever dreamed it could. She could taste him, feel him against her, her own body responding completely and wonderfully. His hand pressed her hips against his, and she could feel his response, every bit as complete as hers.

It was right, so right, and the changes she'd tried to make in her life came together so perfectly she could have cried. She felt his hand move lower on her back, his other hand at her throat, and the taste of him filled her. Dennis was everything she'd dreamed a man could be, and she'd finally found that out.

She felt Dennis gently ease her back, his hands shifting to her shoulders. As she opened her eyes, the world exploded. She stared into a face roughly chiseled, framed by sandy hair that had never seen a razor cut, and narrowed eyes lost in the shadows of the night. The face of a complete stranger.

"Oh, my God," she gasped as she free-fell into a parallel universe where everything was an insane mirror image of reality.

The only sense of reality she had was his hold on her. The rest was madness. As crazy as her reaction to this man's kiss. God, the kiss. She jerked back, freeing herself of his hold, and fought the overwhelming urge to scrub her lips hard enough to banish the memory of what had just happened.

Instead she hugged her arms around her middle and stared at him. Even in the gathering shadows of the night, he seemed to be all planes and angles, his features compelling in some way. Then she saw his mouth, a suggestion of a smile at the corners. She swallowed hard. His mouth. The kiss. She held herself more tightly, more than embarrassed by the disaster she'd participated in these past few minutes.

"I'm so…sorry," she managed to say around the tightness in her throat. "This was all a mistake." She knew that was the height of understatement. "I thought…" She swallowed hard. "You aren't…"

He leaned back against the railing of the deck and cocked his head to one side. His eyes narrowed even more, the look unsettlingly speculative, before he spoke in a deep, rough voice that somehow fit him. "Obviously, I'm not."

She grasped at anything to stop the thought that he wasn't nearly as handsome as Dennis—but he was as sexy as hell—and the thought that came right on its heels. No kiss from this man would ever be labeled as "nice." Not even close. And that scared her to death.

She felt her heart still pounding wildly in her chest, and prayed that it would settle down so her body could forget what had just happened. Forgetting wouldn't be that easy. She couldn't remember ever being kissed like that before, or responding so eagerly and completely. Not even with Robert.

Robert. Definitely Mr. Wrong. Exciting, sexy, fun, but so very wrong. This man had the same look and, heaven knew, he was having the same effect on her. She hadn't changed as much as she'd thought. She pushed her hands behind her back, gripping them together so tightly that she could feel her nails cut into her palms. She welcomed the sensation. Anything to divert her attention from the man in front of her.

Then it hit her that she'd made a real mistake, but he must have known. He'd known and gone right along with it. A flashing memory of his body against hers came with a clarity that cut right through her and produced an anger that she grabbed at with both hands. He'd not only gone along with it, he'd enjoyed it!

"Why did you do that?" she asked.

"Have you looked in the mirror lately?" he murmured.

She wasn't going to let him flirt like that and get away with what he'd just done. "I was mistaken, but you knew all the time. You knew, and you…you…"

"Kissed you? Of course I did. You walked in here, threw yourself at me and what was I supposed to do?" He shrugged, the denim of his jacket straining across his broad shoulders, and that unsettling trace of a smile was back. "I'm only human, and certainly no saint. And you might keep in mind that I didn't attack you. On the contrary—"

"I didn't attack you," she said quickly.

"Then what do you call it?"

Damn that smile. "Mistaken identity," she muttered. "I mistook you for a gentleman."

She regretted the words as soon as they were out of her mouth. His rough laughter only made things worse. "Well, I'd say you really were mistaken."

"Obviously," she whispered. "Why are you here?"

"I guess you wouldn't buy it if I said I loitered on decks waiting for women to throw themselves at me?"

"Aren't you ever serious?" she muttered as her jaw began to clench.

"Not if I can help it. Being serious seriously impairs a person's ability to have fun. And if you can't have fun, why bother?" He came toward her, wiping out any safety buffer she'd built between them in less than a second. "Don't you agree?"

Melanie stared at him, the low glow of the fire in the house touching his face with deep shadows at his jaw and eyes. It flickered over his lips and that persistent smile. "Why are you here?" she asked again, sidestepping his question completely.

Sam hadn't heard her come in. He'd been too intent on the view and its inherent sense of freedom. Suddenly her voice had been there, smooth as silk and so sexy that his whole body had responded. Her touch had not only startled him, but had instantly aroused a response that defied logic.

Then he'd turned. He'd only briefly glimpsed a face that could have belonged to an angel, an angel who was circling his neck with slender arms and pressing her angelic body against him. Offering him her lips. He had only had a fleeting instant of hesitation before he'd taken what was offered. He didn't regret his action at all.

Now he was looking into huge eyes filled with shock and indignation. And looking at lips that were still so tempting that he had to lean away from her before he reached out to taste her again. His responses to her came with such impact that he tried to regroup.

He took the time to look right at her. Tall, slender, a vision with short dark hair framing a delicate face with eyes shadowed by improbable lush lashes. Despite the veil of mists and night, he could tell that high color dotted her cheeks. And despite the fact they had no contact now, he couldn't get past the effect she had on him.

"Okay, seriously, I guess I owe you an apology," he muttered, wondering how the distance that she put between them only made things worse. It just gave him a better view of her. The sweep of her throat, the way her soft, white pullover clung to small, high breasts. The way the dark slacks showed off legs that seemed to go on forever, and the fact that she was only five or six inches shorter than his own six feet, three inches.

He saw her take a deep breath, her breasts lifting with the action, and watched as her tongue quickly touched full lips that didn't look as if they had any lipstick on at all. For an instant he thought of his lips, that the lipstick could be there, but he didn't test that theory. He folded his arms across his chest and watched her take a sharp breath before she said, "I can't believe anyone would do something like that."

"Me, neither," he countered with what he hoped was control. Because he didn't feel controlled at all.

She held up one hand, palm out toward him, as if to ward him off. "Are you the real estate agent?"

"No, I'm not," he managed, keeping a quip to himself that if she thought he was a real estate agent and kissed him like that, what would she do if she'd thought he was the owner of the house? "She'll be back in a few minutes. There was a call." He nodded toward the house. "All I know is, she said she'd be back in a bit." He narrowed his eyes a bit more to try to lessen the impact of the vision in front of him. "Let's hope you weren't planning on greeting her the way you greeted me. Now that could be a disaster."

The color in her cheeks deepened again. Dammit, she

was blushing. He couldn't remember the last time he'd actually seen a woman blush. An endearing trait, and sexy as all get-out. He was thankful that the air was chilly on the deck and what light there was came from the fire behind her.

"I thought you were someone I knew who was meeting me here to see about leasing this place."

"You're half right."

"What?" she asked softly.

"I'm here to see about leasing this house. But I don't know you. Let me introduce myself." He held a hand out to her, wanting to feel her again, to sense her skin against his. "I'm Sam Harrison." She looked at his extended hand, but didn't move. "We *are* going to be civilized about this, aren't we?" he murmured, thinking that being civilized with this woman was the last thing he'd put on his agenda. "Shake hands and come out fighting?"

Sam wished that he had a clear look at her. That he could see her without the shadows of night blurring her features. She still didn't move, but he didn't pull his hand back. "Well?" he said softly.

She kept her arms at her sides, her eyes narrowed. "This isn't a prizefight. It's a house, for Pete's sake."

"And I'm being polite about it," he murmured, a little baffled by his own reactions, the man who had never needed or wanted any connections in his life suddenly wanting another connection with this stranger... "How about you?"

"Oh, shoot," she muttered, putting her hand into his.

After the kiss, he hadn't been sure what to expect when he felt her slender fingers wrap around his palm with a surprisingly firm grip, but it wasn't that his world would tip precariously off center again. That shook him on a level that he'd never known before. Before he could figure out what was happening, she jerked back from the contact.

Then he realized that she'd said her name, that he'd heard it, but he didn't have a clue what it was. "I'm sorry?" he said, his voice vaguely rough. "You're..."

"Melanie Clark," she repeated as she moved away from him.

Melanie. He watched her go to the railing, then touch the damp wood with the tips of her slender fingers. Jealousy of an inanimate object was so absurd, yet he almost wished it was him she was touching, that her fingers were brushing his skin again.

He jerked his thoughts back to rational patterns as quickly as he could, and asked something he was really curious about. "Just who did you think I was?"

She saw her hands still, then slowly curl around the damp wood. She didn't turn from the sweeping view as she spoke to him. "My boyfriend. I was meeting him here to look at the house. I thought you...well, I expected him to be here."

Boyfriend? He should have known she wasn't greeting any real estate agent with a kiss like that. Of course she had a man interested in her, a man she'd kiss with all that passion and abandon. Damn him, he thought. Hoping his expression was neutral, as he asked, "Then he's the one interested in the house?"

"Yes, he is," she murmured, her voice a whisper on the growing chill in the breeze. "He should be here any minute." She lifted one hand and pushed back the cuff of her sweater to glance at a watch that glowed blue. "In fact, he should have been here by now."

What man wouldn't be early to meet this woman?

"He's running late," Sam said, and added mentally, The fool.

"He's never late."

Sam watched the way she lifted her face ever so slightly into the growing breeze. The sweep of her throat was delicate and inviting, and the idea of tasting the skin there was starting to play havoc with his body again. "He's never late? That's pretty absolute, don't you think?"

"Not for him. If he says he'll be somewhere, he is."

He didn't point out the obvious to her. For some reason he felt petty attacking the man, and was all too sure that his motives would be very evident to Melanie. "The traffic's pretty rough out there, with the holidays and everything," he said with what he thought was great restraint, then wondered why he was making excuses for some man he wouldn't mind never showing up.

He heard her sigh before she turned and glanced right and left at the sweep of the house. "He's going to love this place when he gets here. It's absolutely beautiful."

"Absolutely," he echoed as he watched her carelessly brush at her hair. "So, you were meeting him here to give your stamp of approval on his choice?"

She glanced at him. "He asked me to look at it with him."

"Angela, the real estate agent, said that it was available for lease right away, fully furnished. I had no idea that anyone else was interested in it."

He wondered just what color her eyes were. With the shadows so deep, he could only tell she was looking at him. Although the way his body was responding to this woman, the dark wasn't all bad.

"Neither did I," she said softly, once again hugging

her arms around her middle. He didn't miss the slight shiver she couldn't suppress.

"Even California gets chilly in December. Why don't we go inside where it's reasonably warm to wait for the others to show up?"

"Sure," she said, then came toward him, stirring the air as she passed. The night, the ocean and a subtle sweetness mingled in the chilly air. He braced himself before following her into the huge central room. God, she affected him so profoundly that he barely understood it. What he did understand was that the man coming to meet her here was a boyfriend, not a husband or even a fiancé. Another thing he understood was that his stay in Santa Barbara might be very interesting indeed, after all.

Chapter Three

As Sam stepped into the warmth of the room and as Melanie crossed to the fireplace, he said, "I hope your friend has another house in mind, because as soon as Angela gets back, I'm taking this one."

Melanie hesitated, then stopped and turned to him. "The Realtor promised it to you?" she asked.

He shrugged as he moved closer to her, fascinated by the way the flickering firelight touched the delicate hollows at her cheeks and throat. "Well, no," he admitted, stopping a few feet from her. "But since I was here first—"

"This is the first time you've been here?"

"Yes. But I was here well before you showed up and, I might add, I was definitely here before your friend."

"But he was here yesterday," she said, resting her hands on her hips. "If we go by 'first come, first served,' the house is his."

He almost smiled at the way she tipped her head slightly as she spoke. "But who says we go by 'first come, first served'?" he countered, crossing his arms at his chest. "What if we go by 'first one here with the cash'? I've got the cash and I'm here. Ergo, I—"

"I think we should wait for the others to get here, and then we can iron out the ground rules."

"You and I can negotiate, can't we?" he drawled, deliberate suggestiveness in his tone.

He definitely liked the way her face colored slightly before she said, "The house isn't for me. So, I don't see how—"

This was getting better all the time. "So, you're not moving in here with your very late friend?"

"Not that it's any of your business, but I'm not."

Relief was there immediately. He didn't like the idea of her sharing the bedroom with its flowing views and deep shadows, making love. "I just assumed that—"

"That's your problem. You shouldn't assume anything until you know all the facts."

"Such as?"

"You don't know me, or what my relationship is all about."

That was very true, and right then he did know two things about Melanie Clark. First, he was going to find out everything about her. And second, her tardy boyfriend was going to have a hell of a fight on his hands when and if he got here.

Sam was going to enjoy this immensely. This woman brought out more than lust in him. She stirred something in him akin to that adrenaline-pumping feeling of knowing he was up against formidable odds to make a stunt work, but also knowing in the pit of his stomach that he could do it. He moved a bit closer to her. "Then why don't you tell me all about your relationship?"

"Excuse me?" she asked, her color deepening again.

"How serious is this relationship?"

"None of your business," she said quickly and with undisguised defensiveness.

"Then how can I do anything but speculate when there's no way for me to get the facts from you?"

"Mr. Harrison, I—"

"Sam. Just call me Sam."

"Mr. Harrison," she said firmly. "We're here about this house, not about anything else."

"Oh, really?"

He could see that she was getting a bit angry with him, and he actually liked the way her eyes brightened as she said, "I think you should go and look for another house. This is a wonderful city, and there are lots of houses you'd like in it."

"How would *you* know what I like and don't like?"

"Logic. If you like this place, there's lots of other places you'll like. I mean, it isn't as if you're buying it or anything."

"Are you telling me that there are clones of this place up and down the coast?"

"Darn it, why are you—"

"'Darn it'?" he asked, his smile growing. "I haven't heard an adult say that for..." He shrugged. "I can't remember the last time I heard it used."

"Some people don't have a need to use profanity," she muttered, and walked away from him.

"Excuse me?" he said as he turned and followed her across the room to an arched doorway opposite the hearth. "Dammit, are you saying that I've been using profanity?"

She didn't laugh at that at all. "Use of profanity is the sign of a limited vocabulary," she said over her shoulder as she stepped into the shadows beyond the door.

Sam knew that direction led through a dressing room on either side of a short hallway into the master bedroom suite. He ignored a certain sense of emptiness around him as soon as she was out of sight and went after her. "What does that mean?" he asked as he walked through the dressing area.

He stopped at the entry to the bedroom and saw her immediately, standing by the foot of the huge bed across from a series of French doors that led out to the rear decking. The light from a partial moon peeking through dark clouds in the early evening sky filtered into the space, and the sight of her backed by misty glow enthralled him. He stayed where he was, just looking at her.

The room was perfect for her. It was a room where she should be held and explored and loved. Wrong thoughts to have, he conceded quickly as the visions floating in his mind made his body tense. He leaned against the door frame as she crossed to the French doors to look out at the rainy ocean view.

"Are you going to explain what that means?" he asked again.

"I think you understand it perfectly," she murmured.

"I understand perfectly that I want this house. It's wonderful."

"I won't argue about that. It's terrific," she said. "Can you imagine this place all done up for Christmas, with lights and a huge tree, and the fire in the fireplace scented with pine?"

The holidays weren't even in his thought processes. They never had been. "I never paid much attention to the holidays." He usually just ignored them, unless his mother was around and he felt he had to do something. "But I'd guess you pay attention to them."

"With eight brothers and sisters, it's hard to ignore Christmas."

There were more like her at home? "Eight?"

The sound of her sigh seemed to fill the corners of darkness in the room. "Nine, counting me. And you're an only child, right?" she asked, touching the glass in the door with the tips of her fingers.

"Very singular," he said. "But I didn't know it showed that much."

"Just a lucky guess," she murmured as she slowly turned back to him.

He had the sudden feeling she was laughing at him. He wished he could see her, really see her, because he wanted to see her smile. "You have to admit that it's not usual, having that many children," he said, just to keep the conversation going.

"Not usual, but very natural," she murmured.

"Is your very late boyfriend one of a brood, too?"

Laughter did come then, softly running through him and surrounding him with a sense of joy that stunned him. "Oh, no," she said, then stunned him even more, but not with her humor this time. "Dennis Benning is certainly one of a kind."

The name hung in the shadows all around Sam, pushing back all the feelings that had been so close to the surface just seconds ago. He couldn't have heard right. "Dennis Benning?" he repeated, hating the name even as he said it out loud.

"Do you know him?"

Sam stood straight, every good feeling dissolving with sickening speed. "Investments, money, been in Santa Barbara for years?" he asked, enumerating some of the things his mother had finally told him about his father. He hoped against hope that there would be a full denial coming any minute now, that Santa Barbara had a slew of Dennis Bennings living in the city.

But he was wrong. Dead wrong. "Yes, that's him. You know the family?"

Fate had played cruel tricks on him before, but this was the worst of all. Out of all the women in this city he could have met, he'd met and fallen hard for the one his long-lost father was involved with. The idea sickened him so much that he had to swallow hard to get out words. "I've heard of him."

"Most people around here have," she said. "And right now he *is* very late. I wonder—"

"Hello, is anyone in here?" a deep voice called from the other part of the house. "Mel? It's me."

Melanie moved quickly, hurrying across the darkened room. She brushed past Sam in the doorway, the fleeting contact as elusive as the touch of an errant breeze. Sam didn't follow her right away. He stayed by the doorway, needing to regroup, to figure out what was happening to his world and how to face that world when he walked out into the other part of the house.

"Dammit," he muttered, his vocabulary totally limited by frustration and shock. His so-called father. Here. A man he'd planned on meeting, on seeing and walking away from. Now he was just around the corner. The man who had never touched his life in thirty-seven years, never wanted to, and that man brought disaster. He wasn't only here when he shouldn't be, but he was with Melanie.

He braced himself, ready to get it over with. As he turned to walk back through the dressing area, he saw a low light flash on beyond it. There were murmured voices as he headed toward the light, and his thoughts refused to focus. Suddenly he was at the archway, about to step into a room where Fate was having fun at his expense.

In the middle of the room he saw Melanie with a man. But this man couldn't be Dennis Benning. He wasn't nearly old enough. Maybe in his middle thirties at the most, and close to Sam's own build and height. He even had the same coloring. Melanie was holding the man's arm as she turned, and he saw in that moment that her eyes were amber, the color of topaz. Eyes that sent his world into a dizzying tailspin.

She seemed to move closer to the man, almost pressing her cheek to his shoulder. "Dennis, this is Sam Harrison. Mr. Harrison, Dennis Benning."

If this was Dennis Benning, then there had to be more than one Dennis Benning in Santa Barbara. The odds of that happening, despite his own wishes, weren't great. But if they were related... Related. Suddenly Sam thought he understood. His stomach clenched and his mouth felt dry as he finally managed to ask, "You're Dennis Benning's son?"

The man nodded. "Yes, you know Father?"

His son. The same build. The same hair color. Around the same age. God help him, but a day that had started out making sense suddenly slipped from one form of madness to another type altogether. He wasn't looking at his father, but at his half brother.

He looked at Melanie, the soft overhead track lighting showing the delicate lines of her face, a faint sprinkling of freckles across her nose, and veiled eyes. His earlier responses hadn't diminished. And dammit, she was holding on to Dennis Benning as if she loved him.

For one horrendous moment he felt his hands tighten into fists that wanted to strike out. Sibling rivalry? Was that what this was? The urge to punch Dennis's lights out, to take that smug smile off his face—that Benning face. That urge grew when he saw Dennis rub his hand on Melanie's shoulder. Sam only knew one thing clearly right then; he had to get of there, and get out as soon as he could.

Melanie held on to Dennis, relieved that he'd finally come, a rock in her sea of confusion. Yet she was unable to ignore Sam as he walked into the living room. Nothing about the man was ignorable and that fact only made her more thankful for Dennis. Steady, dependable, reliable Dennis, who didn't make her think wild and crazy thoughts that she knew would only get her into trouble.

The kiss was still seared into her mind, that spontaneous response to Sam's mouth on hers, and she cringed at the images she remembered. She'd been there, done that and lived to regret it. Robert was still fresh in her memory of regrets. Her hold on Dennis tightened before she looked right at Sam, who was just a few feet from her.

Mr. Wrong, big as life and twice as sexy…and someone the old Melanie would have been drawn to like a moth to a flame. A flame that could burn and destroy. She met the intensity in those navy blue eyes, and saw Sam clearly in the overhead light. Now she could see fine lines fan at the corners of those eyes, and she was a bit thankful that his dark brows shadowed his expression. Darkness was preferable for her with this man.

Through the shadows, she had felt the strength of that gaze, but now it was making her mouth go dry and something in her tensed to the point that she felt a bit nauseated. But, thank God she had control, and she'd learned her lessons well and was being sensible. The kiss was an aberration, because she'd thought he was Dennis. That was the only reason it happened. One thing she had to thank Robert for was making her grow up and take charge of her life instead of leading it full-tilt into danger. And as she took a tight breath, she knew that Sam Harrison was very dangerous for her. A very dangerous man indeed.

She watched him nod to Dennis when she introduced them, but before she could explain that he was here about the house, too, a woman burst through the front doors. With flame-red hair, the stranger came in as if she owned the place. She was dressed all in black, from slacks, to a suede jacket, to boots that added three inches to her slender height. A startlingly pretty woman.

"Hello, hello, hello," she said breezily in a throaty voice as she crossed to the three people. "I'm Angela, your facilitator." She beamed at them. "That means I'm here to help all of you...with this house." She glanced at Sam. "Mr. Harrison, so sorry I had to leave," she said, then turned to Dennis and Melanie. "And I'm very glad to finally meet you two."

Melanie had heard of human whirlwinds before, but had never actually met one. Now she had, in the form of a beautiful woman. As she looked into her eyes, for a fleeting moment she felt as if she knew her, that they'd met somewhere before. Maybe the boutique? A customer?

Before she could mention it, Angela was smiling brilliantly at Dennis. "Mr. Benning?"

"Yes," Dennis said, letting go of Melanie to hold his hand out to her. "I'm sorry I'm late. I got held up at the office and—"

"No problem," she assured him as she took his hand in both of hers and her smile deepened. "We're all here now, intersecting, as it were, and that's all that counts."

"'Intersecting'?" Dennis repeated with a frown.

Before Angela could explain her odd usage of that

word, Sam broke in abruptly. "I'm sorry. I have to get going."

Angela turned to him. "But the house, you barely had time to see if it fit you, if it was just what you were looking for."

Sam never looked at Melanie, but she had the strangest feeling that he was talking to her as he spoke to Angela. "It's a great house, and I want it. I'll take it at the price you quoted."

"But I haven't had a chance to even look around," Dennis said quickly as he frowned at Sam. "It looks like a great house to me, too, but I need time to look around. I had no idea that this was going to be a competition. You never mentioned—"

"It's not a competition," Angela broke in. "I just thought Mr. Harrison should see what my company has to offer. As to the house—"

"I told you on the phone I was in a hurry." Sam cut Angela off this time. "That I need to get settled so I can concentrate on work. This has the space, the isolation and location. I want it."

"Of course, of course," Angela said with a touch of patronizing that Melanie could tell rankled Sam just a bit. "I thought you could both look at it, and with any luck, one of you would take it. It's been empty for a while, and the owner is anxious to have it occupied again. I had no idea that both of you would want it." That smile came again. "Whoa, I have an idea. Why don't you both fill in applications, and we'll leave the decision up to the owner?"

Sam exhaled on a hiss, and Melanie felt Dennis tense a bit. She had a flashing image of the old West and two men in a showdown, and she didn't understand that at all. It was just a house. Both men started to speak at the same time.

"Let me talk to—" Dennis said, as Sam said, "If you'll give me a number—"

Angela held up one hand. Staying remarkably calm in the center of a potential storm, she shook her head. "I am the owner's representative, and I am very sure we can settle this amicably. After all, we're all adults here, and it isn't as if we're talking life and death. It's just a house."

Both men frowned at her words, then each stepped back half a pace. For a moment it was as if Melanie was watching the action in a mirror, reflections that mimicked the reality of each man. It startled her. Then Sam broke away completely.

He started toward the door, speaking over his shoulder. "You're right. It's just a house. But I need it and don't have time for this. I've got an important appointment." He reached for the door handle, then stopped and turned, casting a slanting glance over his shoulder. "You know where I'm staying," he said. "Fax the application to me, and I'll get back to you right away." Then he was gone.

As the door shut behind him, Melanie took the first easy breath she'd drawn since she'd opened her eyes after the kiss. Her chest eased, and she touched her mouth with fingers that were slightly unsteady. She'd survived and done the right thing. She felt much safer now that she was in control, and it was all over. Sam was gone, and she was here with Dennis. The way it should be.

"That guy seems pretty intense about a house," Dennis muttered.

Intense? Melanie knew just how intense Sam could

be. "You weren't backing down, either," she said without thinking.

"I won't be railroaded," he said. "Not by anyone." He touched her cheek, his contact jarring her slightly. "You like the house, don't you?"

His touch felt oddly cold and she almost recoiled from it before she caught herself. "Yes, I...I like it."

"It's just what I've been looking for." He grinned, a very boyish expression of delight. "Dammit all, it feels like I'm finally getting my life in order...the way I want it to be." He actually laughed at that. "And it only took me thirty-five years to figure out what I *really* wanted."

Melanie looked at Dennis and admitted it had taken her twenty-seven years to figure out where she was going. Twenty-seven years to finally find a man she could respect and care for, and she wasn't going to let a chance encounter with a stranger mess things up now. No way.

ANGELINA STAYED with Melanie and Dennis for a bit, then handed the key to Melanie to put in the lock box when they left, excusing herself for another appointment. She almost danced as she walked away. Things were going so right for her at the moment. Melanie was attracted to Sam. Sam was attracted to Melanie. The kiss had all but melted the world down around the two of them. A great start.

Pure luck that Melanie had thought Sam was Dennis, but it had worked out so well. Dumb, stupid luck that had paid off big-time. And she was going to take advantage of it. Thank goodness Dennis wasn't madly in love with Melanie, after all. His luck with the Clark sisters wasn't very good, but at least it was clear that his heart wasn't at peril. It would all work down the line for everyone.

She went out into the chilly mists, ready to put the next step of her plan into action—if only she had a next step to her plan. Things were moving so quickly that she was pretty much playing this assignment by ear, improvising as she went. Right now she needed some perfect reason to bring Melanie and Sam together again, to get them to intersect as soon as possible.

If she had read Sam right—and she was good at reading these humans, even if she did say so herself—he wanted Melanie badly. But now he knew about his half brother. It was all on the table, so to speak, but the man hadn't backed down. The instant he'd realized who Dennis Benning was, Angelina had felt the gears kick into place. The sudden flare-up of rivalry between the two men had been so thick it could have been cut by a knife.

Sam may have gone off to think, to figure things out, but he was still in the fray. Right then, Angelina knew exactly what to do: use the rivalry over the house. That was the common denominator.

Suddenly she had another great idea. As she looked around in the misty winter night, she amended that. Not just great—perfect! She started for the gates. What a coup for her if she could change this mess that the Council had made into a success for everyone involved.

The toe of her boot caught on the uneven stones in the path, and she barely kept herself from pitching forward by grabbing the top of the open gate. There was a whispered voice in her ear, Miss Victoria's voice. "Pride goes before a fall."

She gripped the gate and looked over her shoulder, but no one was there.

Drawing her hands back, she brushed them against her sides and whispered into the chilly air, "Yes, ma'am. I understand." Then she ducked her head and moved quickly out onto the graveled parking area by the stone fence.

She moved past the three cars and onto the pavement before she took a couple of deep breaths and paused. She was unnerved that the Council was so bothered by its mistake that it was monitoring her so closely during her assignment.

And her toe hurt from the impact of the stone she'd tripped over. She looked down at her scuffed boot, then realized that she was getting more help than even Miss Victoria knew she was offering. Angelina pointed one finger at the irregular ground near the gates, then moved away from the house and started down the road.

Calling a taxi was out of the question. Time was of the essence, so she walked up the narrow road through the mists until she was out of sight of the house and, with a nod of her head, she went after Sam.

As she transported herself to the hotel, she thought about learning to drive. In this world it seemed a human necessity, especially in California where you couldn't go anywhere physically without a car. She really should master it when she had the chance. There couldn't be that much to it if just about any human could do it.

She looked down, and could see Sam at the door to his hotel room on the tenth floor. Humans were such an odd species, she mused. Falling in love, something that should be the easiest of all things to accomplish, was one of the hardest things humans did.

This case was a good example of just how confused humans could get. As Sam closed the door behind him, she hovered nearby and waved her hand in the direction of the phone on the desk by the windows. It rang immediately, and Sam crossed the suite to answer it.

She didn't bother listening to the woman on the other end. She knew what was being said and she could almost feel the pressure the words were putting on Sam. A nudge to keep him on track. He was being told that the production company wanted to verify that he would be ready to start the job the day after Christmas. The main star of the movie wanted to start his work a month ahead of time, so it was imperative that Sam's crew have their work completed on time.

"He was summoned to Tibet on New Year's to talk to his spiritual advisor?" Sam asked. "What in the—"

He listened again, then exhaled harshly and said, "Just let me know the dates." As he hung up, the fax machine beside the phone beeped once and paper started forth. Snapping on the low desk lamp, Sam reached for the two sheets of paper. He read them, murmuring as he laid them on the desk, "That seals that."

Angelina knew she'd done it. Sam had to have that house. Period. And he wanted it. It was perfect for him, and he'd find out that Melanie was perfect for him, too. She'd make very sure that he wouldn't walk away from Melanie a second time.

Chapter Four

Sam hated being pressured, but that's exactly what had happened since the moment he'd turned and seen Melanie standing before him. First, it had been good pressure, meeting a beautiful woman who rang every alarm in him. The pressure of playing "the game" with her, talking and getting to know all about her. That, he could deal with. But it had gone downhill when Dennis Benning had appeared.

Melanie and Dennis. His half brother. Dennis had Melanie, and he wanted the house. He'd had a silver—no, a golden—spoon in his mouth since he'd been born. No scrimping and saving, no mother working twelve-hour days. Sam took a breath to ease an odd tightening in his chest. No, Dennis didn't need that house, and he didn't deserve Melanie.

He leaned forward, pressed both hands to the desktop and slowly rotated his head to ease the tension in his neck. He'd prepared himself to see the father, but he hadn't been prepared for something like this. A part of him. He slowly raised his head and looked out the expanse of glass to the night outside.

Part of him. He couldn't deny that that fascinated him. When he'd been a kid he'd thought about having a brother, but that had been a fantasy. Then an hour ago he'd looked into the eyes of that brother, just before he'd walked away. Dammit, he wished he hadn't reacted on such a gut level. That thought brought a rough chuckle. Gut level? With Melanie it had been lower than the gut.

He couldn't forget that moment when he'd turned and taken what she'd offered. And he couldn't forget looking his brother in the eye.

He glanced down at the faxed sheets on the desk. On the top was the realty logo, then a phrase under it in a flourishing script: *Let Angela Make The Connection For You.* There was a single paragraph about three more homes on the ocean that Angela had found for him, but two weren't available for viewing until after the holidays. The other wouldn't be available until well into January.

Picking up the sheets, he read the handwritten note. "Here's the application and a list of beachfront property. The selection is very low right now, but will be better after New Year's. Send in the application, or call me and we'll make the right connection for you. We'll find whatever you need." A single *A* was scrawled under it.

Sam tossed the papers onto the desk as his mind formed one clear thought about what he really needed. But he had neither the house nor Melanie...at least, not yet. The image of the beach house was there, and the sense of freedom he'd felt on that deck. Then the woman. The kiss, the taste of her invading him. His world being rocked.

Life wasn't fair, but then again, Sam had never expected it to be. One thing he knew for sure, he never gave up...on anything. Maybe he'd call the real estate agent to see if she knew where he could find Melanie Clark. He picked up the paper, but her phone number was blurred. He remembered that she'd given him her number and he'd written it on a card in his wallet.

Reaching into his back pocket, he uttered a low curse. For a second he almost thought he'd heard someone laugh, the sort of laugh of a person very pleased with something. He looked around the empty room and shook his head. The sound was in his mind, but his wallet not being in his pocket was very real.

"I'LL GET the application in tomorrow first thing," Dennis said as he and Melanie stepped through the front door of the beach house. "The more I see of this place, the more I want it."

They hurried through the light mists to the gate and out onto the parking area. Melanie hurried to her car and opened the door. Before she got in, she turned and Dennis was there, one hand on the door, the other on the frame to his right. "What do you think? You were awfully quiet in there."

She looked at the house through the blur of the windshield, at the way mists were swirling in a light breeze around coach lights set in the stone wall by the gates.

"It's great," she said softly, thinking of how the house could come alive if Christmas lights were strung on the wall and outlined the peak of the roof. Mostly, if there were people to fill the emptiness inside.

When she realized it wasn't Dennis she was imagining in the house, she tried to cut off her thoughts. She closed her eyes for a brief moment before looking back to Dennis. "You're getting wet. You need to get going."

"I'm fine. Besides, this isn't rain, it's just a bit of

humidity in the air." He grinned at her. "I'm just excited about this place. I hope I can get it."

"Don't worry. You've got the edge."

His smile slipped a bit. "What did you mean, I have the edge?"

"I just meant that you're a Benning. In this town, that counts for a lot."

Dennis touched her arm as a dark frown smothered the smile completely. "Mel, that sounded just like my mother."

She covered his hand with hers, and was taken aback by how cold he felt. "I'm sorry." She was, but more for being distracted by thoughts she had no business entertaining than by what she'd inadvertently said. "That was the wrong thing to say, wasn't it?"

"Listen, Mel, we've talked about this before. I am who I am, but I won't be a clone of my parents. I don't want the sort of life they have. I never did want it. I love them, but that doesn't mean I have to be a *Benning* at all."

His hand moved out from under hers to touch her cheek as he finished saying, "You've always understood that about me and I like that about you." His fingers traced the line of her jaw. "We've gotten so close, and I've made changes. Changes I know are right. Like finding you again."

She understood all too well reinventing one's self. She also understood how precarious the process could be. She'd been doing so well until Sam Harrison had brought out the old Melanie full-force for a wrenching moment. But she'd managed to sidestep the trouble. She'd regained sanity and pulled herself up short.

"I should never have said that," she said. "I just meant that your family's been around here for a long time, and that your references will be impeccable." His finger gently cupped her chin as she spoke. "You've got your own business and contacts in the city. And Mr. Harrison...well, I doubt that he can match that."

"Okay, I'm being too sensitive. I'm sorry. Let's get on with this and forget about the past," he murmured. "Okay?"

She tried to focus on Dennis, on his blue eyes, not darker blue eyes, and on his touch, not a touch she'd felt on the deck. Yes, the past was better forgotten. She whispered, "Absolutely. The future is what counts."

"Amen," he breathed, then studied her for a long moment before saying something that brought the past back with biting clarity. "This house could be a beginning for us, a place where neither one of us has a past."

Her mind was playing perverse games with her, taunting her with the image of Sam on the deck in that moment when she'd known he wasn't Dennis. In the dark bedroom, him at the door, telling her that he wanted the house and asking about Dennis.

"The...the house is very nice." She took a breath, fighting the remembering that was plaguing her.

"Yes, and this is quite a change from the place in the hills." He chuckled softly as his hand skimmed under her hair to cup the back of her neck. "And that won't be lost on my mother. She'll have a fit that I'm leasing and not buying, and that it's at the beach. I can hear her now, 'Dennis, it is so common to live in a place like that.' Her nose turned up, of course."

"She won't like this, not any more than she likes the idea of you dating Reggie Clark's sister, will she?" she asked, aware of how close Dennis was now.

"My mother has her opinions. But they're hers, not mine." She knew he was going to kiss her before he moved even closer and whispered, "Not mine at all." Then his lips touched hers.

Gently, softly exploring, with warmth and sweetness, and in a heartbeat, Melanie's mind became downright cruel. She was suddenly kissing Sam Harrison again, and there was nothing gentle and soft about it. The contact seared through her, and she moved closer to him, wanting to inhale his essence, to know the man in ways that frightened her. But when she shifted closer, winding her arms around his neck, it was Dennis who pulled back.

Dennis, who shakily exhaled and hoarsely breathed, "Whew," jarred her back to reality as he held her from him. "That sure takes care of the chill around here."

This time when she opened her eyes, she was facing Dennis, not Sam, and her face burned with an embarrassment and anger at herself that almost choked her. She could barely look at Dennis. She hadn't meant to do that, any more than she'd meant to kiss Sam on the deck. It shook her how wrong she could be time after time.

She touched her tongue to her lips. "I have to go. I—I have to get back to the shop. Gwen's watching it for me, but I have to close up. Reggie and Ben are bringing Mikey by for a while so they can buy some Santa presents for him."

Dennis framed her face with his hands. "How about dinner later on?"

She should. She should be with Dennis and calm down and center herself. But she couldn't. "I don't know how long Reggie and Ben are going to be. And Mikey...well, I don't think it would be a good idea to take him to dinner with us."

"You've got a point there," he said, but smiled when he said it. "Why don't I come by later on tonight?"

"I'm going to my parents' house to decorate the tree after work."

"We always had a decorator come in to do our trees. It sounds downright homey to do it yourself. Would you mind if I came to watch?"

"Sure, come on by, if you want."

He surprised her by not hesitating. "I'll meet you there in a couple of hours. How's that?"

"That's fine, as long as you're sure you can take the full impact of the Clark clan. Everyone's going to be there to go and get the tree and decorate it."

"Oh, I'm building up an endurance for all of it. In fact," he said with a slow smile that came precariously close to the sort of smile she'd noticed with Sam, "I'm getting to enjoy it a bit."

"Well, you *have* changed," she murmured.

"So have you," he said, giving her a thankfully quick kiss before he drew back and let her go. "And I like this new Melanie a lot."

She could feel the chill of the night around her as he released her, and she got into her car. She pulled the door shut, and was thankful when her car started on the first try. With one look at Dennis in his Jeep, she backed out and headed up the road toward the main highway.

Dennis pulled up beside her at the stop sign, and with a wave, turned left onto the highway. As she lifted her hand to wave back at him, she realized she was holding a key. She lowered her hand and looked at the key resting in her palm. Angela had given it to her, but she didn't remember holding it. Until now.

Had she been that distracted? She shook her head. She hadn't locked the gates or the door. As Dennis disappeared down the road, Melanie made a U-turn and headed back to the house.

She parked by the gates, left her car idling with the headlights on for extra illumination, and got out. As she went to the gates, she stumbled over something on the ground. She looked down at a black square on the loose gravel, and when she crouched to reach for it, she realized it was a wallet.

Picking it up, she felt the well-worn leather, damp from the light rain, then turned it toward the headlights and flipped it open. There were credit cards in one section, at least six of them, and a thick packet of money in the bill section. In a clear window on one side, she saw a driver's license with a small colored picture.

There was no way she would mistake the man in the photo for anyone else. Or the effect on her of just seeing his image on the license. Samuel Bradley Harrison— with his eyes narrowed, his hair longer than it was now, his expression as unreadable in the frozen frame as it was in person. And just as compelling.

She quickly read the facts. He was thirty-seven, six foot three, and she didn't need to read that his eyes were blue or his hair blond. She looked away from those eyes, quickly closed the wallet, then hurried over to lock up the house. When she was done, she put the key in a lock box on the gate. As she closed the container, she was taken aback to see her hand was slightly unsteady.

Quickly, she got into her car, tossed the wallet onto the passenger seat and left. She was thankful that it was only the wallet she'd found at the house and not the man himself. As silly as it was, she could almost sense him in the car, and all she had was the small square leather container.

Driving onto the highway, she decided to call Angela,

then drop the wallet off at her office so she could give it back to Sam. There was no reason to see Sam again, she told herself. No reason at all.

AN HOUR LATER Melanie closed up the boutique for the evening and knew she had to take care of returning the wallet. She couldn't ignore it anymore. All the customers were gone, and the old bungalow that had been converted into an upscale specialty store, with brass racks of vintage clothes and showcases of antique and collectable accessories, was finally quiet.

She glanced around the store, which looked like a Victorian wonderland. Tiny, twinkling white lights were everywhere while the soft strains of classical Christmas music filtered into the shop through hidden speakers. A living tree decorated with blue and gold ribbons sat in a brass pot in the middle of the space.

Ben and Reggie had dropped Mikey off so they could go shopping, and he was being unusually quiet, sitting on the floor by the drapes to the dressing rooms, constructing castles out of empty jewelry boxes. His face was intent under a cap of blond hair as he built turrets that surrounded a dump truck. From nowhere he started singing his own version of the music on the sound system, "Deck the Halls." In a piping voice, he sang, "Deck the balls with bouts of folly."

Bouts of folly hit a little too close to home after the day she'd had, and she felt her smile falter just a bit. She crossed to the delicate Queen Anne desk near the Christmas tree and opened a side top drawer to take out the wallet. Putting it on the desktop, she reached for the phone, and put in a call to the real estate office.

There was only one ring before it was answered brightly by a woman. "Merry Christmas, and let us make the connection for you. This is Agnes. How may I help you?''

"I need to get in touch with one of your Realtors. Angela?''

"I'm sorry, but she's not here right now.''

"It's important that I reach her as soon as possible. Do you have a number where I could reach her?''

"I'm not sure where she is or how to locate her,'' Agnes said. "But if you want to leave a message, I'll make sure she gets it.''

Melanie dropped the wallet onto the polished wood top of the desk, then turned her back on it and closed her eyes. "Do you have any idea when you can get the message to her?''

"I don't. Angela keeps odd hours, and it's the holidays, too. But I'll give it to her as soon as I can.''

At the same time she realized Mikey had stopped singing, she heard the chair by the desk scrape on the hardwood floor. Opening her eyes, she turned to the sound, and Mikey was there in his denim overalls and red-striped T-shirt, standing on the chair as he grabbed for the wallet.

She reached for it, too, but she wasn't fast enough. With a squeal of victory, Mikey tossed it into the air. It flew up, spun around and, as it rotated, opened, and showered credit cards, money and pieces of paper all around.

"Oh, shoot,'' she muttered.

As something sailed past Melanie's face, she heard the woman on the other end of the phone say, "Miss? Miss? Is something wrong?''

Mikey scrambled off the chair and dropped to his knees, reaching for the scattered contents on the polished hardwood floor.

"Miss? Miss? Hello? Are you there?"

"Oh, yes, I—I'm here," she said as she dropped down beside Mikey. As she caught the phone between her ear and shoulder, she grabbed at the scattered contents. She had thought there was a lot of money in the wallet, but now she could see there had to be well over a thousand dollars. "I really need to get hold of Angela as soon as possible."

"I'm sorry, but I told you, if you leave a message, it will be delivered."

She pushed the money into the wallet, then reached for a one hundred dollar bill Mikey was trying to push into his pocket. "That's not yours, buster," she muttered as she took it away from him.

"Excuse me?" the lady on the other end said.

"I was…isn't there *any* way to reach Miss…" She had no idea what Angela's last name was at all.

"No."

She sank back on her heels as Mikey brought her credit cards and slips of paper, offering them to her with solemn earnestness. She took them, and tucked them back into the wallet.

"Miss, maybe if you explained the problem to me, I could help. Angela and I work very closely together."

"Okay," she said as she slipped the credit cards into the holders in the side of the wallet. "I was at a house today and a client of Angela's dropped his wallet. I wanted to get it back to him as soon as possible."

"A client?"

"Mr. Harrison, at a house on—"

"The house on Mar Vista Way?"

"Yes, that's the one."

"Angela had me fax Mr. Harrison an application for the lease. He's staying at the Reef Hotel. I'm sure it would be greatly appreciated if you could take the wallet to him at the hotel.''

She looked up as Mikey crawled out from under the desk and came over to her, offering her one last item from the wallet. She took it, and looked down at a picture that was faded and worn-looking, as if it had been carried in the wallet for a very long while. But even in its ragged condition, the beauty of the woman in the small photo was unmistakable, from a feathery cap of dark hair to luminous eyes that sparkled with endearing humor that curved full lips.

She turned it over and saw the inscription—For My Sam, With All My Love—in delicate script. A woman who loved him. She looked at the woman again, at the soft humor in her eyes, and knew without a doubt that Sam was the reason for that smile.

She slipped the picture into the back of the wallet, behind the money, then stood and gripped the phone with her free hand.

''Do you know where the Reef Hotel is?'' the woman on the phone asked.

''Yes, I do.'' She was vaguely aware of Mikey off to one side playing kick-ball with the empty jewelry boxes.

''With all that money in it, I know Mr. Harrison must be concerned. I'll let Angela know that you're personally taking the wallet to Mr. Harrison this evening.''

That was the last thing she wanted to do. ''Oh, no, I'm not—''

''A very Merry Christmas to you,'' the woman said, then hung up.

Melanie held the dead phone for a moment, then redialed the Realtor's office. A busy signal beeped in her ear, and she finally hung up. She stared at the wallet in her hand. There was no way she was taking this to the hotel. She would leave a message for Sam at the hotel, then send the wallet with a messenger in the morning. It would be over and done, neatly, cleanly…and safely.

As Mikey pushed his dump truck into one of the dressing rooms, Melanie dropped the wallet onto the desk and wished that she had a safe. What with all that money in it— Suddenly she realized what Agnes had said. ''With all that money in it…'' But how had she known about the money? Melanie didn't remember saying anything about it to her, but then again, she'd been so distracted she might not remember.

A crash, followed by a blood curdling scream, exploded from the dressing room, and Melanie ran toward the sounds. She burst into the small cubicle to find Mikey sprawled on his back on the floor under a heavy bentwood rack. There were two huge holes in the plaster wall where the rack had been, and a nearby chair was on its side.

Years of being the second oldest in a large family kicked in, and she quickly looked for blood as she tugged the heavy rack off of the screaming child. She had a blurred impression of there not being any blood as Mikey scrambled up and threw himself into her arms. She hugged him and spoke soothingly to him, mentally berating herself for being distracted. She knew if you gave a child a chair, they'd find a way to use it for something, and odds were that something wouldn't be at floor level.

''I falled,'' Mikey sobbed into her shoulder as she carried him back into the closed shop. ''I falled boom.''

''You sure did, sweetie,'' she whispered, patting his back as she crossed to the desk. She sat him on the desktop to take a better look. The last thing Reggie needed right now was to come back from a shopping trip to find a child with a lump on his head or black eye or a split lip or something equally horrible.

But as she smoothed back the fine blond hair from his little face, she was thankful the only marks from his encounter with the rack and chair were a tearstreaked face and a shaky bottom lip. "You're fine, champ," she said, wiping at the tears on his face.

Mikey looked down, and grabbed the wallet again. "Melly, see," he said as he held it up to her.

The damn wallet. "Thanks, champ," she said as she took it from him and moved it to the other side of the desk. She'd call the hotel as soon as Ben and Reggie came for Mikey, leave the message, then lock the wallet in her cash box until tomorrow.

When the phone rang, she caught Mikey in her arms, balanced him on one hip, then reached for the receiver with her other hand. "The Place. I'm sorry, but we're closed for the evening."

"Miss Clark? Is that you?"

"Yes."

"I was hoping I'd be able to catch you. This is Angela. I met you at the beach house."

"Oh, yes, thanks for getting back to me."

"Excuse me?"

"About the wallet Mr. Harrison lost."

"I'm sorry, I didn't know about it. Mr. Harrison lost his wallet? You're helping him look for it?"

"Oh, no, I found it after he left the house."

"Lovely. That's wonderful. He must be thrilled that it was found so quickly."

"He doesn't know yet." Mikey squirmed, grabbing at the receiver, and she moved her head to one side to avoid his little hand. "Just tell me where your office is and I'll drop it by when I leave here."

"Oh, no, that won't do. The office is closed. I think you need to take it to Mr. Harrison at the hotel right away."

Oh, no, she wasn't going to do that. "I'm sorry, I'm busy," she said as she tried to untangle Mikey's fingers from the phone cord. "I'm waiting for someone, and they won't be back for…" She glanced at the clock by the entry door. "Another hour, at least, then I have plans that can't wait." Melanie closed her eyes for a moment.

"Maybe they'll get there sooner than they thought," Angela said.

"I don't think—" As she opened her eyes, her words stopped. She blinked at Ben and Reggie at the door, getting ready to knock. They saw her, waved, and Mikey spotted them right then, too.

"Mommy, Daddy!" he squealed, squirming so much Melanie put him down and watched him run for the door.

"Miss Clark?" Angela was saying in her ear. "Are you there?"

"Oh, yes…um, could you hold for a minute?"

"Are you going to take the wallet by the hotel?"

"I'm not sure…" She motioned to Reggie that she'd be off the phone as soon as possible. "Mr. Harrison might not even be there."

"Then leave it with the concierge. They're quite trustworthy."

She saw Mikey grab for the door handle and swing on it, trying to open it. "Okay, I'll do that."

"I knew you would," Angela said, then hung up.

Melanie put the phone back. "You knew I would?"

she muttered as she started for the door. That was
strange, because she hadn't known she would until
she'd actually said the words.

Chapter Five

Melanie had barely opened the door before Mikey threw himself at Ben and was swept up in a bear hug. "Sorry, I couldn't get off the phone," she said as Ben and Reggie came into the store and she shut the door on the chilly night outside.

"So, did Aunt Mel survive Mikey?" Ben asked with a grin at Melanie over his little boy's head.

"Aunt Mel has survived a lot more than just one little dynamo. We had a minor incident, a run-in with a coat-rack and a chair, but other than that, everything was just fine."

"I falled." Mikey captured Ben's face between his two tiny hands and spoke solemnly. "I went boom, Daddy."

While Ben smoothed back Mikey's hair with one hand and said, "I bet you did," Melanie looked at a very pregnant Reggie. The woman who never wanted children was well and truly married and expanding the family. People changed. Reggie was living proof of it.

"I thought you weren't going to be here for a while," she said.

"So did I," Reggie said. "But we got right to the store and there was a power failure. They had to close up early, so no shopping. Didn't your lights go out here?''

"Not even a flicker," Melanie said.

"Odd." She sighed. "Actually, I'm exhausted, so it wasn't all bad." She leaned toward Melanie and whispered, "I think I'll take Mom up on her offer and let *her* find the perfect p-r-e-s-e-n-t for M-i-k-e-y, then I'll wrap it.''

"Sounds like a plan."

"Yes, it does." Reggie looked past Melanie, then crossed to the desk. As Melanie turned, she saw Reggie pick up the wallet. "Did a customer leave this?"

"No, not a customer," Melanie said quickly, crossing to Reggie. "I found it earlier today."

"Where?" Before Melanie could reach for it, Reggie had the wallet flipped open and was looking at the driver's license.

"At a beach house up by Gross Point."

"It says he's from Los Angeles," Reggie murmured. "And..." She uttered a low whistle. "Good heavens, look at this pile of bills. There must be four or five hundred dollars here."

"Twelve hundred, to be exact," Melanie said, and would have taken the wallet then but Reggie shifted to lean back against the desk to study the license. "A beach house? He's obviously rich. And he's not badlooking."

That was like saying a Rembrandt wasn't bad art, but Melanie wasn't about to argue about that. Instead, she took the wallet out of Reggie's hands and flipped it closed. "Don't be so nosy."

"You met him at a beach house? What beach house?''

"Reg, it's a long story, and I don't have the time to

go through it all right now. Besides, I need to get it back to him."

"All the way to Los Angeles?" Reggie asked.

"No, just to the Reef Hotel. He's staying there."

"The Reef? Whew, more money. You're meeting him there now? I thought you were going to Mom and Dad's for the tree trimming? Now you're running off with this guy?" She frowned. "I don't like the sound of this, Mel."

Melanie was vaguely aware of Mikey and Ben picking up the empty jewelry boxes behind her. But she never looked away from Reggie and that tinge of disapproval—no, maybe disappointment—on her face. "It's not like that," she said.

"Mel, I'm not judging anything. Believe me. But you said you were—"

"Changing, growing up, getting beyond leaping before I looked? That I was getting past men like Robert? I am, and I have. I just found the wallet. I'm taking it back, then I'm meeting Dennis at Mom and Dad's and having a terrific night decorating some tree that's going to be two feet too tall to even fit in the living room."

"Okay, okay," Reggie said. "I believe you."

"Reg, don't look at me like that," she muttered in a low voice to try to exclude Ben from this conversation. "Just don't."

"Like what?"

"Like you're thinking, 'Poor, Mel, another potential mistake, another bomb.' That look."

At least Reggie had the decency not to try to deny it. "Okay, I admit it, I was just hoping...well, you and Dennis, you're..."

"Dennis and I are just fine."

"Are you sure?"

"Good, great, terrific. Is that enough for you?"

"Of course it is. All I want is for you to be happy."

"Hey, you two. We need to get going," Ben said.

"Okay," Reggie agreed. Then, catching Melanie in a hug, whispered in her ear, "Who would have thought you'd get it all together and find out Mr. Perfect is perfect for you?"

"Yeah, who would have thought?" Melanie breathed as Reggie stepped back and turned to Ben and her son.

"Okay, guys, we're out of here. Let's blow this pop stand." She took Mikey by one hand and Ben caught the other. "We'll see you and Dennis at Mom and Dad's," she said to Melanie as they headed for the door.

"See you there." Melanie followed them to the door and let them out.

With a wave, she watched as they got into Ben's car at the curb, then she pulled down the door shade and locked up. She crossed the room, got her purse from a cabinet in the back storage room, pushed the wallet into it and grabbed her short corduroy jacket. Without a backward glance, she left the shop to go to the Reef Hotel.

SAM WAS ANNOYED and angry and impatient and frustrated as he rode down on the elevator to the lobby. He'd left messages for Angela on her voice mail, but none had been answered in the past three hours.

He'd used the time to try to figure out just where he was going to go with the sudden news of a brother; how he was going to contact the man who was his father. The only thing he knew clearly now was that nothing was over. Nothing was finished. Not with Dennis, or his father, or with Melanie. He wouldn't let it be over until he decided it was over.

But the first thing he had to do was find his wallet. There weren't many things in this life that were important to him, but there was something in his wallet that he didn't want to lose, that he couldn't replace.

He stepped out of the elevator into the cavernous lobby with its thirty-foot ceilings, crystal chandeliers and elaborate antique furnishings. It was as impressive as any hotel lobby could be and made even more so by the twenty-foot-tall Christmas tree that dominated the center of the marble-floored area.

Sam was a bit startled that the sight of the Christmas tree brought back the image of Melanie talking about having eight brothers and sisters and them celebrating Christmas. The woman had a sneaky way of coming to mind at the oddest times and staying there. He turned to start for the side entrance and valet service, but knew that the woman could do more than just pop into his mind without warning.

She could materialize, too.

Unless he was imagining it, she was standing at the concierge's desk, bundled up in a white corduroy jacket, speaking intently to the person behind the counter. The sudden sighting stopped him in his tracks for a minute. While he'd been thinking about her upstairs, he'd almost convinced himself that his response to her at the beach house had been an aberration. That it had been a product of the surprising kiss and their isolation and setting.

But that thought died instantly. It wasn't the case at all. Just the sight of her touched him on so many levels he could barely breathe. In that moment he could have hated his newly discovered brother. Damn Dennis Benning. He had everything, even her. That thought started him in her direction. There was no ring, no engagement, and as far as Sam was concerned, Dennis wasn't going to get Melanie Clark without a fight.

As he neared where she stood talking to the concierge, he saw his wallet in her hand resting on the marble desktop. She had his wallet. Taking a tight breath, he went closer, hoping that his voice and expression were as neutral as possible. There was no way he wanted her to look at him and know that his thoughts were heading straight to the bedroom with her, not yet. He'd never been an actor, but suddenly he hoped that years being around actors had somehow rubbed off on him.

He came within a few feet of her, inordinately aware of the curve of her slender hips in the dark slacks, of the overhead crystal light catching at the highlights in her hair and her slender fingers holding his wallet. He caught a suggestion of the sensual floral fragrance that he knew clung to her. He remembered it from the kiss, when she'd been so tightly in his arms.

He watched her for a long moment, just enjoying the sight of her within arm's length before he finally said, "Hello, there."

She turned, and for a moment she just stared at him, those incredible amber eyes widening with surprise. Then she drew the wallet to her middle and pressed it there with both hands.

"Oh, it's you," she breathed.

"Just me." He found a smile that came with ease around this woman. "And just you. But try to control yourself this time. This hotel is pretty damned conservative."

She blushed and he was fascinated by the way she lowered her lashes just a bit. "Oh, for Pete's sake," she muttered.

He held up one hand and clicked his tongue. "Please, no strong language. Now, what are you doing around here?"

Her tongue touched her full bottom lip and his body responded eagerly to the vision. So eagerly that he shifted and cut it off as soon as it began. "Your wallet," she murmured as she held it out to him.

"Where did you find it?" he asked as he took it from her. Even though he made no direct contact, he felt the heat of her touch lingering in the leather.

"On the ground by the gate at the beach house." When he flipped it open, she said quickly, "Oh, everything's still there. It just sort of got dropped and…well, I put everything back in it."

He saw the picture nestled behind the bills and didn't look any farther. When he glanced back at Melanie, there was still a touch of color in her cheeks, and the overhead light exposing a pulse beating at the hollow of her throat. The movement fluttered quickly, almost a match for his own heartbeat.

"Thank you," he said. "I really appreciate this."

"I thought you'd need it."

"An honest woman," he murmured with a slight smile. "I like that."

She shrugged, an endearing gesture that caught his breath in his chest. "Well, now that you have it, I'll be going."

He could feel her need to bolt, to run for some reason, and he didn't want her to go, not yet. Whatever quirk of Fate had brought her here had answered his wishes, and he wasn't going to let it end this easily. If she was here, she wasn't with Dennis. His chest tightened at the thought of her being with Dennis, and he found himself talking quickly.

"Miss Clark, let me buy you a drink. That's the least I can do after you going out of your way to bring my wallet back to me."

"I don't need a reward for doing the right thing," she said.

"But wouldn't you like one?" He caught the suggestion of a smile at the corners of her full mouth, and he wondered what he'd have to do or say to have the expression fully realized. He knew that he wanted to be there when it happened, and to be the reason for the smile. "How about a hot toddy at the bar?"

She tipped her head slightly to one side, her lashes sweeping lower on her eyes, considering him intently. "You know, I've heard about hot toddies, but I've never known what they were."

"I don't know, either, but they always sound good." He was thankful she hadn't taken off, but the longer she stayed, the more he could feel his body responding to her closeness. A pleasure and a pain, both at the same time.

"I don't think so. I'm not much of a drinker," she said.

"Then how about some soda or hot chocolate?"

"Thanks, but no thanks."

"No vices at all?"

"I have to admit that I'm more or less a caffeine addict."

"Okay, how about some cappuccino or espresso?"

"I really appreciate the offer, but I can't. I've got plans and if I don't get going, I'll be late."

He wasn't going to beg. "Sure, plans, I understand. I guess I'll have to owe you one. I'm going to be around here for a while, so just let me know when you want me to pay you back."

She hesitated, then said something that really took him off guard. "If you're set on paying me back, there *is* one thing you can do for me."

"Really? What can I do?"

"Let Dennis have the beach house."

He didn't know what he'd expected, but it wasn't that.

"What?"

"It's important to him," she said.

From somewhere he felt anger surfacing. The man who had all the money he wanted, all the family prestige he could use, who'd had a father all of his life, and now had this woman, was using her to get a house. It didn't sit well with Sam at all. "Is that why you brought my wallet back here, to talk me into letting Benning have the beach house?" he asked, anger fringing his words.

"No, of course not. You said you owed me and I thought I'd ask. That's all. Forget it."

"Give me one good reason why I should let him have it."

"You said you owed me."

"That's between you and me. It's got nothing to do with Benning."

She crossed her arms at her chest, a defensive move that wasn't lost on him. "Well, the house is important to him and he's important to me."

"It's important to me, too."

"But—"

"Can I tell you a basic truth about me?"

"Could I stop you?"

He let that pass. "I usually get what I want if it's really important to me."

Melanie looked up at Sam, the overhead light vaguely

shadowing his eyes, but taking away none of the intensity she could feel in his gaze. Nervously, she touched her tongue to her lips, and knew that this man probably got "who" he wanted, too. "Why is that house so important to you?" she asked, her voice sounding just a bit weak in her own ears.

"Why's it so important to Benning?"

Ever since she'd turned and seen him standing there, looking cool and casual in jeans and a denim jacket, the light catching at the gold in his hair, she'd felt on edge. Now she felt positively frayed. She'd just wanted to get in and out and never see him again. But now he was no more than two feet from her, challenging her on every level as they talked. "I hate that," she muttered.

"What?"

"Calling people by their last names."

"Okay, why is it so important to Dennis...or do you call him Denny or Den?"

She ignored that sarcasm, too. "Because he wants to move, and he found it, and it's perfect for him."

"And it's not perfect for me?"

"I don't know you. I know Dennis."

His eyes narrowed. "Have a drink with me and get to know me," he murmured.

That jarred her. Getting to know him. That was one thing she didn't want to do. "I told you—"

"I know, you've got plans. And you know Dennis."

She had no idea where his confrontational attitude came from, but it was getting stronger all the time and she knew she should just shut up and walk away.

"Mr. Harrison, forget I said anything about anything. Now, I have to go."

"Sure. Thanks for bringing my wallet, and tell Dennis that the house will go to the better man, just the way most things do in this life.''

She could feel a resentment in Sam when he talked about Dennis that made no sense. She reached for her purse on the counter, slipped it on her shoulder, then pushed her hand into it to find her keys. ''I'll let him know,'' she muttered as she rummaged in her purse.

He studied her for a long moment, then nodded slightly. ''Thanks again.''

''You're very welcome,'' she said as she tugged her purse off her shoulder and opened it to peer inside. She couldn't see her keys. She'd wanted to make a quick exit, but that wasn't going to happen. ''Oh, shoot,'' she muttered.

''That sounds like there's a problem.''

She glanced up at Sam, thankful he wasn't any closer to her with that kind of smile on his face. ''Actually, there is a problem. My keys.'' She turned and, on a clear spot on the concierge's desk, upended her purse. Everything tumbled out.

Her wallet landed with a thud, followed by a flutter of papers, a little calculator, packets of flavored instant coffee, a lipstick she seldom used, receipts for gas and groceries, and a small address book. But no keys.

''Any kitchen sinks in there?'' she heard Sam murmur, so close to her left side that she could have sworn she felt the vibration of his voice against her shoulder. A strange sensation ran along her spine as she reached inside the purse again without looking behind her. It was empty.

It took her off guard when Sam reached around her and picked up a loose photograph that had fallen to one side, a picture of her family around the Christmas tree last year. It was the first year Ben and Mikey had been with them.

"Whew, you weren't kidding about a big family, were you? You can barely see the tree for all of them."

She quickly stuffed the address book, receipts and lipstick into her purse without looking to her left at all. "Eight brothers and sisters and all their partners. It just keeps expanding."

"Did someone get your family wet?"

She turned to him, almost hitting her arm on his shoulder as he stepped back, the picture still in his hand. "What are you talking about?"

He looked at her over the picture. "You know that movie where the dad gets his kid a cute little furry pet from a store in Chinatown. But he's given the warning never to get it wet. Then, of course, since it's a movie, the kid gets it wet and it starts multiplying and multiplying, and no one can stop it. Or maybe the warning was about feeding them after midnight. I don't remember, but the outcome was the same. Millions of furry little things taking over the world."

Despite everything, Melanie could hardly contain a bubble of laughter that rose precariously close to the surface. Quickly, she reached for the picture and pushed it into her purse. "You're saying my family looks like gremlins?"

"Not at all. They're a very nice-looking...group. I was just referring to the multiplying part."

"Trust me, my parents planned it that way. No water was involved or eating after midnight...that I know of."

His smile was as quick and brilliant as summer lightning in the dead of night. "Kinky. Water and food after midnight," he murmured, the smile deepening to something suggestive and disturbing.

The jolt in her that that smile produced, made her turn self-protectively back to her purse on the marble desktop. "People always think big families are strange," she muttered. "They always make jokes about rabbits...or furry things, and think that every kid was there by accident. Not many people are comfortable with big families. Dennis sure wasn't at first, that's for sure."

As she grabbed up the coffee packets, papers and calculator, and put them back into her purse, she realized she was babbling, but her nerves were shot. Being this close to Sam was making things much worse. "I told you before that he's an only child and he didn't understand about big families. And his parents...well, they think it's absolutely pagan to have more than one child."

"His parents?"

Finally tucking her wallet into her purse, she turned to Sam, infinitely relieved that he'd moved back just a bit. "They seem to be of the opinion that one has a perfect child, singular, and that's it." She wasn't going to tell this man all about Reggie and Ben and Mikey. "The point is, they aren't people who like confusion or discord or...children, for that matter."

He frowned at her, making the smile a thing of the past so perfectly that she wondered if it had ever been. "They sound like real winners," he muttered. "How do you deal with them?"

"I don't. I mean, I haven't. I haven't ever met them." She looped her purse over her shoulder and would have left to see if her keys were in the car if Sam hadn't effectively been blocking her exit with his body. A body she didn't want to have any more contact with at all, so she didn't move.

"You've never met them? I thought you and Dennis...that you were together?"

"We are. I just haven't had a chance to get together with them yet. But I will...soon." She glanced at her watch. "Oh, great, now I'm really late."

"Ma'am, is there something wrong?"

She was startled by the concierge. She'd actually forgotten anyone was there but Sam. "I can't find my keys." She looked at him. "Did you see any keys lying around here? They're on a ring with a large brass *M* on it."

"No, ma'am, I'm sorry. I haven't seen them."

She reached into her pocket, took out one of her business cards, and wrote her mother's phone number on the back of it before handing it to the man. "If anyone finds them, could you call me at this number tonight, then the one on the front after that to let me know?"

"Yes, ma'am, of course."

She turned back to Sam. "I just hope I left them in the car and didn't lock the door."

Sam moved to one side and she thought he was going to finally let her go, breaking this off so she could breathe without this tightness in her middle. But that was too much to hope for. Instead he said, "I need some fresh air. I'll walk you out."

The man was like a magnet, not about to let go. "Sure," she murmured, and started for the doors, not having to look to her left to know that Sam was right there with her, step for step. She could sense him at her side, and even though he didn't touch her, she found herself trying to move a bit farther from him as they stepped through the open entry doors.

A day that had been misty and damp had turned cold, the mists had changed to a very light rain. She headed for the side parking area beyond the valet parking service. Sam was right there at her side as she stepped off the curb onto the blacktop.

She wended her way through the first parking area and into the second one before Sam spoke again. "Where did you park? In Los Angeles?"

"In the next section over. That's the closest I could get."

"That's what valet service is for," he murmured.

"If you've got the money," she said as she kept walking. "I wasn't about to pay for that when I was just running in to leave your wallet, then leave. The attendant wouldn't let me park my car there, so I found a parking spot. I think he knew very well that I didn't belong at a place like this."

"Why not?"

She cast him a slanting look. "I certainly don't look like the kind of person who would carry over a thousand dollars in my wallet."

He was closer now, so close she could almost feel his body heat brushing her hand as she walked. "Well, you'll soon be very welcome here, won't you?"

"Why?" she asked as she spotted her car.

"You marry Benn—Dennis, and you'll be part of that monied crowd. Hell, you'll be the toast of that monied crowd. You'll either be lucky or damned by being a Benning."

Chapter Six

"Lucky or damned?" Melanie frowned at Sam, the light rain darkening his hair and the shoulders of his denim jacket. "What are you talking about?"

Sam shrugged. "When you marry Dennis, you'll be a Benning, part of *the* family in this town. Either you'll be right up there enjoying all the perks, or you'll go crazy after a while and want the hell out of there."

She wiped at her face, at the rain that was chilly against her skin. His words shocked her. "Who do you think you are?"

"Hey, don't attack the messenger because you don't like the message. I'm just giving an opinion about your possible marriage to Dennis."

Marriage? She tried to see herself as a Benning, but couldn't. Then again, Dennis wasn't actually a Benning anymore, either, except in name. "Then you really don't know what you're talking about. Dennis isn't like that. He's not a snob. He's the fairest, nicest person you'd ever want to meet, and he works hard running his own business."

"A business his father gave him?"

"No, of course not." She was one aisle away from her car now and headed for it without looking at Sam.

"He's worked hard to get where he is and he's done it all on his own."

"What business?"

"His own law firm, with a growing clientele, and a good life."

"He sounds like a real gem," Sam murmured.

As she got to her old compact, she stopped at the passenger door and turned to Sam. The lights in the parking area drained all color from the night, and Sam was a man of blacks and whites. Stark and strong. Etched clearly, yet with his eyes lost in the blackness. A dangerous man. Very dangerous. "Dennis is wonderful," she said, and turned to try the door. It was locked.

She bent and cupped her hands on the closed window to look inside, but there were no keys in the ignition or on the seats. "Oh, great." She straightened. "They aren't there."

"You don't have an extra set hidden somewhere on the outside of the car?"

She looked at Sam. "I only had one key left. I've lost a few here and there, and I kept meaning to get duplicates made, but I've been so busy with my business and everything, I didn't do it."

"Then you've got two choices."

"What are they?"

"You can call a locksmith to come out, open it, and make a new key for you."

"What's the second choice?"

"I can break into the car and hot-wire it for you. Dubious talents carried over from my misspent youth."

"A talent for breaking and entering and hot-wiring?" she asked.

"Part of the package of black leather jackets, rolling

my own cigarettes, and not having a car. So I sort of borrowed them, and since the keys weren't readily available, the logical thing was to learn how to hot-wire them.''

"Rolling your own cigarettes and stealing cars?"

"The smoking was a six-month period in my senior year of high school, before I came to my senses and decided that my body was trying to tell me something when I coughed until I almost passed out. And I never stole a car, I borrowed it and only kept it as long as I needed it.''

"Semantics."

"Maybe, but I'll tell you that I held the record on the East Coast—ten seconds flat back then, for getting into a car and getting it started. Do you want me to demonstrate on your car?''

She held up one hand. "No. No. No. I'll take your word for it. I've done enough impetuous things in my life, so I think I'll go the traditional route and call a locksmith.''

"It's your choice."

"Definitely the legal way with the locksmith."

"Okay, then let's go back to the hotel and give him a call.''

Melanie started the trek back, her hair clinging to her skin, and the chilly breeze getting more brisk. She stared ahead of her at the multistoried hotel, its Christmas lights draped elegantly along the lower lines of the building. But she couldn't ignore the man who stayed right beside her. Finally she blurted, "You were joking back there, weren't you?''

"About what?"

"About stealing cars?"

"I told you, I *borrowed* them, and actually, hot-wiring has been a plus from time to time in my business.''

''What business is that, chop shops and robberies?''

A chuckle came, soft and sensuous through the rainy night, but she kept walking and never looked away from the hotel ahead of them. ''No, I'm an action coordinator.''

''And that's a euphemism for what?''

''I layout and set up stunts in movies and television.''

She could easily see him leaping from windows and diving off tall bridges. ''What are you doing in Santa Barbara? This isn't Hollywood.''

''It's trying to be Hollywood north, courting production companies, hoping to get business up here. An independent company I've worked with off and on came up here for a production they're involved with. It's cheaper and it's different, and the city practically bribed them to seal the deal for an action/adventure shoot. So, this is where I have to work.''

''You actually do stunts?''

The chuckle was louder this time. ''Do I *look* insane?''

She didn't look at him, but kept going, not about to say what he looked like to her at all. ''Then what do you do?''

''I develop them, lay them out, work out the details, guide them through it, and mesh it with the rest of the action in the movie. I'm like a dance choreographer, but besides using people, I use cars and speeding trains and boats and explosions.''

The man had an edge, and none of this surprised her at all. ''It sounds dangerous.''

''It can be, but if you do it right, and get lucky, things usually go well.''

"And if you don't get lucky?"

"Then it's like anything else in life, you get a kick in the butt and hope you survive."

"You must get paid very well for what you do."

"Well enough."

"You can afford to stay at a place like this," she said as they approached the circular drive in front of the hotel. "It's the best hotel in the city, so why don't you just stay here while you're working in Santa Barbara?"

"A hotel is just a bunch of boxes. I can't do my business in a box. I need the beach house."

She glanced to her right, to his strong legs striding by hers, but kept her eyes from going higher. She was uncomfortable enough as it was with the man without really looking at him again. "Why?"

"I need the isolation and privacy because working out the stunts gets pretty noisy at times, and it takes a lot of space. The sand's ideal for practicing falls and working out logistics." He took a harsh breath. "I also just plain like it there. I like the ocean. I always have, and I've been away from it too long. All I've seen for the past six months is a very old river, crowded by a huge city that's swarming with people. I'm ready to take a break for a while before heading back to the real world."

"What old river?" she asked as they neared the entrance again.

"The Seine."

She stopped under the ornate overhang that protected the entryway to the hotel. "The Seine, as in Paris, France? That river?"

He skimmed his hand over his damp hair, spiking it a bit by the action, then he pushed his hands into the pockets of his worn jacket. "That's the one."

"You were in France?"

"Unless there's another River Seine."

"Of course there isn't. But then again, you couldn't prove it by me. I've never been outside of this country. Oh, I've been to Tijuana, but that doesn't count, I don't think."

"Why not?"

"You can drive to it."

"So, if you can drive somewhere, it's not real traveling? That rules out a lot of places."

"I meant, you take the Concorde to Paris, but you can't take it to San Francisco."

"You've got a point there." He rocked forward on the balls of his feet slightly, narrowing that protective buffer between them. "Actually, I think that traveling to Europe is overrated."

"Easy for you to say. You've been there, done that."

"It gets old. And you find yourself just waiting until you can go somewhere else."

"You mean, you get homesick?"

"No, not that. You just get the need to keep moving, to go someplace else, someplace new."

"How does your family feel about moving around like that?"

"That's not a problem."

"They travel with you?"

"No, there is no family."

Melanie remembered the woman's picture in his wallet. The woman with the beautiful eyes. "There isn't anyone?"

"No."

That was all he said. A single word. No elaboration. Dammit, she didn't want to know anything about this man anyway, or about the woman with the laughing eyes. But for some reason she didn't understand, she kept going down a road she knew she shouldn't be on. "Just like that, no?"

"What do you want to know? If I'm married? I'm not. Never have been, and probably won't ever be."

"Why not?"

"Now that's something only my analyst, if I had an analyst, could answer. I guess the easy answer is, I don't want to be married. I'm sure as hell not good at sticking around."

Robert had been married, but said he didn't feel married. Sam and Robert blurred together, and she withdrew more from the feelings the man could stir in her. "That's more than I needed to know," she murmured.

"I thought you wanted to know."

"You were wrong," she lied, and wished it was true.

"My mother used to always say I was painfully honest. She seemed to think that wasn't an entirely desirable trait."

"Sounds as if she's a smart lady," Melanie said.

"She was." His expression tightened perceptibly. "She passed away last year."

"Oh, I'm sorry."

It startled her when he reached out and gently touched her chin with the tip of his finger. The first real skin-on-skin contact she'd had with him since the kiss, and it set off alarms in her. Just a fleeting touch, and she felt her breathing stop. Instinctively she drew back from it. "Don't be. As you said, you don't know me," he said.

"I just meant—"

"I've told you a hell of a lot more than you ever wanted to know, and you're expected somewhere. You're late and you need to get a locksmith out here."

She looked at him, and wondered if there was such a thing as an honest Robert? A man who was in for the short haul and told you right up front. That would be a novelty to her. But at least she knew where she was going with Sam. And that was nowhere. She turned away from him and headed for the entrance. "Yes, I do."

Melanie went into the lobby and spotted the pay phones by the elevators, off to the left. She crossed to them, called her automobile club and was promised that a locksmith would be out to help her in about two hours or less. *Great.* Tonight was going from bad to worse rapidly. She told them where her car was parked, then hung up.

She looked up and Sam was there, leaning against the wall, just watching her. "Well?"

"They're coming out, but they can't be here for at least two hours." She gripped her purse to her side. "I'll have to get a taxi, I guess."

"That won't work. The taxi line out front was totally empty when we came in. You might have quite a wait for one."

"Oh, shoot." She sighed as she glanced at the huge clock suspended over the reception desk. "It's already nine o'clock."

He stood straighter. "I'll take you where you need to go."

"Oh, no, I couldn't—"

"Of course you could. I'm here with a car, and I've got absolutely nothing to do right now. I'd like to get out of this box for a while, as fancy as it is, and you're late."

She wasn't sure at all about being in a car with him. "But you must have things to do."

"Nothing at all."

The man seemed bigger than life out in the open, but in a closed car.... Everything about him, every reaction she had to him, was intense and instantaneous, and made her feel totally out of control. She hated it. "I could call someone to come and get me."

"Why?"

"Why not?"

"I'm here with a car. Why get someone else out in this weather when you don't have to?"

She knew how foolish it would sound to say she'd wait for a taxi that might never come, or wait here for two hours for the locksmith to arrive, or call someone all the way down here to pick her up when he was right here with his car. She swallowed and bit back everything else she wanted to say to protest and did the sensible thing. "Okay, thank you." She could do this. "Just let me make another call." She *would* do this, and walk away.

Sam motioned to the phones. "Go right ahead and make your call." As he watched her dial the number, he congratulated himself that he'd managed to prolong this time together without too much effort. He'd gotten his wish—more time with her—and he wanted that. But he also had to admit that what she'd said about Dennis and the Bennings had piqued his curiosity.

They didn't like kids. They were a power to be reckoned with. She'd never met them. That seemed odd in itself. Just about as odd as him volunteering to deliver her to Dennis. That was the downside of driving her in his car. But he'd take it, because he'd have her all to himself during the drive. Not a bad trade-off.

"Hi, there. It's me," he heard her say into the phone. "I'm running late, and I knew you'd be worried."

She touched the polished face of the phone with the tips of her slender fingers and smiled. Something in him resented that smile coming so easily for, he assumed, the man on the other end of the line. "I can't wait to do the tree, but I lost my keys and...never mind, it doesn't matter. I'll get there as soon as I can."

She nodded and when she spoke again Sam's twinge of resentment was gone, pushed aside by jealousy. "I love you, too. See you soon."

When she hung up and turned those huge eyes on him, he knew that jealousy was very real, jealousy that his brother had this woman caring about him.

"Ready to go?" he asked a bit abruptly.

"Yes."

She moved closer to him, and for a split second it seemed as if she was going to walk into his arms, that he was going to feel her against him again, and inhale her scent. But that madness evaporated when she walked right past him to head for the exit. He followed her, saying, "We need to go out the side door."

Without warning, she changed direction, cutting right in front of Sam. And the impact was there before he could stop it. He reached out for her, keeping her from tumbling to one side by pulling her against him. And the madness was reality.

Every spot her body touched his felt as if it seared him. Her scent permeated his being. Then she was looking up at him. "Oh, I'm sorry," she gasped. She was so close, he could literally feel the warmth of her breath caress his face.

That moment froze in time, its effect on him as potent as the moment she'd kissed him on the deck at the house. But this time he saw every detail of her face, the way her lips were slightly parted, her delicate nostrils flaring with each rapid breath she took, the way her eyebrows arched, those golden eyes a man could get lost in.

The busy lobby might not have existed. All there was, was Melanie, and the feel of her in his arms. Then it was gone as suddenly as it had happened. She pushed back, both hands flat on his chest, giving her leverage, and leaving him feeling isolated in a way that clutched his chest. He made himself release her, pulling his hands away to push them behind his back so he wouldn't reach out for her again. Touching her was something he wanted to do so badly that he ached from the need.

"Valet parking, right?" she asked.

He didn't miss the way she moved even farther from him. "Yes," he murmured.

Without another word she turned and headed for the side exit. He watched her for a long moment, then followed through the doors and out into the chill and dampness of the night. He narrowed his eyes, trying to lessen the impact of her image on him as he stopped beside her under the shelter of the portico.

She glanced to the main entrance, her purse clutched to her middle. "Look, there's an empty taxi."

Before he knew it, she was turning toward the main entrance. She had barely started off when the doorman waved to it and blew his whistle to summon the cab. Melanie stopped as the taxi pulled up in front and a tall, red-haired woman hurried out of the hotel and got inside.

"Too late," Sam drawled.

Melanie walked back to where he stood on the curb. "Shoot," she muttered.

"I bet you say 'fudge' and 'darn it,' too."

She looked at him blankly for a moment, then a smile flickered at the corners of her mouth. "That's only when I get really mad."

The valet came up to them, and Sam handed him his claim check. As the man jogged off into the light rain, Sam looked at Melanie and knew that he wanted to touch her again. But the only thing he could think to do was to hold out his hand. "Let's make a deal. You give me plenty of warning before you get *that* mad, okay?"

She acted as if he hadn't offered her his hand to shake, not even looking at it as she kept her grip on her purse. "Sure, of course," she said, then turned to look out at the parking area.

The coldness of the night seemed to be everywhere as he withdrew his hand, and he hated it. The rain fell in a steady pattern, and there was at least two feet of space between him and Melanie. But it felt like miles. Miles that he wasn't at all sure how to erase.

"I thought it never rained in Southern California," he commented just for something to say to fill a growing void.

"Oh, it rains, okay. Santa Barbara has its floods and its droughts and its fires and its storms and its mudslides and its earthquakes."

He didn't doubt the earthquake part. This woman could cause an earthquake for him just with her touch. "A regular disaster area," he said as the car pulled up in front of them.

The attendant jumped out and when Sam and Melanie got inside with the doors shut, it felt as if the world was gone. All that remained was Melanie near him, and the fact that for a few more minutes, she was here with him. Sam put the car in gear and drove off into the misty night.

ANGELINA WAS SATISFIED as she watched Sam and Melanie drive off. Fireworks, skyrockets, the earth moving—the connection between the two of them was obviously potent. Now if she could get Melanie past that fear of making another mistake because of her emotions, and get Sam the chance to be with her longer, she'd be home free.

She turned from the retreating car and quickly materialized in the lobby. Crossing to the concierge's station, she dropped the key ring with its brass *M* on the marble desktop and smiled at the man standing there.

"I found these in the door of a car in the parking lot. I thought the owner might have asked—"

"Oh, yes, ma'am. She was here just a few minutes ago. In fact—" He looked out the doors. "She just left." He reached for a business card on the desk. "I'll get in touch with her and let her know her keys are here."

"Good, you do that," Angelina said, then walked around the corner out of sight. With a slight nod of her head, she was off to catch up with Sam and Melanie.

Sam drove silently, while Melanie tried to press herself into the corner of the passenger door. Sam wanted her. Angelina could feel his need, but she could also feel Melanie's fear. If Sam reached out in any way right now, Melanie would probably jump out of the car. Humans were such a perverse lot. They couldn't see the logic of what was right in front of them. They thought they understood life and what they needed, but they didn't have a clue.

Clueless in Santa Barbara, Angelina thought as the

silence between Melanie and Sam stretched uncomfortably and became almost painful. Humans. Couldn't they even help themselves a bit? Even if they just talked, it would be an improvement. She closed her eyes for a moment and wondered why there wasn't a "talking pill" in her little bag of tricks.

"Excellent idea," Miss Victoria said from somewhere in Angelina's mind. "Excellent, indeed."

MELANIE COULD BARELY breathe in the car. *Stupid, stupid, stupid.* She closed her eyes tightly, but opened them quickly when she had a rushing memory of Sam's hands keeping her from tumbling when they'd collided in the lobby. Talk about the old Melanie. An accidental contact and her whole being had jumped to attention, ready to run headlong into danger.

She took a breath, reasoning if she could just get to her place without anything else happening she was home free. No talking, no interaction. That was the safest way to handle this situation.

But even as she made the plan in her mind, she found herself with the oddest urge to talk to the man. She had no idea what she wanted to talk about, but she had a real need to hear voices and break the strained silence in the car.

"It's a terrible night, isn't it?" she heard herself say.

"It's damp, all right," Sam murmured.

Okay, the weather was a safe topic. She could handle that. "I wonder if it's going to keep raining." She sounded so inane, but couldn't stop. "I personally love rain, when you're inside, dry and comfortable." The next thing she knew, she'd be talking about the barometer, but she could feel his eyes on her and his words stopped her cold.

"If you're in bed, making love, rain makes great atmosphere."

Wrong, wrong, wrong. With this man, there wasn't even any safety in talking about the weather.

Chapter Seven

Melanie stared at Sam for a long strained moment while she tried to think of something to say. But before she could think of anything, Sam spoke again. "Isn't that what you had in mind? The rain beating on the windows, a huge bed, a fire in the hearth?"

"No, I didn't," Melanie muttered, not about to admit that the images he painted were making her heart speed up.

"Right?" he asked.

"What?"

"Do I go right here?"

She gripped the purse on her lap tightly and mumbled, "Yes, right." She stared straight ahead into the light rain, not even trusting herself to talk about directions.

Words chased through her mind, words on top of words, words that she'd love to say to him. Telling him he was smug and suggestive and he was doing it deliberately, but something in her knew that she'd never win a battle of words with this man.

Insanely, she wondered if she touched her tongue to her lips, would she still taste Sam there even after all these hours? She knew it was crazy, but she deliberately bit her lip and kept her eyes ahead of her.

"How long have you known Dennis Benning?" Sam asked abruptly as they climbed into the hills.

His voice startled her, and she had to take a deep breath before she could manage to respond with, "A year and a half or so."

"You've been dating that long?"

She tried as hard as she could to focus on Dennis, so it was upsetting when she could barely retrieve a mental image of his face. "No. He dated my older sister last year for a while, until she met her husband. I never thought Reggie and Dennis fit together. Actually, I used to call Dennis 'Mr. Perfect.'"

His wry chuckle only made her nerves tighten more. "Mr. Perfect? Why doesn't that sound complimentary?"

"Because at the time, it wasn't. He was so uptight and driven to be a Benning, and he didn't want kids. I don't think he even liked kids. Shoot, just thinking about all of us used to make him run for cover."

"You think he's changed?"

"Yes, and so have I."

"How has Melanie Clark changed?"

Her grip on her purse tightened so, her fingers tingled. She actually formed the words to tell him she didn't want to talk about herself at all, but when she opened her mouth, words she hadn't thought of saying to Sam tumbled out. "I used to be flaky. I was going from job to job whenever the spirit moved me. I didn't have a clue what I wanted to do with my life, and I made horrible choices."

"Such as?" he asked as he drove up the coast.

There was no way she wanted to talk about the Roberts in her life with this man. So she fudged a bit and changed direction. "I picketed a slaughterhouse once. I was in a sit-in protest for three days, until the police came in and arrested the whole lot of us."

"You aren't the sort who throws paint on fur coats, are you?"

"I would have, back then, probably. Anything I felt strongly about, I got involved in. I was a vegetarian. I still am, actually. I didn't, and still don't, eat any real meat, just some fish and chicken now and then."

"Fish and chicken aren't real meat?"

"Well, certainly not like beef or veal or lamb. There's no inhumane slaughtering process involved."

"I guess that's a matter of opinion, especially if you happen to be a fish or a chicken," he murmured. "So, you stood up for your beliefs. Is that flaky?"

"I could have done it differently. I wouldn't call it brilliant to get arrested and sit in jail for twenty-four hours. I went to the protest on a whim. I jumped in with both feet, or rather, sat in, and did it because it was exciting and different."

"That's bad?"

"It's not smart. I should have been more calm and rational about it."

"Let me get this straight. Now you're building a dull life with Dennis?"

She should have known better than to tell him anything, but that didn't stop her defending herself and defending Dennis. "I never said dull. I used the words *smart* and *rational*. Dennis is very smart and rational."

"Not a touch of flakiness?" he murmured.

She had to bite her lip hard to keep from screaming. The man never quit, and never stopped nudging at her with his words. "None. Turn left here."

As he made the turn, he asked, "So how did you go about achieving this degree of unflakiness?"

She could hear the tinge of humor in his tone. "I'm not trying to be funny. This is serious."

"Of course, and it's rational," he said. "So, now you're not flaky?"

"It's an ongoing process," she said, meaning to cut off the discussion right there. But she'd barely taken a breath before she started explaining again. She didn't understand any of this. "Right now, I'm in the process of buying my own business. The woman I worked for wanted to sell it. She and her husband retired to Florida, and I thought it was a good idea. I've even got a little house behind the store. So I'm working hard, especially now with the holidays. I think before I leap, and I consider everything and make smart choices."

"It sounds like you're trying to reinvent yourself."

That's exactly what she'd been doing until Sam had burst into her life and brought back the old over-the-top reactions. But this was just a minor glitch, a bump in the road. "I guess that's it."

"Has it been that hard for you? You sound exhausted from the effort."

"It's hard, but I've great role models, like my sister Reggie. She's changed her whole life and it's great."

"Is this a family endeavor? You don't like what you are, so you set about changing everything about yourselves?"

"No. Reggie didn't know she needed to change. She was so sure she wanted this antiseptic life, a quiet, uncluttered relationship. She thought Dennis was so perfect for her. But in the end, she got a very cluttered relationship. Dennis was out, and Ben was in, along with his little boy, Mikey. From what I heard, the Bennings almost had a seizure when they came face-to-face with Mikey. They are very conservative, very proper, very socially correct."

"They sound like cold fish," he said, his voice suddenly tight and clipped.

Melanie shifted in the seat and smoothed the leather of her purse with the tips of her fingers. "As I said, they're socially correct and upscale and rich, and they can be anything they want to be. Thank goodness, Dennis doesn't want all that."

"He doesn't?"

If she was going to be babbling like this with Sam, it made her feel stronger to talk about Dennis instead of herself or her family. "He loves his folks, but he's changed a lot since the time he met Reggie. Dennis and I sort of coincided with...oh, I guess you'd call it our moments of clarity. You know that moment in your life when you suddenly know exactly where you're going, what you need, and how you have to change to get it? Maybe like the moment when you decided not to hot-wire cars anymore."

"Who says I ever had that moment?" he murmured.

"Well, you don't go around hot-wiring..." She hesitated, then mumbled, "At least, you shouldn't."

"I don't, unless there are special circumstances. Tell me more about this moment of clarity."

She exhaled, grabbing at the image of Dennis and not of Sam as a teenager hot-wiring cars. "I told you Dennis and Reggie broke up, and I thought he was out of our sphere of existence. I'd made a very bad choice in that time." Remembering Robert really helped her put things in perspective. Robert the Creep. A result of acting on impulse. Yes, that put everything into perspective for her.

"You ate real meat?"

"I wish that was all it was."

"Oh, I see," he said softly.

She looked at him, at his blurred profile and was taken aback to find him glancing at her for a long moment. Then he turned his eyes back to the road ahead of them. "You see what?" she asked.

"A bad choice, as in Mr. Wrong?"

Damn him for guessing so accurately. "Yes. To make a very long, gruesome story short, I came to my senses, ran into Dennis again right after it happened, and he'd changed so much. He was…well, less driven to be a Benning and he was starting his own law firm, and he was so…so…solid and sure."

"Solid and sure are good?"

"Very good." She knew that sounded boring, but it was so familiar and so reassuring. "He's dependable and sweet and grounded."

"And that's what you're looking for in a man?"

"Yes, it is. Someone who's not afraid of commitment, who can say the word without breaking out in hives, and someone who's honest and upright."

"One out of three isn't bad," he said.

"Excuse me?"

"I'm honest. But I'd probably have a hell of a case of hives, and I have been known to borrow other people's cars. I guess I'm failing the test."

She didn't want to hold him up to any measure of suitability for her. That wasn't even a consideration. "It isn't a test."

"So you and Dennis are together now? You're both changed people, not a case of hives in sight, and he's got a yen for a beach house because he's homeless at the moment?"

"He has a house in the hills, a modern thing all done in black and white marble, in a very upscale, private, gated community."

"Don't tell me. His parents picked it out?"

"No, of course not, but they approved of it." She spotted their turn. "Left here," she said, then kept talking. "Now he's decided to make a change. He's loosening up, and the beach house is just what he had in mind." She felt on solid ground now, as if she could finally think clearly. "It's perfect for him."

"I agree the beach house is perfect. That's why I want it."

"As soon as your job's done, you're leaving, aren't you?"

"Absolutely."

"But Dennis has roots here. Go right." When he made the turn, she said, "He's lived most of his life in Santa Barbara."

"Oh, I get it. He should get it because he's part of a Santa Barbara dynasty?"

"Turn right here," she said. "Dennis is hardly part of a dynasty."

"A socially acceptable local family. Is that better?"

The tinge of sarcasm in his tone gave her even more focus and just a touch of anger. "I don't know why you have to be so sarcastic about Dennis and his family. You don't know them, and they're nothing to you."

"What I want to know is, why should I let Dennis have that house, when he has everything else he wants in life?"

"You don't know what he has in this life."

"It's pretty obvious what he has."

She chanced another look at Sam, and tried to keep her focus. "What's obvious?"

"Money, position, protective parents."

She could almost laugh at that. "Wrong. His parents are smothering parents, and the only position he has is attorney or lawyer, whatever you call it."

"And he's poor?"

"Of course not. But he's not rich. He doesn't take money from the Bennings."

"If you say so." She saw him flex his fingers on the steering wheel before he said, "It's obvious that he approves of this new person you've become."

"We get along just fine, thank you."

"I've got the feeling he wouldn't have gotten along with the old Melanie."

"*I* barely got along with her," she said in a low voice.

"Was she all that bad?"

Crazy and uncontrolled. "She needed to grow up and quit being so impetuous and so trusting and so…"

"Whew, Mr. Wrong was really Mr. Wrong, I take it?"

"More than once," she said with all honesty.

"You never said if you've been married."

"No, thank goodness."

"So 'commitment' isn't in *your* vocabulary, either, is it?"

"On the contrary, it's right there. It's important to me, very important to me. That's why Dennis is so important to me. I'm just thankful I never made mistakes as permanent as marriage." The last thing she wanted to do was to tell Sam all of her mistakes, and she forced herself to stop this ridiculous soul-baring. "Let's just leave it that that sort of trouble is in my past. It's over and done."

"The old Melanie sounds like fun to me. Living for

the moment, a bit wild and crazy. I'd say you were never dull...back then.''

And always stupid, she thought as she pushed closer to the door. The old Melanie would have plunged head-long into a relationship with a man like Sam without a backward glance. A man who wouldn't even be there the next time she turned around. The type of man who scared her now. ''You're not dull, are you?''

''God help me, I hope not. I tend to jump into things, go with the flow and see how things end up. Life's made to be lived.''

''With no rules, no restrictions?''

''The two ugly R-words,'' he muttered.

''But what if things go wrong, if you...''

''If I get hurt?''

''Or if you hurt others?''

''I wouldn't do that. I'm always up front about what's going on. And if I get hurt, that's life. I pick myself up and move on.''

''So you live life the way you want to live it and damn the consequences?''

''Everyone does up to a point, some more than oth-ers. People like the Bennings are experts at living life the way they want to without worrying about the con-sequences. You've obviously chosen to live life the way you think you should.'' Then he took her completely off guard. ''But the real question is, are you happy with what you've chosen?''

'''Happy'?'' she echoed. The word almost sounded foreign to her at that moment.

''Happy. As in 'Hey, hot damn, life's great and I'm doing exactly what I want to do. I'm having a terrific time, and I'm really alive.'''

She hadn't thought in those terms for so long she

wasn't quite sure what to say. "Sure, of course," she murmured. "I'm happy."

"Then it's right for you."

It was supposed to be right, so it *was* right. "What's right for you?"

He took a harsh breath before saying, "Several things."

"Like the beach house?"

"Yes. But it's not just a whim for me, like it is with Benning, who has this idea he wants to change his life so he's changing his location."

"That's not fair at all. Dennis has a right to do whatever he wants to do without you judging him."

"Of course he does. And he's got the money to put some muscle behind it, too."

"Well, you're not exactly poor."

"No, I'm not, but I'm not in the range of the Benning trust, either."

"That's hardly a consideration in this. It isn't as if Dennis is going to bribe the real estate agent or something."

He laughed out loud at that, a sharp sound that took her totally off guard. She almost smiled when he said, "Ah, the Benning mob, applying muscle to the deal, and they have their own lawyer."

"The Bennings would die if they heard you say that."

"I bet they'd die if they found out they could be in line to be grandparents to a brood of grandchildren."

"What?"

"I assume that you want a lot of kids when you're married. So do they have a clue that there's going to be a boom in the Benning population? Not just their one perfect child?"

That sobered her up right away. Children? Of course she wanted children, maybe lots of them, but the idea right then seemed off-kilter. "I told you I haven't even met them yet."

"Oh, yes, I remember. Dennis is hiding you from them."

"That's ridiculous. It just hasn't been the right time yet."

"Sure, of course."

The man could infuriate her as easily as he could stir her, and that made her feel very edgy. She looked out at the night, into the cold and dark, and wished that she didn't sense heat so close by in Sam. Thankfully, she saw the street that cut off of the main highway and up into the hills. "Turn here," she said. "Then go to the first stop sign, then left, two blocks down, another left, then the street is the third on the right. It's a short turn onto a dead end."

"Come again?" he asked.

"I'll tell you when to turn so you won't get lost."

"Another thing you should know about me is, I've got a great sense of direction. I never get lost."

Now that she was almost home, she felt as if she could breathe a bit better. This was almost over, and it wouldn't happen again. "I bet you're never wrong, either?"

"Actually, I thought I was wrong once, then I found out I was wrong. I wasn't wrong."

She laughed at that, a bit nervously, but welcomed the bit of humor to help things out. "I asked for that, didn't I?"

"Walked right into it," he murmured.

Sam drove up the road, the sound of Melanie's laughter still ringing in his ears. Dammit, he liked that sound.

He also liked that edge in her voice when she felt she was wronged in any way. And the way she got flustered when he teased her. He liked the scent of her in the car, shutting out the chill and dampness and the night outside.

The drive had gone better than he'd hoped after the initial silence, with her talking and giving him glimpses of herself that only added to his fascination with her. Also, getting a better idea of his brother, who was either a saint or boring as hell. Either way, Melanie stuck up for him, and seemed overly protective of him. Sam wouldn't have minded her being that way about him.

"Here," she said. "That's the street."

Sam turned where she pointed, but the neighborhood he saw through the rain-streaked windows wasn't anything like he'd imagined a Benning would live in. There was no gated entry Melanie had spoken about, and no upscale houses. From what he could see, there were rambling bungalows set on large lots and a narrow street lined with ancient sycamores and towering eucalyptus trees.

"All the way to the end," she said. "The house with the red lights all over it. Francine decided to do a red Christmas this year."

He saw the house, a hulking two-story with pitched eaves and dormers all outlined with red Christmas lights. Even the driveway was lined by looping strands of lights, and the trunks of the trees were wrapped with them. A red assault to the eye and the senses. "Francine?"

"My sister. She decided that she wanted to make a unified statement the way my brother did with his blue year. He even managed to cover the lawn with blue lights and it ended up looking like an airport runway."

"This is your house?"

"It's my family home." She sat forward as he pulled into the driveway. "And it looks like they're still out getting the Christmas tree."

"How can you tell?" he asked as he pulled up beside a spacious wrap-around porch and under the partial protection of one of the eucalyptus trees laced with red lights.

"If everyone was here, the curb would be lined and the driveway would be packed. But my mother's car's the only one here."

So that meant no Dennis, at least for now. "I thought you were going to Benning's house?"

"No, he's going to meet me here, so he either went with the others, or he's running late."

"Mr. Perfect is late again?" he asked as he stopped behind the sedan and let the car idle. "I thought he was never late?"

"I should have never told you that," she muttered.

He flipped the car into neutral and turned to Melanie. The red glow cast flickering shadows over her face, emphasizing the delicate hollows at her cheeks and throat. Dammit, she was beautiful, even with that touch of disapproval he could see in the set of her mouth. "Sorry, that just slipped out."

"You're the only man I know who says he's sorry but never sounds like he is." She reached for the door handle. "I need to get inside."

"Wait," he said, and when she turned back to him, he didn't have a clue what to say to her to keep her here with him.

"This tree thing, do you do it every year?" he asked to prolong the contact, not because he had any desire to know about Christmas trees.

"Yes. We have a friend who has a tree farm and he lets us have the pick of the crop. We go together, pick one out, cut it down, then drag it back here. It's a tradition, and the Clark family is very big on traditions for each and every holiday."

"What about on New Year's?"

"On New Year's we always have bacon, lettuce and tomato sandwiches along with ginger ale for the kids and champagne for the adults while we all watch the ball fall at Times Square at midnight."

"You all go to New York?"

She laughed at that, and he knew he could never hear her laughter too often. "No, of course not. We watch it on television. What do you do on New Year's Eve?"

He shrugged, the memories of past New Years fuzzy at best. He couldn't even remember where he'd been last New Year's or who he'd been with. It hadn't been worth remembering at all. So he told the truth in part. "It depends where I am and who I'm with."

"I guess that would make a difference," she murmured.

He looked at her, at the sweep of lashes as she studied him, and the way her hand worried the door handle. Oh, yes, that would make all the difference in the world if he was with her. He'd remember that. "You know, you had me fooled back there."

"Me?" she asked. "How?"

"The way you were talking about your past, about your wicked, wild ways, I thought you used to be the rebel, the one who went her own way and let the consequences be damned."

"I never meant—"

"Now I find out you're very old-fashioned and traditional, from tree cutting to BLT sandwiches on New

Year's Eve. The things you're still doing. I fail to see any big change in you.''

"It's more inside than outside."

"Oh, yes, your penchant for Mr. Wrongs."

"That's something else I wish I'd never told you," she sighed.

"Everyone makes bad choices from time to time," he observed. "That just means that you're human."

"Sure, and most humans should learn from them," she said. "It took me a while, but I finally got the idea."

He hated the idea of there being a procession of men in her life, men that hadn't known what they had with her. God, he barely knew her at all, yet he understood clearly that she was made to be loved. And every atom in his being wanted to know what it was like to make love with her.

"Why was the last Mr. Wrong so wrong?" he asked, to cut off those thoughts.

"I hate talking about this, and it's getting late."

"Humor me. Explain it to me."

She sighed heavily. "Okay, then I have to get inside. Robert was a stained glass window-maker, very talented, very bright. He came into my life like a bolt of lightning. I thought he lived at his studio, and that he was open and honest."

He could hear the tightness in her voice. "He wasn't Mr. Perfect?"

"He was perfectly wrong. He forgot to mention that he was married and there was a two-year-old son at home with his dutiful, trusting wife. Perfectly wrong."

"Then Dennis came along?"

"Yes, Dennis." He saw the softness of a smile touch her lips. "Now, thanks for the ride, but I—"

Without thinking, he moved, touching her shoulder,

and she seemed to freeze with one hand holding her purse and the other on the door handle.

He felt the dampness of the corduroy of her jacket and under it, she tensed. He definitely saw the smile disappear completely and he knew right then that there was no reason to be coy about any of this. Not when he knew when she got out of this car, she was gone. Unless he did something to change that.

"Don't go."

Chapter Eight

Melanie stared at him silently, the twinkling glow from the lights exposing the shock on her face. "I—I have to go," she stammered.

"Wait." Sam forced himself not slip his hand higher to cup the warmth of her throat against his palm. "I need to ask you something."

She shifted, breaking their contact. "What could you possibly ask me that you haven't already?"

"Come with me? Let's get out of here and go and find a nice private place where we can really talk."

The only sound in the car was the idling engine, the rain on the roof, and a soft, shuddering sigh from Melanie before she breathed, "Why?"

"I must be doing something wrong if you have to ask that after that kiss."

"The kiss was a mistake."

"Some mistake," he muttered.

"Well, just because it...it got a bit out of hand, that doesn't mean it was right or made any sense. Things happen, and they can seem...like more than they are, and you can get fooled and you can ruin what you already have."

"How do you even know what they are unless you're willing to find out?"

"I…" She exhaled, a soft, shuddering sound. "I thought you were Dennis. I really did. I'm sorry, but it was a terrible mistake."

"Why don't I believe that you're sorry?" he murmured.

"I am, believe it or not, and I can't go anywhere with you because of some misunderstanding."

He felt oddly isolated, almost as if he'd been set adrift, but he didn't have any idea what he was isolated from, or where he'd been pushed away from. Whatever was going on, it was a totally new experience and distinctly distasteful to him. "Don't you believe in Fate? In something beyond us, making things happen for a purpose?"

He heard her sigh, then say softly, "I guess so."

"Okay, we agree on that."

"But there's also coincidence and happenstance. That doesn't make it important or significant."

"Oh, doesn't it?" Whatever was happening with Melanie wasn't something he could pass off as unimportant or insignificant. "What if it's not all of that? What if it wasn't a mistake? What if it was part of a master plan to…" He groped for the word. "To change your life or my life? Period. What if it was an opportunity to find something we otherwise would have missed out on?"

"And what if it was what I said, a huge mistake? Dennis is coming soon, and I've got plans, and—"

"Oh, Dennis," he muttered.

"Yes, Dennis. You know that I'm seeing him, and that he's…he's…"

"Perfect? Yes, I've been told that repeatedly. Please,

don't go through that again." Enough was enough. "I can see where this is going, and believe me, I don't have any desire to be on anyone's list of Mr. Wrongs."

"Oh, for heaven's sake, you always take things wrong. You're the one who brought it up, not me, and I'm not good at explaining—"

He laughed, a rough, humorless sound that cut off her words. "Oh, you're very good at it. You're getting your life in order...a life with Dennis. I understand that. No problem. Sorry I asked."

She was motionless for a moment, and for a second he had the oddest feeling that she wasn't nearly as certain about her refusal as she wanted him to believe. Or she wanted herself to believe.

He realized how wrong he was when she said, "You're not sorry, but thanks for the ride," and opened the door.

Sam looked away from her as she got out, and stared at the rain streaking the windshield as he muttered, "You're damn right, I'm not sorry."

He didn't know if she heard him or not, but the door slammed shut and he watched as Melanie hurriedly cut across the glow of his headlights. He had that fleeting image of her: the mists of rain all around her, her purse clutched to her middle. He deliberately cut that vision short by looking down at his hands, which gripped the steering wheel so tightly he was a bit surprised that he hadn't snapped the cheap plastic.

That was that. She was gone, and any chance of anything more with her was gone, too. Dennis would show up, sooner or later, and she'd have her sane, sensible life so she could go on with the traditions for years to come. Bitterness rose in his throat. And she'd do all that with his brother. What couldn't be, couldn't be, and he'd never been one to brood about what life gave him.

He backed out onto the street and as he drove away from the house strung in red lights, suddenly understood what she'd been talking about earlier. That second of clarity, an experience that shook him to the core. He knew right then that this woman had brought to life a need in him that he'd never before experienced, but she wouldn't be the one to satisfy it. Maybe it never would be satisfied.

As he headed away from Melanie, he had the fleeting wish that whatever quirk of Fate had been at work to bring her into contact with him would somehow work again. Right then a clap of thunder rattled the car and lightning flashed across the heavens. But no giant hand pulled him backward, and no miracle zapped Melanie back into the car.

At that moment he decided he wasn't going to see Dennis Benning again, either father or son. Whatever had happened, it was over and done. This had been a glitch in time, a blip. And he wanted it put behind him as quickly as possible. He pressed the gas pedal and headed back to a life that until that afternoon had been enough for him. It would be again.

MELANIE RAN into an oddly quiet house. "Hello!" she called, and glanced into the living room. The huge space that ran the front of the house was cluttered with half emptied boxes of Christmas ornaments alongside furniture moved to accommodate the Christmas tree spot by the windows. But there was no scent of popcorn in the air, or even a wood fire in the empty stone fireplace on the far wall. "Hello! Hey, is anyone here?"

"Up here, Mel!" her mother called from somewhere

on the second floor. "I'm giving Mikey a bath. The others all left to get the Christmas tree over at Devlin's."

Melanie took off her jacket and hung it over the newel post at the foot of the staircase, then shook the clinging raindrops from her hair. "It's raining. They'll never be able to get one picked out and cut and bring it back tonight. It's already almost ten o'clock!"

"You know your dad. He says they can, so they went to get it about half an hour ago. Devlin left the gates open for them."

"Is Dennis with them?" she called.

"No, he hasn't shown up yet. Oh, there was a call for you about fifteen minutes ago, though. Someone from the Reef Hotel about your keys. The number's by the phone down there."

She crossed to the phone on a small table by the staircase. "What did they say?"

"That your keys were there, and that you should call and let him know when you'll be back to get them. His name was George Something-or-other."

"Thanks. I'll give him a call," she said as she glanced at the note and dialed the number.

When she got George on the phone, he promised that he'd keep them at the desk until midnight when his shift ended, then they'd be locked up in the safe until tomorrow morning at ten. She told him she'd be there before midnight, then hung up and tried to call Dennis at work. When it rang six times then flipped to his voice mail, she knew he was on his way and hung up. Right then a car pulled into the driveway and as she glanced out the steamy windows, she could see a single set of headlights glowing through rain that was coming down steadily now. Dennis was finally here.

"Mom, Dennis is here. I'll get him to drive me back to the hotel to get my keys."

"Sure, but be careful driving," her mother called. Melanie heard Mikey squeal before her mother added, "By the way, what were you doing at an expensive place like the Reef?"

"It's a long story. I'll fill you in when I get back," she called. Quickly she slipped on her jacket, grabbed her purse, and noticed the umbrellas in the stand by the door. "I'm taking the yellow umbrella, okay?"

"Sure, just be safe, sweetie."

"See you in a bit," she called, then snapped up the umbrella and went out onto the porch. She crossed to the steps, opened the umbrella and hurried down them into the rain, running for the headlights stopping by the porch side.

AFTER JUST A FEW MINUTES of winding back and forth through the drenching rain and the narrow streets, Sam knew he was lost. He slowed the car to a crawl, trying to make out street signs, but nothing looked familiar. As he'd left Melanie's, reason told him that if he was headed down, he'd be headed in the right direction out of here. But even after two streets "down," when he'd turned at a stop sign, he hadn't been any closer to the main highway or the ocean.

As he turned left, he looked ahead of the car and knew he wasn't lost anymore. Through the rain, he could make out the watery red glow of Christmas lights strung over a rambling old house and entwined in the trees that framed the driveway.

He'd gone full circle and ended up on Melanie's street, heading straight back to where he'd started from. He'd never had a problem with directions before, and he couldn't begin to think how it had happened this time.

As he pulled into Melanie's driveway to turn around, the front door of the house opened. He saw someone on the porch with a bright yellow umbrella. Using the umbrella as a shield against the falling rain, the person was running toward his car.

As he put his window halfway down, the runner slowed and he didn't have to see clearly to know that Fate, luck, or whatever you wanted to call it, had done it again. But there was no way that Melanie was going to believe he hadn't planned this. She'd never believe that this was an accident, that he'd gotten lost and ended up back here.

He watched as Melanie slowed as she got close enough to recognize his car. It didn't take a mind reader to know what she was thinking when she realized it was him in the car. But that didn't kill the pure pleasure he experienced from just looking at her and hearing her say, "You?" as she came closer.

She was a shadowed image in the night under the umbrella, blurred by the rain and the flashing red glow of the Christmas lights. And lovely, devastatingly lovely. He had to fight to keep his voice casual as he spoke. "Yes, it's me. The one with the great sense of direction."

He felt the rain on his face as it invaded the car, but he barely noticed it. He watched her frown and knew what was coming before she actually uttered the words. "What's going on? You said you never got lost."

"Well, I lied. I'm lost. I can't find my way out of this place. I feel like a rat in a maze going around and around."

"A rat. A good analogy," she said without a smile.

"I told you I don't lie, and I didn't do this on purpose. I'm lost, well and truly lost."

She took another step toward him, and the umbrella blocked a bit of the rain. "Are you?"

He wasn't a man to defend himself well, because he'd never felt the need to until that moment. "Yes, I am. So, what are you doing out here?" he asked, even though he was certain he knew the answer to the question.

"They found my keys at the hotel, and I need to get down there before midnight. I thought you were Dennis."

"Again? This is getting to be a habit, isn't it?"

He knew she was blushing, even if the red lights hid it from him. He could tell by the way her eyes narrowed and her mouth tightened. "No, it's not," she said, exasperated.

"Sorry," he murmured.

"Oh, please," she muttered.

"Okay, let's start again. What's going on?"

"They found my keys at the hotel, and I was going to get Dennis to take me back to get them."

"Dennis isn't here yet?"

"No, he's not."

"I guess punctuality isn't part of his perfection."

"It's not his fault with this weather and all."

"You forgot the holiday traffic, too."

"I'm not defending Dennis to you," she muttered, and took a partial step back. "I don't need to."

"No, you don't. Besides, my first priority is getting out of here before I get old enough to draw Social Security."

At least the talk about Dennis had distracted Melanie

for a moment; she wasn't challenging him about being here.

"What do you want? Do you want me to write you out directions or something?"

Right then he knew what he wanted, and it was simple. He wanted her. "I've got a deal for you. You need to go to the hotel, and Dennis isn't here with his car. I need to get back to the hotel, and I'm not going to get there without someone showing me the way. Why don't you get in, show me the way back, and we'll kill two birds with one stone?"

"Oh, no—"

"Melly?" someone called out to her, and Sam looked at the house, at a woman in the doorway, the lights behind her silhouetting a tall, slim build. She was holding a child in her arms. "Dennis just called. He got tied up at the office and since it's so late, he went right home and he's not coming by after all."

"Thanks, Mom," she called.

The woman and child ducked back into the house and closed the door.

"That settles it. Dennis isn't coming, and I'm here. How about a ride back to the hotel?"

She shook her head. "I don't think that's such a good idea."

He'd never come close to begging a woman to be with him, but Melanie seemed to bring him to the brink of begging as easily as some women made him smile. "I need help, you need a ride. You get in. I get to the hotel in this lifetime. You get your keys and everyone's happy."

"Nothing's that simple," she said. "Especially not with you."

"Why not?"

"It's just not."

"I promise you, it is." He knew that was a lie. Nothing about this woman was simple. "Just a ride. That's all I'm offering. You've made yourself very clear about how you feel."

She twirled the umbrella. "You accept that?"

He'd told her he never lied and he'd meant it. But with Melanie he was doing a lot of things he'd never done with a woman before. "Absolutely," he said, shocked that the lie didn't choke him completely.

"Then I'll take you up on the ride."

"Good," he said, feeling as if a heavy weight had been lifted off his shoulders. "Get in, and let's get going."

"Can you wait while I talk to my mother for a minute?"

"Sure."

"I'll be right back," she said, then turned and hurried back to the house.

He watched her go, and suddenly his world seemed to settle. Despite the dreary night all around, he had the oddest feeling that the sun was just about to come out. And whatever form of Fate or luck had been operating today, it was back full-force. "Thanks," he murmured to the empty car, and hoped that now that he'd been given another chance with Melanie, he could manage to get past the protective barriers she'd built.

MELANIE THOUGHT of going in the house, locking the door and never going out again. But she knew she couldn't. She wasn't sure that she bought the idea that he'd gone around in circles and gotten lost, but then again, she wasn't at all sure she bought the idea that he'd come back just to seduce her. That last thought was harder to ignore.

"Melanie, what's going on?"

Her mother's voice startled her as she stepped inside and closed the door on the night. She glanced to her right, into the main part of the living room, and saw her mother sitting on the floor with Mikey, untangling strings of Christmas lights. At least, her mother was untangling them. Mikey seemed to be intent on taking every bulb out of every socket and stuffing it into a huge dump truck he had balanced on a box beside him.

Melanie was always amazed at how young her mother looked. Not like a grandmother at all. It also amazed her at how sure and secure her mother seemed to be about her life and the choices she'd made. Melanie propped the umbrella by the door and crossed to crouch in front of the little boy and her mother.

"He's a handful, isn't he?"

"He's a joy." Her mother handed Mikey a hopelessly tangled set of lights. "Here, get the bulbs out of these, if you can." She looked back at Melanie. "So, are you going to tell me what's going on?"

Melanie rocked back on her heels. "It's a long story, but the man who gave me a ride from the hotel got lost and ended up back here."

"Melly, a red one," Mikey said, shoving a bulb at Melanie. "Frannie needs red."

"Let's save it for her," she said, taking the bulb and setting it in the dump truck with the others.

"That's another thing. You never said why you were at the hotel. That place is so expensive. Why, your father and I have never even been past the lobby in that place."

"Neither have I. I was doing someone a favor and

lost my keys, and this…this man offered me a ride. Now he's going to run me back there to get my car.''

"Melanie, why do I have the odd feeling that there's something going on here that you aren't telling me about?'' She grimaced. "Sort of like the old days.''

Melanie didn't want to talk about the old days. "Mom, don't fret. I'm fine.''

Her mother lifted one eyebrow speculatively. "And everything's fine with you and Dennis?''

"Fine, fine, fine.''

"That's wonderful. He's very nice, and he seems to bring out the best in you.'' She handed a bulb to Mikey without looking away from Melanie. "I've been meaning to tell you that I'm really proud of you. Who would have thought my Melly would have her own business, and have a man like Dennis who adores her.''

"A man who isn't going to bolt and run away, or who isn't married?'' Melanie asked with a tinge of bitterness.

"I didn't mean that. You know that. I just want the best for you, and if you love Dennis, I'd say that's pretty good.''

For a second she wished she could tell her mother about what had happened today, but that thought was gone as quickly as it came. No, her mother had met her father, fallen in love and made a life. So simple. So direct. So perfect. She envied that, and knew it wasn't the time to tell her mother how close she felt to the edge.

"My life's just fine now,'' she murmured, then stood. "I have to get going.''

"How long will you be?''

Melanie hesitated, then said, "It's getting so late, I think I'll just go straight home. I have to open the store at nine tomorrow because of the extended hours for holiday shopping."

"You know, that might be for the best. I don't think they'll be able to bring the tree in the house tonight, anyway, not with all this rain. They'll have to prop it up in the garage just to dry it out a bit. Why not come by tomorrow evening and we'll do the tree trimming?"

She agreed without any protest. "Okay, it's a deal. I'll even pop the popcorn."

Mikey jumped up. "Popcorn?" He grabbed his grandma's hand. "Come on, Mamaw, come on. Popcorn! Please?"

"Sure, sweetie, we'll make a bit just for you and me," she said as she got to her feet. She smiled at the little boy as she reached for his hand. "Can you believe he's so wide awake at this time of night? I thought the bath would settle him down."

"He's a live wire, all right."

Mikey tugged at his grandma's hand. "Come on, Mamaw, popcorn."

"Okay, popcorn," she said. But before she let Mikey drag her to the kitchen, she looked at Melanie. "Be careful, sweetheart."

Melanie had the oddest feeling that her mother was warning her about something besides the weather, but she couldn't know. Although when she'd been growing up, Melanie had always thought that her mother knew more than anyone should know about her mistakes and foolishnesses. "I will be," she murmured. "See you tomorrow evening."

While her mother and Mikey went into the kitchen, Melanie crossed to the phone, called the automobile club to cancel her first call, then reached for the umbrella and went out into the night. Every step she took felt as if she was going toward something that she should be running from. But she could be mature and responsible. She would be at the hotel in fifteen minutes, and this would all be over and done.

She hurried down the steps and ran for the car idling in the driveway. She skirted the front of the car, cutting through the shimmering light of the headlamps. When she got to the door, Sam pushed it open from the inside. Folding the umbrella, she scrambled in and slammed the door quickly on the night and the storm.

As she pushed the umbrella to the floor by her feet, she sat back, but didn't relax. Every atom in her being was aware of Sam so close to her. Nervously, she ran a hand over her damp hair, then said, "Let's go."

"Just tell me how to get out of this maze."

That was the easy part of this whole thing. "No problem."

"Easy for you to say," he murmured as he backed up and out onto the street. "So, where were your keys?"

"I don't know, but they were apparently found just after we left."

"It was a lucky break they were found at all." He stopped at the end of her street. "Okay, where to, lady?"

She gave him directions, and as he turned onto the next street, she said, "Basically, just keep going down and you'll get out of here, sooner or later."

"I thought that's what I did before," he said. "But all I managed to do was go around in one giant circle."

Melanie looked at Sam in the blurred shadows and for a moment she could have sworn she was looking at Dennis. Then she noticed the differences, the slight sharpness to Sam's chin, the casual way his hair was brushed back from his face. The hair was a bit too long for Dennis. Yet it was odd how much alike they could seem, given how very different the two men were in reality. That kiss had been reality, a reality she wished she could forget completely.

"What?" Sam asked, startling her slightly at the sound of his voice.

"Excuse me?"

He flashed Melanie a quick look. "You were staring. I just wondered if something was wrong."

"I—I wasn't staring," she lied. "I was concentrating on the directions. This storm is getting pretty bad." And being in the car with him was a definite mistake. She could have waited until morning to get her keys and retrieve her car. "I didn't even know we were going to get rain, let alone this. I'm sorry I dragged you out into the storm in the first place."

"You hardly dragged me out here, and I told you, I owed you for getting my wallet back to me intact."

"That's a lot of money," she murmured as she strained to see into the stormy night.

"The money's not important. But other things couldn't be replaced."

She knew without asking that one of those things was that picture of the woman with the laughing eyes. "Left, here," she said, barely seeing the street in time for him to make the turn.

They took two more turns before Melanie realized something wasn't right. There were no lights at all, and she felt disoriented. This street was narrow, winding downward, and almost obliterated by the night and rain. "Oh, shoot," she muttered.

"Oh, no, that language again. What's wrong?"

"I don't think we want to be here. We should have

hit the highway by now, but this…'' She strained her eyes to make out anything. ''We can't be, but it looks like we're on the backside of the hills. But we can't be.''

He slowed down. ''Okay, just tell me how to correct it.''

''We need to turn around, go back to the first turn we find, then go south. That should take us in the right direction.''

''Are you sure?''

''Yes. Of course. At least, I think so.'' But she wasn't sure at all. ''I mean, if the first street is Shepherd Way, we're okay, and if we can get to Blair, we're home free.''

''Okay, I trust you,'' he said, easing into a U-turn and heading back up the hill to make the right turn. As soon as he started to make another right, she knew it was completely wrong. ''No, not this—'' she started to say but was cut off when they hit a bump that jerked them to one side, forcing the car to glide toward the far edge of the road.

Chapter Nine

As the car came to a stop, the motion didn't. She could feel the car tipping to her right, and it took her a second to realize that they were sinking. This couldn't be happening. The car couldn't be stopped here, in the middle of a storm, slowly sinking into the mud.

Sam hit the gas, but the tires only spun while the engine roared. As the engine slowed to an idle, and the night and storm surrounded the car, he muttered, "Tell me you know where we are and that there's a gas station just around the corner."

"I wish I could," she said, and meant it. "I wish I could."

When the car lurched slightly to the right again, Melanie held her breath until it stilled. Sam pulled the emergency brake on and turned off the ignition, then rested both hands on the top of the steering wheel as he leaned forward and squinted out the window. "We aren't going anywhere."

Melanie sank back in the seat, clasped her hands together in her lap, and stared out at the night and storm. "This can't be happening," she lamented, feeling incredibly trapped.

"It not only can, but it is." The growing wind shook

the car again, making it shudder. "You wouldn't happen to have a cell phone would you?"

"I don't. I mean, I do, but the battery was dead and I left it in the car."

She felt Sam shift in his seat as he spoke. "Then we're here until the rain lets up enough for us to go and find help, or someone comes by."

Melanie moved closer to the door, pressing her shoulder against the frame, and stared hard out at the black blur of the night. "You didn't have to do this," she muttered.

"What?"

"This. Couldn't you just have run out of gas or something simple like that?"

She didn't expect him to laugh, but he did. "Oh, boy, are you wrong. I didn't plan this. I didn't get us lost, or try to get us stuck in the mud out in the middle of nowhere."

She glanced at him in the shadows. She'd been lied to by the best, and believed them...for a time. She had a gut feeling that this was planned, but that didn't make sense. No more sense than the feeling that something was very wrong, besides the fact she was trapped in here with this man. "You didn't?"

"I told you, I don't lie." He sighed, a rough sound in the confines of the car. "If I was trying to get you alone to seduce you, doing it like this in a car wouldn't be on my list. Not in the top ten."

She had a flashing memory of his comment about being dry and warm, with a fire in the hearth. She shivered and hugged her arms around herself to control the action. "Mine, neither."

Lightning ripped through the skies, and as the rumble

HARLEQUIN®

AN IMPORTANT MESSAGE FROM THE EDITORS OF HARLEQUIN®

Dear Reader,

Because you've chosen to read one of our fine romance novels, we'd like to say "thank you"! And, as a **special** way to thank you, we've selected <u>four more</u> of the <u>books</u> you love so well, **and** a beautiful Cherub Magnet to send you absolutely ***FREE!***

Please enjoy them with our compliments...

Candy Lee

Editor,
American Romance

P.S. And because we value our customers, we've attached something extra inside ...

EDITOR'S FREE GIFT SEAL — THANK YOU

PEEL OFF SEAL AND PLACE INSIDE

HOW TO VALIDATE YOUR
EDITOR'S FREE GIFT "THANK YOU"

1. Peel off gift seal from front cover. Place it in space provided at right. This automatically entitles you to receive four free books and a lovely Cherub Magnet.

2. Send back this card and you'll get brand-new Harlequin American Romance® novels. These books have a cover price of $3.75 each, but they are yours to keep absolutely free.

3. There's no catch. You're under no obligation to buy anything. We charge nothing — ZERO — for your first shipment. And you don't have to make any minimum number of purchases — not even one!

4. The fact is thousands of readers enjoy receiving books by mail from the Harlequin Reader Service® . They like the convenience of home delivery...they like getting the best new novels BEFORE they're available in stores...and they love our discount prices!

5. We hope that after receiving your free books you'll want to remain a subscriber. But the choice is yours — to continue or cancel, anytime at all! So why not take us up on our invitation, with no risk of any kind. You'll be glad you did!

6. Don't forget to detach your FREE BOOKMARK. And remember...just for validating your Editor's Free Gift Offer, we'll send you FIVE MORE gifts, *ABSOLUTELY FREE!*

This charming refrigerator magnet looks like a little cherub, and it's a perfect size for holding notes and recipes. Best of all it's yours ABSOLUTELY FREE when you accept our NO-RISK offer!

of thunder followed, Sam said, "So, how far would you guess it is to the nearest phone?"

"I don't know. I've lived here all my life, and this place doesn't even look familiar to me."

"Then we're really up the creek, in more ways than one," he concerned.

"I can't believe the way today's gone," she said, chancing a look at him. She'd tried to do the right thing, but no matter what she did, things just seemed to happen that messed up every good intention she had.

"It's been strange, hasn't it?" he mused, slanting her a glance through the shadows. She looked away quickly. "Interesting, but strange."

"If you didn't do this all on purpose, then there has to be some sort of conspiracy."

"Sort of what I said before about some higher power?"

"No, of course not." Even when she wasn't looking at him, he still affected her. Just his voice in the close confines of the car played havoc with her nerves. She stared determinedly at the windows as they steamed up. God, she wished she was anywhere but here. "Just dumb coincidence, probably."

"Sure, dumb stupid luck," he said on a rough whisper. "Mistaken identity, lost wallet, lost keys, miserable weather, bad directions, and sinking mud."

There was another crash of lighting followed by rolling thunder, and at the same moment Melanie felt the car shift more to the right. She bolted upright. "What's happening?"

"We're sinking more," Sam said with what she thought was remarkable calm. "Don't worry. It can only go so far."

Melanie pressed back further into her seat. "We'll never get out of here."

"Never say never," Sam murmured.

ANGELINA WAS ZAPPED AWAY from the scene in the car before she could take a breath, and when she appeared in front of Miss Victoria, her head felt ready to explode. She bit her lip hard as she looked at the tiny lady sitting in the midst of the virtual meadow.

Pale eyes narrowed behind the rimless glasses, and bright color touched her cheeks. Annoyance in Miss Victoria? This case was bringing out a lot of firsts for both of them. Angelina took a step back on the soft bed of flowers at her feet.

"Angelina," Miss Victoria said tightly. "We are not amused. We have told you and told you that there are limits to the situations we can engineer to expedite our assignments. And goodness knows that we do not advocate using contrived situations or coincidences freely. We must use control and manipulate humans with great insight and care."

"Ma'am, I don't know what—"

Miss Victoria waved her hand and the space to her right filled immediately with the picture of the night storm and the sedan sitting awkwardly in the soft mud on the roadside in the hills. "We have said, time and time again, that the elements have to be used sparingly. Even then we do not approve of inflicting inconvenience, or even danger."

They couldn't think Angelina had produced this storm! It had been Fate, not her, something she used, not produced. "But, ma'am, I didn't—"

Another voice—a voice she had only heard once before, in the very distant past when she'd first started on her assignments—interrupted her. The voice came from nowhere but was everywhere. Neither male nor female, it was the all-encompassing voice of the head of the Council.

"Angelina, we wish to underscore the immediate need to rectify this situation, however we do feel that you are starting to think in human terms, and that is inherently dangerous in this business. You must elevate yourself above the mundane, the obvious, the contrived. Even the humans are beginning to feel that something is at work in their lives, that they are being manipulated. That will not do."

"Oh, my," Miss Victoria murmured, waving a hand faintly in front of her face. "That is just what we were saying. It will not do, Angelina. It will not do."

What did they want? She was working on the fly here, without the usual time to put things in order to set lives in motion. She thought she'd been doing a remarkable job with what she had to work with. She looked up at the blueness over her. "But I don't have the time to—"

"There is no excuse for thinking as a human. None at all. We will expect you to do this in a manner that leaves no questions in the humans' minds, but brings them irrevocably together. We do not want coincidence and manipulation to abound to the point that even a human can figure out that what happens is not the natural course of events."

Angelina frowned, then sensed that the Council head was gone. She looked back at Miss Victoria. "Ma'am, what is going on? You know that I'm working blind on this, that if there hadn't been a mistake—"

Miss Victoria shook her head and held a finger to her lips. "No, we do not want to go into that right now.

We just wanted to remind you that this is a very important assignment and that you have been chosen to…take care of it.''

To clean up the mess, Angelina thought, and quickly tried to cover it with, ''I appreciate your faith, ma'am.''

Miss Victoria eyed Angelina. ''Pride is not an attractive thing. One must be humble and know that no matter how well we think we are doing, humans have a way of causing grievous errors in their lives.''

''Yes, ma'am.'' She cleared her throat. ''Ma'am, I was wondering about Dennis Benning.''

''What about Mr. Benning?''

''You're certain that he will eventually be happy?''

''Yes, Angelina, blissfully so, or at least, as blissful as a human can be.'' She glanced at the scene of the night and storm. ''My, my, my,'' she murmured. ''We think it best that your efforts are channeled into a more positive path.''

The scene to the right was suddenly ripped with lightning, and Angelina could momentarily see Melanie and Sam isolated in its brilliance. Sam was looking at Melanie, but she wouldn't look at him. She was fighting this with every atom in her being. Stubborn indeed.

''We know the adage about life-and-death situations bringing humans closer together,'' Miss Victoria said. ''But sometimes that intense emotional upheaval causes more problems than it's worth. We do not want anyone put in harm's way. Danger is not—''

''Danger?'' Angelina asked, confused. All she'd done was have Sam pull over and sink in the mud to force Melanie to be with him for a few more hours. To give Sam plenty of time to melt Melanie the way he'd done on the deck when they'd kissed. ''I don't understand how this—'' she started to say but was cut off as lightning struck again.

"Oh, no," she breathed as she understood completely.

"Go now!" Miss Victoria said. In an instant Angelina was zapped back to the rain and the night and Melanie and Sam. She climbed onto the trunk of the car nearest the roadside, then materialized to use her weight as balance. As another bolt of lightning ripped through the heavens, she just hoped that she could get everyone out of this in one piece.

MELANIE WAS UPSET about being stuck in the mud, but as the brilliance of another bolt of lightning exposed everything around them, she knew that being stuck in the mud was the least of their worries. Her throat tightened with fear, and she could barely rasp out, "Oh, oh, shoot!"

The darkness came back full-force, but the light had been there long enough for her to see where they really were. On the edge of a drop-off that tumbled down into a gully of oaks and brambles…at least thirty feet below.

"Lightning can be pretty awesome," Sam was saying. "But we're okay in here."

"Oh, no…no, we aren't," she whispered, and slowly recoiled in horror, pressing back from the window until she felt the console cut into her hip.

Sam moved behind her, one hand touched her shoulder, and his breath ruffled her hair when he spoke. "Of course we're okay." His fingers on her tightened slightly through the bulky jacket. "We're lost, but high and dry for now."

She reached blindly for his hand on her shoulder, and gripped it tightly. "No, we're…we're going to die."

His chuckle jarred her. "Oh, come on. It's not that bad," he said. Then lightning flashed again, and the scene to the right of the car was exposed for one horrifying moment. This time she knew Sam saw it. He uttered a wrenching epithet in her ear, then said in a rough whisper, "Don't move. Don't move at all."

She couldn't have moved if she'd wanted to right then, especially when the car groaned slightly and slowly tipped even more toward the drop-off. "What...what should we do?"

"Get the hell out of here," he rasped, his fingers tangling tightly with hers.

"How?"

"I don't know."

"But you've done things like this in the movies, haven't you?" She couldn't take her eyes off the dark void outside the rain-streaked window. "How did you do it then?"

"I hate to point this out, but this isn't a movie, and there isn't a script to follow."

"But, can't we..." Her voice died out when lightning struck again, exposing the drop, and was quickly followed by rolling thunder that vibrated through the car.

Sam took a harsh breath, then spoke in a quick, low voice. "Okay, this is the plan. We need to get as much weight as possible on this side of the car. You come backward, slowly, over to my side, then we'll ease out my door." His hand released her, then slipped his arm around her waist until his forearm was pressed tightly to her waist. "Slowly, love, very, very slowly."

"I-if...we move..."

"If we don't move, we're in real trouble. Just ease on back. Come on, I'll help you. Just take it easy."

She took a shuddering breath as Sam pulled slightly

at her middle and she inched backward. Somehow, she managed to get over the console to find herself sitting on Sam's lap, caught between him and the steering wheel.

For a second she was looking into his eyes, inches from his face, and the heat of his breath offset the horrible chill that had taken over her body. "It's going to be okay, love," he whispered hoarsely. "I'm going to open the door, then—"

His words were cut off when the car suddenly lurched, angling farther downward with a horrifying groan. Melanie grabbed Sam, wrapping her arms around his neck and burying her face in his throat.

"Oh, God, Sam," she gasped. She felt everything around her, the steering wheel biting into her hip, Sam's hold on her, and his pulse beating wildly against her cheek.

"We don't have much time," he whispered.

She couldn't have moved right then if she'd wanted to. Despite everything, in that moment she felt an inexplicable sense of safety with Sam, that no matter what, he'd get them out of this.

"Okay, I'm going to try to reach the door and get it open. That should help with the weight distribution and give us a couple of extra seconds."

She kept her hold on him as he shifted slightly toward the door. She could feel the straining in his neck and shoulders, then there was a blast of cold and rain and the louder sounds of the storm.

"Got it," he breathed into her hair. "Listen to me. Ease back and out of here."

"What about you?" she whispered against the heat of his throat.

"I'll be right behind you, love."

"W-we can do it together." She wasn't sure she could let go of him, even to make her escape.

"No, we can't. I'll help you out the door. Once you're out, grab the top of the door and push down as hard as you can. Put as much weight on it as possible. Do you understand?"

"Yes."

His hold tightened for a moment. "Promise me one thing?"

"Anything."

"If you feel the car going, let go and get the hell away from it."

"No. If you're not out, I—"

"Promise to get the hell out of here, and don't worry about me."

"Sam—"

He shifted, catching her face between both hands and forcing her to look right at him. God, the sight of him right then twisted at her heart, a mingling of fear and need that was unexplainable.

"No, you listen to me." His hands were shaking. "I have no intention of dying like this, in this place, right now. Now just do what I say."

She knew a wrenching fear for him that almost nauseated her. "You'll get out, won't you?"

He studied her intently, then his hand moved to her cheek, the tips of his fingers rough on her skin. "Damn straight I will," he rasped, then abruptly touched her lips with his. The contact was nothing more than a fleeting touch, but Melanie felt as if some irrevocable bond had been forged between them.

"Now go," he breathed.

She reached behind her with one hand, felt the cold, wet handle of the door, and grabbed it. Very carefully, she eased back as Sam all but lifted her away from him and through the open door. Somehow she made it. She was out in the cold and rain, her feet on the blacktop where water ran like a river around her shoes.

She grabbed the open door, turned and held it tightly with both hands, leaning on the top of it with all of her weight. The metal edge dug into her middle through her heavy jacket as she watched Sam move, easing carefully back. Then he was out of the car, grabbing at the door himself to get his footing on the asphalt.

There was a flash of lightning behind him and for one insane moment Melanie thought she saw someone. Someone at the back of the car, a shadowy figure sitting on the trunk. Then it disappeared. She blinked, and in that moment everything started to happen in a blur of speed.

Sam lunged at her and the car lurched up and out of her grip. But Sam, holding her by her upper arm, was jerking her back with him toward the center of the road. In a flashing second she saw the car tip farther and farther toward the abyss, the driver's side door slamming shut from the force of the upward angle. Then the car was gone, disappearing into the night without a sound.

The next thing she knew Sam had her in his arms and was holding her to his chest, his arms shaking as they circled her. She was surrounded by his sure strength, and she held on to him for dear life as the night raged around them. They'd made it. They'd survived.

Sam held on to Melanie, with the rain streaming around them, and all he could think of was the feel of her in his arms. It felt so right, it was almost frightening. Almost as frightening as the feelings he'd had moments ago in the car. A raw fear for her, a fear that he couldn't do what he promised, that they wouldn't get out of there in one piece.

Now the fear was dissipating and in its place was another fear that he was getting in far too deeply with this woman. He wanted her. That was a given. He wanted to spend time with her. He had no reason to deny that. But beyond that, he just plain wanted her to be right where she was forever. And that shook him to his core. He'd never let himself need anyone on that level before, and he wasn't sure he should now.

He closed his eyes tightly, resting his chin on her wet hair and barely noticing that the rain was beginning to subside. He just let the feelings of relief and the rightness of holding her filter into him. That was about all he could absorb at that moment.

"Oh, my God," she breathed against him, her voice vibrating against his chest. "We could have…just…just fallen over the side."

He could feel the trembling in her and his feelings shifted to an almost suffocating surge of wanting to protect this woman from every bad thing in the world. He could barely breathe as she slowly eased back and tipped her head up to look at him.

Rain spiked off her lashes, and the look in her eyes echoed the fear and shock deep in his own soul. He knew he was holding her as much to support himself as to support her. His eyes flashed to her softly parted lips, the way she was breathing in short, soft pants, and a confusion that he'd never known before assailed him.

As she slowly pushed away from him, and her hands left him, the confusion only grew. He'd always been the one to walk away when it was time to go. He'd learned a long time ago that connections were fleeting, that you enjoyed what was good, then left. But something in this woman with amber eyes threatened to break all his tried-and-true rules. Walking away from Melanie Clark when the time was right wouldn't be easy at all.

He swiped at the rain trickling down his face. "Now I know why I don't do stunts anymore. I don't have a death wish."

He watched her clasp her hands tightly in front of her, then her eyes widened again. "Oh, God, my purse…" She looked toward the chunk of embankment that had fallen away with the car. "It's…it's down there."

The rain was light now, but steady, and the lightning, when it struck this time, was a distance off. The colorless glow exposed Melanie to him, her flinch at the sudden light, the way her dark hair clung at her temples and neck…and the trembling in her chin.

"And we aren't," he reminded her. "We can get your purse later when they pull the car out. But right now we need to get out of the rain and find a phone."

She turned back to him, but the shadows were heavy and he could barely make out her blurred features as she moved a bit farther back from him. "Yes…of course. A phone."

He wanted nothing more than to hold her again and be assured that she was whole and safe right here. But he knew how selfish his motives were, and he couldn't do it. So he swept one hand out to his right. "Does this look familiar to you at all?"

Melanie glanced up and down the road, then to the vast expanse of what looked like bramble and scrub on the opposite side of the road. She took a step in that direction, then said softly, "I don't believe it. It can't be." She walked the rest of the way across the road and looked out across the space beyond. "I don't understand."

He went after her. "What going on?"

"It's the vineyards."

What he'd thought was scrub and bramble was really grape vines strung on low supports. "As in wine?"

He could see her nod. "But they're north of where we were, and on the backside of the hills. On the opposite side to the coast."

"I guess we really were lost," he murmured as she turned to him in the night.

"Sam, we couldn't get here from there. I mean, the roads, it would be hard in the daylight to find the back way here. I used to get lost just trying to do it in the daylight, and at night, in this storm, we couldn't have…"

"But we did."

"But how?"

He looked down at her and said softly, "Fate, chance, a higher power. Whatever you want to call it."

He could see the way she stared at him, then she said tightly, "More dumb, stupid luck."

"I won't argue the point for now. If you know where we are, do you know where to find a phone?"

She looked up and down the road, then back at him. "A phone could be miles from here. There aren't any houses around and when you drive through here, you can go forever without seeing anyone but farm workers."

"Then I guess we should start walking."

She sighed, a soft, shuddering sound, then started off down the road with a muttered, "Dumb, stupid luck. All of this is from dumb, stupid luck."

In the rainy night, he went after her, and knew that he'd never give the credit for finding Melanie to dumb, stupid luck. It felt more like a miracle to him.

Chapter Ten

Melanie walked down the road, her legs still rubbery and barely supporting her. But she had to keep moving as her clothes got more and more soaked by the steady rain. She couldn't stand still with Sam and be safe. The dark night, this man, and herself. The combination was way too dangerous, and that danger had little to do with what had just happened with the car. So, she kept moving.

When he fell into step beside her, she didn't look toward him at all. Now it was worse than at the hotel, that sense of him so close to her, that fear that their arms might accidentally touch. She jammed her hands into her pockets, pressing the soaked corduroy of her jacket into her stomach and kept her eyes on the dark road ahead of them.

The fiasco with Robert had made her realize her problem was that she moved too fast, got into things before she knew what she was doing. After today, she wondered if that still held true. Had it only been six hours at the most since she'd first met Sam? Six hours that had rocked her life and set it on its ear.

"Hard to believe, isn't it?" Sam asked.

For a moment she thought the man could read her

mind, too. "What can't you believe?" she asked without looking at him.

"That we're so close to a major city but there hasn't been a car come past, and there aren't any houses anywhere around."

"Hard to believe," she murmured. Just about as hard to believe as her insane reaction to the man beside her.

Lightning ripped through the sky and she stumbled as rolling thunder came right after it, crashing through the night. Before she could catch herself, Sam had her by the arm, holding her securely and not letting her tumble forward onto the pavement. All she could think about was an anchor. And the idea of Sam as her anchor scared her.

She jerked away from his support, and spun around to face him. Her nerves were shot and she could barely think straight. His touching her was too much for her to take right then. "Don't," she snapped.

He was close to her, maybe a foot away, and she could see that he was looking at her the way he had when he'd been studying her intently: his eyes narrowed and his jaw set. "Don't what?"

"Don't touch me again." She knew how stupid that sounded, and the rain felt cold on the heat that burned in her face. "Just don't touch me!"

"The next time, do you want me to let you fall?"

Melanie exhaled, annoyed that she felt so unsteady and scattered. "That's ridiculous," she answered.

"I'd say standing in the middle of a deserted road in the middle of a rainstorm telling someone to let you fall is well beyond ridiculous."

His voice was low and edged with a jarring sense of humor that was hard for her to endure. "Forget it," she muttered. "You never understand what I'm trying to say to you." She turned from him to keep walking.

"I'll be the first to admit that I don't know a lot about you," Sam said, falling into step with her again.

"Thanks for admitting that," she said, trudging on down the road.

"You're welcome," he drawled, but didn't stop there. "But one thing I *do* know is that, for some reason you've decided that life isn't to be lived and, God forbid, enjoyed."

"You can't stop, can you?" she said, not about to look at him.

"I feel compelled to point out something that is so obvious, yet which you can't seem to see yourself."

She stopped and faced him, anger giving her a degree of self-protection at that moment. "Who appointed you the person to set me straight on life?"

"I guess I appointed myself, because God knows, Dennis isn't doing his job. If he cared about you, he'd—"

"Stop, stop, stop," she retorted. "Just stop."

"Can't you see what I can see and what I can feel? You're shutting yourself down just because you've had some bad experiences with men who didn't know anything about who you were or what you were. Dennis sure as hell doesn't understand—"

Before she had even formed the thought, she hit Sam as hard as she could across the face. The impact of the slap shocked her, and when she pulled her hand back, her palm tingled from the blow. She stared in horror at Sam who didn't move. He didn't even touch where she'd hit him.

"Oh, God, I never..." She closed her hand into a fist. "I'm so sorry, but I—"

"You're not sorry," Sam said in a low voice. "Neither am I."

She stared up at him, nothing making sense to her in that moment.

Sam slowly lifted his hand to finger his face where she'd hit him, and he actually smiled down at her. "It's good to know that Robert the Sleaze didn't kill all the passion in you."

Melanie tried to block his words as the memory of Robert saying, "You're so dammed passionate, Melanie. You're made for fun, for pleasure, but not for the long haul."

She'd realized the moment she'd heard Robert say the words that she wanted to love someone desperately, to be in for the long haul, to have the house and kids and a love that went on and on and on. And she'd found that with Dennis. Everything she needed. Everything. No matter what this man said or how foolish her thoughts got from time to time.

Meeting Sam was nothing, it couldn't be. He was the equivalent of what she'd been six months ago. In for fun, then gone. Never sticking around. Not what she needed at all now. A man who could stir her, anger her, laugh at her, then walk away.

"Robert was a jerk, but so are you," she snapped. "And you're right about one thing, I'm not sorry I hit you." With that, she turned and started down the road toward a curve in the downgrade.

"I was just telling you the truth," Sam said as he fell into step beside her once again and raised his voice to be heard over a peculiar rushing sound that was getting louder and louder all the time.

"Baloney, it's your version of the truth."

"'Baloney'? That's a new one. You must *really* be mad."

"You're just—" Her words were cut off as Sam grabbed her by the arm and jerked her to a stop so abruptly that it wrenched her shoulders and neck.

That was it. She yanked against his hold, but he didn't let go. When she looked up at him, she could see that he was looking past her. Following his gaze, she understood why he had stopped her.

Through the night and rain she could see what looked like a barrier across the road, and it took her another second to realize it wasn't a barrier anyone had put there on purpose. It was a two-foot-high wall of mud being pushed onto the roadway by rushing water.

The mudslide, heading in the direction of the bank on the far side and into the ravine, grew even as she watched, cutting off the road completely. The water was a torrent as it flowed around it and out of sight. There was no way to get over it, or through it, or past it. If Sam had talked about a curse being on them, rather than a higher power, she would have agreed instantly. "Darn it," she breathed.

"Damn is more like it," Sam said beside her. "Southern California with its flooding and mudslides." He finally let her go. "But, all things considered, it's probably a blessing in disguise that we didn't get this far."

She hugged herself to try to stop the trembling that was growing deep inside her. "We might not have been able to drive past, but we'd be dry in the car."

"I think we would have run right into the slide and gone over the side with it. We'd be in the car, all right, but at the bottom of the ravine. High and dry would be debatable."

He was right, and that admission made her shiver violently. She hugged herself, her fingers digging into her upper arms through the wet material of her jacket. "What now?" she whispered.

Sam was so close she could feel him at her shoulder. "We need to get around this some way, or go back and start at square one again."

She wiped at her face as she looked to her left, at the rise that went up into the vineyards, the rise that had a huge, gaping chunk of earth washed out of it now. "We can't get around it."

"You're right. So I guess we head back." He turned, looked around, then said, "Or maybe not. We could climb the slope into the vineyard and walk around the slide."

She looked again at the steep, gouged bank. "We can't climb that slope."

He'd barely touched her shoulder with his fingers, but it startled her and she turned to face him. "We'll go back a bit, where it's less steep. Okay?"

"Sure," she said, then headed back up the hill.

Around the bend of the road, the slope grew more and more shallow and was dotted with scrub brush and weeds. Sam stopped and looked up to where it was maybe three feet high. "Here. We'll give it a shot." He motioned to the slope. "Want to go first?"

"Sure," she said, and moved past him to grab at the thick shrubs by the roadside to pull herself up. Her feet slid on the mud and then she felt Sam's hands span her waist.

"Don't get crazy," he said. "I'm only doing this to get this over with." He lifted her with an ease that was startling, and she was at the top, staggering forward into the vineyard.

She righted herself, then turned as Sam got to the top of the bank and managed to get on level ground. He wiped his hands; his hair was plastered to his head from the rain, and his clothes, totally soaked, clung to his body. "What do you think that is?" he asked, pointing behind her.

She turned and had to shield her eyes from the rain with her hand before she could make out a dark shape about two hundred feet from them across the vineyard. "A building of some sort? What do *you* think?"

"It think it looks promising," he said, moving past her into a narrow row between the vines that led in the direction of the building. "Let's hope someone's there, or at least that there's a phone."

Melanie could feel her feet sinking into the earth as she made her way after him through the rain. As they neared the building, she could see it wasn't a house, but a small outbuilding with a flat roof. It looked very low and very dark; a place used by workers in the vineyard.

They broke out of the vines into a clearing of rocky ground with the building in the center. Sam headed for the front door and ducked under the hanging eaves. As Melanie caught up to him, he muttered a curse and let the heavy padlock that secured the door fall against the wood.

"Dammit. Locked up tight."

"Darn. Goodness knows how far we are from the main buildings."

"I'm not going any farther," he stated flatly. "I'm soaked through, and the rain's not letting up, so I think it's time to get inside."

"But it's locked and—"

"Another dubious talent I have is getting into places where I want to be but someone else would rather I didn't go.'' He spoke as he turned from her and scanned the area around the building.

"What are you—"

"Perfect," he said as he bent to pick up a large rock that had been propped against the outer wall. "This will do nicely."

"Sam, you aren't going to..."

"Oh, yes, I am," he said as he lifted the rock and hit the padlock with a crashing thud.

"Sam, that's trespassing, or something like that."

"It's called breaking and entering," he said as he hit it again and the padlock flew off into the darkness. "Now it's broken, we can enter."

"Oh, no," Melanie breathed as Sam pushed back the door and disappeared into the building.

She stared at the open door, and his voice came out to her. "Melanie, either fish or cut bait."

"What?"

"Come on inside and be a partner in crime—but a dry partner—or stay out there in the rain until you develop root rot." There was a flicker inside, then a soft steady glow from a single bulb dangling from a low ceiling.

Melanie looked through the door into a small room with plank floors and what looked like stacks and stacks of bound towels lining the walls from floor to ceiling. Towels? She moved closer, stepping over the doorjamb, and the minute she took a breath, knew it wasn't towels. Not even close. The air was heavy with the smell of damp burlap. Bundles and bundles of burlap sacks. So many that there was only about an eight-by-eight foot clear space in the middle of the room.

A gust of wind came up right then, driving the rain

at her back, and she moved father inside and swung the door shut against the cold and night.

"Good choice," Sam muttered. She turned to her left to find him standing beside a plain wooden desk, holding a phone in his hand. "And I believe we have another dose of dumb, stupid luck." He lifted the receiver, put it to his ear, then put it back in the cradle before turning to her. "Then, again, maybe not. It's dead."

She stood there, dripping and cold as she watched Sam try to open the cabinet above the desk. But the doors wouldn't give.

"At least we're inside where it's dry," he said. "Now we just need to get comfortable."

She undid her jacket and slipped the soaked garment off, letting it fall to the floor. But it didn't help. Her sweater was just as wet as the rest of her clothes. Sam crossed to the back wall and started pulling bundles of the sacks down to the floor. With one tug, he broke the ropes holding the burlap together and spilled the rough squares into a pile on the floor.

"Sam, you can't do that."

He stopped and for a minute she thought he was listening to her. But that was short-lived. He'd only stopped long enough to tug off his denim jacket and toss it onto the floor beside the desk. His T-shirt was soaked, clearly defining his chest and shoulders, and she looked away as he reached for another bundle.

"Yes, I can," he said.

She looked down at the growing pile of lose sacks on the wooden floor. "It's one thing to break in to get out of the rain, but you're damaging their property, now."

"I'll retie the bundles when we're done if it makes you feel better."

She bit her lip hard as she looked up at him as he reached for another bundle. The wet cotton strained across his back, showing his muscles as he tossed another bundle to the floor. But this time he didn't turn to break the wrappings off. He let out a low whistle, leaned forward and looked down between the bales and the back wall. "Well, I'll be damned," he murmured, then reached behind the bundles.

Shivering in her cold, wet clothes, as she asked, "What is it?"

He tugged upward and pulled out a bedroll tied to a knapsack. He laid the bedroll on the top bundle, undid the strings and, as Melanie moved closer to peer around his shoulder, Sam emptied the knapsack. He tipped it up and the contents spilled out.

A pack of generic cigarettes with a lighter strapped to it by a rubber band tumbled out, along with three cans of cheap beer, a package of Twinkies, two candle stubs, some incense and a cassette of some group Melanie had never heard of.

"Well, well, well," Sam murmured. "The quintessential make-out kit."

Melanie shivered as rainwater trickled off her hair and slipped under her collar. "Too bad it doesn't have towels, and a heater."

"I doubt that the people who used this needed a heater," he said softly as he tossed the things back in the knapsack.

Melanie stepped back, the only heat she could feel right then, the fire in her cheeks. When she turned, her feet tangled in the loose sacks and she plunged forward into the stack of rough burlap. "Shoot, shoot, shoot," she muttered as she pushed up with her hands, then twisted around and ended up sitting in the middle of the sacks.

Sam stood over her. He skimmed his wet hair back from his face, a face that was smiling down at her. "See, I let you fall. I do as I'm told."

"Oh, just...just..." She tugged at her shoes, which were oozing with water, to get them off. "Just be quiet."

"Sure, no problem, as long as I can get out of these wet clothes."

Her eyes shot up to him, but he wasn't looking at her now. He was tugging his T-shirt out of the waistband of his jeans. "But it's cold," she said quickly.

"And these clothes are cold, too." He looked down at her as she set her shoes on the floor beside the sacks. "Are you going to stay in those clothes?"

"I don't have any options," she said, then wished she hadn't.

"Of course you do, but you're playing it safe. Sane, I think you called it. And you're going to get pneumonia."

That smile was there again as he leaned back against the bundles and pulled his boots off one at a time. "If I had a talent for tailoring, I'd make clothes out of these sacks, but short of wearing the sacks themselves, we don't have too many options." His hands went to the snap at the waistband of his jeans. "Besides, we've got this bedroll we can share to get warm."

"Oh, no, you don't," she muttered, struggling to her feet. "This has gone far enough."

The snap at his waist was undone, but thank goodness he didn't make a move to take the jeans off. "Now what did I do wrong this time?"

"I'm not about to strip down and share body heat. If you think I am, you're insane."

"That's a shame," he murmured with the ghost of a smile playing seductively at the corners of his lips. "Okay, you tell me what we should do. Eat stale Twinkies for heat, or maybe drink some cheap, warm beer and we might not notice the fact we're freezing? I'm open to any suggestions that don't include lighting up a cigarette or setting bundles of burlap on fire."

"Don't be ridiculous." She turned and padded barefoot across the cold wooden floor to the desk. "I wish this was open," she muttered as she tugged at the cupboard door. "Darn it, anyway."

"Yeah, and dammit it, too," Sam muttered from right behind her. "Why not go all out with your famous 'oh, shoot' while you're at it?"

"You're the expert on swearing around here, and on breaking and entering. How can we get into it?"

"I'll show you," he said softly. Reaching around her, his body pressed along her back as he jerked hard on the door handle. Heat was everywhere for that instant, then with a snapping sound, the heat was gone as the doors swung open and Sam moved away from her.

Quickly she stepped to her right so Sam could get closer to the cabinet. She had no idea what was inside the cabinet. She couldn't seem to focus on anything but the unbearable coldness that was reasserting itself.

"Look at this," he said, and she glanced up as Sam held up something dark green and folded. "No choice of sizes, but these should fit nicely."

She stared at what he held in his hand. "What is it?"

"Coveralls. Probably protection from the staining from the grapes when they're being harvested." He unfurled the coveralls in front of her. "Probably a bit big for you, but it should satisfy your need to be modest."

He came closer to her and held the coveralls out to her. She took the stiff cotton garment from him, then looked around before she looked back at Sam.

He shook his head. "No, there's no way I'm going outside while you change. The best I can offer is to keep my eyes closed or to stand in a corner with my back turned. Take it or leave it."

"Just turn around," she muttered.

"Why don't we both just turn around and get this over with?" he asked.

She nodded. "Okay." He reached for another pair of coveralls from the cupboard, then as he turned away from her, Melanie turned, too, and quickly started to strip.

She was down to her bra and panties when Sam spoke again and startled her. "What's the signal for when we're done?"

"Just say so," she breathed as she grabbed the coveralls and stepped into them. She tugged them up, slipping them over her shoulders, then with hands that were far from steady, did up the snaps. She was just rolling the sleeves up and off her hands when Sam said, "Done yet?"

"Yes, I am," she said.

She turned before Sam added, "Fast. I'm almost done."

His words were too late to keep her from seeing him pushing his legs into the coveralls, or seeing that he was only wearing jockey shorts. She caught the image of his naked back and strong legs before she turned away from him. "Let me know," she said, her voice annoyingly breathless with the words.

"Done."

Cautiously she turned again. This time he had the coveralls on and was doing up the fasteners, covering a chest with a seductive suggestion of dark hair. His eyes flickered up to hers. "Feel better?"

"Drier," she murmured as she wiped at her damp hair.

He went to the pile of sacks, hunkered down and spread them out. The coveralls barely fit him, despite the fact that they were swallowing up Melanie. It wasn't fair at all, she thought as she quickly looked away and down at her hands, that he could do something so simple and look so...so... She fought the one word that came to her. Sexy.

"There we go," he said. When she looked back at him, he was spreading the open bedroll on the sacks like a blanket. "You have your half, and I'll have mine. And never the twain shall meet," he said as he straightened and turned to her. "Go ahead. Get comfortable."

She crossed to the makeshift bed and dropped down onto one side, as far from where Sam was settling as she could. She tugged the bedroll over her legs and sat there, not moving. But Sam wasn't uneasy at all. He stretched out a foot from her and sighed deeply. "It's got to be past midnight, and I'm exhausted."

She was, too, but there was no way she could stretch out alongside this man. So she scooted back until she was against the stack of bales, and wrapped her arms around her legs as she tugged them to her breast. If she moved at all, she'd touch Sam. She didn't want to do that again. She couldn't.

"I can't believe we broke in here," she confessed.

"*We* didn't. I did. When they come to arrest us, I'll

take the fall for you," he said. "Just promise to bail me out if they toss me in jail."

She glanced to her right, slanting him a careful look where he was settling on the sacks. His hands were clasped behind his head and his eyes were narrowed on her. "Sorry, I'm broke. I've put all my money into my business."

"Okay, then I'll settle for visits," he said on a deep sigh, and closed his eyes.

The wind shook the small building and the rain beat down on the roof. "You're just going to go to sleep?"

"Why not? There's nothing else to do, is there?"

"No."

"This isn't exactly my ideal situation in a rain-storm—warm, dry, with a fire going in the hearth."

She closed her eyes and muttered, "It's not ideal at all."

"Amen to that," Sam breathed.

Melanie sat with her eyes closed for what seemed forever, then she heard Sam's breathing, slow and easy, and she could almost hate him for being able to relax. Almost.

Chapter Eleven

Angelina watched the two of them. She was beginning to feel exhausted from the effort of getting them together. Melanie was one of the most stubborn of all the humans she'd ever encountered. Give her a gentle shove ahead two steps and she hurled herself back three steps.

Angelina saw Melanie start to nod, then fall asleep. Slowly, she slid down onto the sacks, close to Sam, but not touching. Then Sam opened his eyes, and for a long, long time, he just watched Melanie from under his lashes. The man was doing so well. For someone who had never wanted to need anyone in his life, he needed Melanie. Angelina could feel that as strongly as she could feel the urgency of the Council to get this settled.

Very carefully, Sam moved closer, cautiously sliding his arm around Melanie and easing her toward him. She shifted, then settled into his hold, her head resting on his shoulder and her hand lying on his chest over his heart.

"Oh, yes," Angelina sighed, but there wasn't a kiss. Sam just held her, then his eyes closed and she knew that they were both sound asleep.

Time lost. Time wasted.

The whole night slipped past, then the storm stopped,

dawn broke and still nothing happened. With her patience near an end, she moved in. She tried to nudge them to wake up, to get on with things, but nothing worked.

Humans! They were so difficult, and from the beginning they'd been like this. Aeons ago she'd had one case that humans still heard about, over and over again, and they loved it. They embellished it, and called it a fairy tale. But it had been real.

She just hoped that she wouldn't have to go to such lengths with Sam and Melanie. She couldn't. Not in this day and age. Besides, Sam wasn't a prince and Melanie had a great family, not an evil stepmother and stepsisters. But as she thought that she remembered… Melanie had reached out to Sam when she'd been terrified in the car as it balanced on the side of the gorge.

Miss Victoria had said life and death was out, but that didn't mean that a little fear would be unacceptable. And Angelina was ready to try anything at this point. She cringed at what she had to do, but, with a wave of her hand, she went ahead with it.

MELANIE DIDN'T REMEMBER falling asleep. But when she woke, she knew exactly where she was and where she shouldn't be. There was an arm around her middle, a heart beating against her cheek, and heat everywhere. Sam. Somehow, she was tangled up with him, sleeping in his arms, and she wanted out of his arms…now.

She could hear his soft breathing, feel it ruffling her hair, feel the rhythm of his heart against her cheek. He was still asleep, thank God. She wouldn't have to face that knowing smile of his, or chance this getting out of hand in any way. If she could manage to get away from him without waking him, she was home free. Just slip back, ease away, get up, and that was that.

But when she would have moved, she felt something at her shoulder, a tickling feeling, as if fingertips were being brushed lightly along the material over her skin. She tensed. He wasn't asleep. He was pretending, and now he was touching her, running his fingers lightly down her upper arm.

She heard him sigh, but the tickling kept up and she eased her eyes open, ready to bolt and jerk away from him. But in the dim light in the workshed, she wasn't looking at Sam or his hand on her, but into the face of the biggest, ugliest-looking rat she'd ever seen in her life. Her reaction was instantaneous and violent, hitting at it with her hand as she twisted and jerked in the opposite direction, right into Sam.

The ringing shrieks in the air were all hers as she frantically scrambled in the opposite direction of the rat as it scurried across the blanket and out of sight on the floor. Then Sam had her caught by the shoulders, and she was sitting in the tangle of bedroll and sacks, her coveralls twisted around her legs.

"What in the hell?" he gasped.

"There...there...a rat," she sputtered, waving vaguely in the direction it had darted. "Big, huge, ugly, and it...it touched me. It was...on my skin...touching me!"

She was shaking all over. When Sam pulled her into his arms, she went willingly. But she didn't expect him to be laughing. She heard the chuckling deep in his chest and felt the vibration against her forehead. Her hands curled into fists and she muttered, "What's so funny?"

"I was just thinking that the rat had good taste if he was touching you."

She jerked her head back, face-to-face with that smile, his features softened by recent sleep and hair that was tousled a bit. His eyes were shadowed, but she knew that they were filled with teasing. And endearing, so damned endearing, even with the thoughts of rats and the fear that still made her heart pound.

"It was horrible," she said with real feeling.

He glanced past her, then his gaze was back on her face. "A field mouse," he murmured. "A small, tiny scared-to-death field mouse."

"It…it was a rat, and it was huge."

"Sure it was," he whispered, and his smile faltered as his hand moved to her cheek. His fingers were less than steady as they feathered across her skin. The touch was nothing akin to the contact from the rat. But it scared her almost as much, and she shivered at the connection. But cold had nothing to do with it. There was heat enough, and it seared through her as Sam gently cupped her chin, then came closer to her.

His lips touched her, a fleeting caress at first, a tantalizing silky heat that drew her like a moth to a flame. She could feel a moan grow in her, and a part of her gave in to something she'd seemed to be fighting all of her life. Right then, the connection between them became explosive, burning away anything that had come before, even the kiss on the deck.

This time she knew it was Sam, that it was wrong, so very wrong, but she couldn't stop it. She couldn't stop the way her lips parted, or the way she circled his neck with her arms and the way she pressed to him. The kiss was almost feverish with an edge of desperation in it. Painful on one level, yet exquisitely stunning on another. The need and the desire. Pain on such a pure level that it was beyond absorbing.

Her body ached with the need for him, and when they tumbled back into the makeshift bed together, she tangled her body with his. His strength was against her, shifting over her, and his mouth moved lower, to the sensitive area by her ear. She arched toward the touch, needing it with a desire that blotted out all reason and sanity.

She heard someone utter, "Oh, God," but didn't know if it was her or him. His lips burned a path on her skin, lower to the neck of the coveralls, then the snaps undid as he tugged at the front, and his lips found the cleavage at her breasts. Awkwardly, he pushed at the cotton material, slipping it off her shoulder, then his hand touched her breast through the thin lace of her bra.

The earthquake he'd talked about happened, rocking her world in a way that both devastated and shattered. All good intentions, all her newfound ability to make wise decisions, were gone in that instant, and she tried to get closer. If she could have, she would have melted into him, become a part of him that could never get out, and the thought settled into her soul.

His fingers tugged the fine material of her bra down and when skin touched skin, fear came suddenly through the passion. Her response was almost wanton, crazed in the need of the man, and the fear tried to fight through the haze. She wanted control, she wanted to be able to stop it, but she couldn't. Her hands pressed to his chest, to the fasteners on the coveralls and she jerked them open. Then her hands were on his chest, and she could feel his heart racing under her palms.

His breath caught when she skimmed her hands lower to his stomach, across soft hair over hard muscles. And she wanted more. Heaven help her, but she wanted much more.

"Stop that, and stop it now!"

At first she thought she'd managed to shout those words, then she realized that it wasn't her at all. She felt Sam freeze, his hand still on her breast, and she opened her eyes. He was over her, the expression in his eyes making her tremble as he looked down at her bare breasts where his hands had teased the nipples to hard nubs.

"What?" she breathed, not understanding.

"You damned kids, I've done everything—" Someone else was there, a booming voice. "Dammit all, you broke the lock again, too!"

Melanie shook, part of her horrified at being found like this, and part of her horrified that she hadn't wanted it to stop. Without a word, Sam reached for her coveralls, tugging them up over her shoulders to cover her breasts. His blue eyes burned into her as he braced himself with one hand and shifted to one side.

Melanie could tell she wasn't the only one who had gotten crazy here. It was very apparent that Sam hadn't been indifferent, and he kept his body angled from the intruder to hide the evidence of just how far this had gone.

Melanie grabbed at the bedroll and looked around Sam to see a man in the doorway of the building. He was a large, barrel-chested man dressed in work clothes and sporting a walrus mustache and gray hair protected by a baseball cap. Suddenly his rage was gone and he was laughing. "Good heavens, I thought you were..." He shook his head. "I had no idea that anyone other than oversexed teenagers ever used this place for making out."

"Listen, we're very sorry about this," Sam said, and shifted more, finally standing to face the man. "I'm Sam Harrison and this is Melanie Clark. We had an accident up the road last night during the storm, and we needed a place to wait out the rain."

Melanie pushed herself up, her legs vaguely unsteady, but as she let go of the bedroll, she managed to stand by Sam's side in the tangle of burlap sacks.

"An accident?" the man asked.

"Our car went off the side of the road, then there was a huge mudslide blocking the road. Sorry we broke in, but it was raining like hell." He motioned around the small room. "I'll pay for any damage we've done."

"Forget that. I've just had such a problem with the teenagers around here breaking in to make out…" He shook his head. "Enough of that. I'm Len Taylor, manager of the vineyard. The important thing is that neither one of you looks hurt."

"No, we got out of the car before it went over the side. But we could use a phone."

The man nodded and turned to the phone on the desk.

"That's dead," Melanie said quickly.

"It just needs a code," he said as he picked up the receiver and hit several buttons. "All we need is those kids coming in here and running up a phone bill." He turned and held the receiver out to Sam. "It's working. Be my guest."

Sam crossed to take the receiver from the man, leaving Melanie standing alone in the middle of the burlap mound. Len glanced at her and smiled. "Those coveralls don't look all bad on you, ma'am."

She brushed at the mussed cotton. "I'm sorry for breaking in like this, I really am. I didn't want to, actually."

Sam turned and asked, "Mr. Taylor, where are we?"

"Sanbourn Vineyards. But if you're getting a ride, you'll need to have them come to the offices on St. Clair Lane." He gave Sam an address, then glanced at Melanie as Sam repeated the directions into the phone. "So, how long have you two been stranded here?"

It felt like a lifetime to her, time enough to almost make a horrible mistake. "Since around midnight."

"Lucky you found this place. You're at least three miles from the main buildings. We just keep this place as a drop-off point for the field workers during harvest, or if we get a freeze." He glanced at the mess of burlap. "We usually use the burlap to protect the fruit."

Sam hung up and turned to Melanie. "The rental company's coming with a replacement car and to take the accident report. We'll be out of here in no time."

Len motioned to the doors. "Now that's settled, let's get going. I'll drive you back to the main office to wait."

Melanie moved quickly to pick up her ruined clothes, pushed her feet into her still uncomfortably damp shoes, then headed to the door and stepped out into the pale light of dawn. There was freshness everywhere touched by the earthy scent of the vines and the sodden ground. A chill in the air cut through the thin cotton of the coveralls as she glanced up at a sky without a cloud in sight. It was almost as if last night had never happened.

But as Sam came up beside her, she was reminded that last night had been real, very real. "Over there," he said as he motioned to a mud-splattered truck behind the building.

Sam watched Melanie hurry ahead of them toward the truck and was thankful his body had relaxed. He'd heard about aching for someone, and always thought that was melodramatic at best and stupidly moronic at worst. But now he knew that it not only could happen, it did happen.

"Sorry about that, son," Len said in a low voice. "Bad timing on my part." He patted Sam on the shoulder. "Hell, I'd be willing to push a car over the embankment to have that little thing so thankful for getting her out safely."

Sam squinted in the clear light of morning at Melanie, who was already at the truck and waiting for them. Gratefulness? Or fear from a rat? That thought sat badly with him. He'd never been one to try to force any woman to be with him, or to take advantage of a woman in any way, shape or form. Thinking that Melanie had to be induced to respond to him like that made him slightly sick.

"We were lucky," Sam murmured.

When they got to the truck, Len opened the passenger door and Melanie scrambled into the cab, scooting over to the center of the old bench seat. Sam didn't miss the way she held her clothes tightly against her, or the way she made very sure that they didn't touch at all.

"So, you two from around here?" Len asked as he drove the truck down a narrow, graveled road that cut through the rolling acres of vineyard ahead of them.

Sam glanced at Melanie, but she didn't offer an answer, so he said, "Melanie's lived here all her life. I'm just passing through."

"Where do you live?" he asked Melanie.

"Over near Kinsley Road. We were at my house, and we got lost trying to get back to the Reef Hotel."

"Good heavens, how in the hell did you get way over here?"

"Dumb, stupid luck," she muttered as she sat straighter and held more tightly to her clothes.

"Luck, indeed," Len murmured, then asked Sam, "The rental company's coming out for the two of you?"

"They said they'd meet me at the main office with a replacement car. I guess they need to take an accident report, too, and have me show them where the other car went over the side."

"I should have called Dennis," Melanie said abruptly.

"A brother?" Len asked.

"No, a close friend," she said. "Dennis Benning."

"Did you say Dennis Benning?"

She nodded. "Yes."

"I'll be damned. Benning's on the board here, one of our investors. He bought in a couple of years back. I'd say this qualifies for a small world sort of thing." Len cast Melanie a speculative glance. "I could be wrong, but I thought Benning had been married for a long time."

"It's his son. I need to call him."

"Sure thing. Just as soon as we get to the offices. No problem. I'm just glad I can help out."

Sam could sense a change of attitude in Len just at the mention of the family. It made Sam feel a bit sick, and he found himself saying, "Doesn't hurt to make a good impression on the big boys, does it?"

"Can't say as it does," Len replied good-naturedly. "No one wants to be on the bad side of a Benning around here."

Sam felt Melanie shift, her slight weight barely moving the seat and the urge to put his arm around her flooded over him. It seemed so natural to just reach out and hold her. That was it. Just hold her, to feel her next to him, to know that she was real and there with him.

He pressed his shoulder against the door and looked out at the series of low adobe-type buildings they were approaching. The bad side of a Benning? Sam knew right then that he was going to be on the worst side of the Bennings. He wasn't about to walk away from whatever he'd found here with Melanie. He wanted her and he'd fight Dennis for her.

That idea stunned him. Fighting with a brother for a woman? He would have laughed if he hadn't been so intensely overwhelmed by the woman so close to him, the woman he'd been holding a while ago and kissing as if it were possible to inhale her essence into his soul.

"Finally," Melanie whispered as the truck pulled up to a mission-style building with a courtyard, an impressive fountain, and an arched entryway.

The physical distance between Sam and Melanie grew when Melanie got out of the truck to follow Len into the building. Emotionally it grew even more quickly. Sam hung back, taking deep breaths of the fresh morning air, letting the resolve to not just walk away from Melanie easily settle into him. Only then did he go after her.

The winery's main building was closed, but he had seen Len and Melanie cross the space used for displaying wines produced at the vineyard and every other possible by-product that could be derived from the business. At the far side of the expansive showroom, Sam saw Melanie and Len enter a side room. He caught up to them as he stepped into what looked like a tasting room. Melanie was on a phone at one end of the wine bar, and Len was standing right next to her.

"Yes, I'm at the main building," she said into the

receiver. She listened intently, and he could see her hand shake a bit as it gripped the receiver. "I know, very lucky. But everything's just fine. I just need you...to come and get me." She nodded silently, then said softly, "Please, hurry." She hung up and only turned when Len spoke.

"You get hold of him okay, I take it?"

"Yes, he's coming for me now." She turned, the coveralls ridiculously large and shapeless on her, yet she looked so appealing to Sam that he felt that need in him again. He wanted to touch her, just one more time. "He said he knew where we were."

"He should," Len said, then looked at Sam. "Coffee?"

"Yeah, thanks," he said as Len crossed to a side door and disappeared through it.

Sam didn't take his eyes off Melanie. "So, Dennis is on his way?"

"Yes." She still had her damp clothes caught under one arm. "He'll take me by the hotel for my car."

"I could have taken you there when the rental company brings the replacement car."

She looked at him, her amber eyes slightly narrowed, as if she couldn't quite look at him directly. "Thanks, but taking a ride from you usually ends in disaster...one way or another."

He flinched inside at her words, but shrugged as if it didn't bother him. "Whatever you want," he said.

"Here's coffee for everyone," Len said from behind Sam. He came into Sam's line of sight carrying a tray. He paused long enough for Sam to take one of the three crest-emblazoned mugs, then crossed to Melanie.

Sam cupped the steaming mug, capturing the warmth from the heavy ceramic, but nothing pushed aside the chill produced in him by the way Melanie had shut down. It was as if she'd never kissed him, as if she hadn't been in his arms, as willing as he was to take things to their logical conclusion. Logical? Not even close to logical, he conceded.

A horn sounded and Len glanced out a side window in the tasting room. "It's your ride," he said.

Sam saw Melanie turn, expectantly, with an undisguised expression of relief in her face. That lasted until Len turned and looked at Sam. "The rental company. Damn, but that's fast service."

Sam took a sip of the hot coffee, then looked at Melanie over the rim. Something in him wouldn't let him just quit. "Are you sure you don't want me to take you back?"

She cradled her own mug, but didn't take a drink. "Yes, I'm sure," she said in a flat tone. "Dennis is coming."

"Great." He crossed to put the coffee on the bar, then glanced at Len. "I appreciate everything you did for us. If there's any charges for what we used, just contact me at the Reef Hotel."

Len waved that aside. "Glad to help. Don't even worry about it."

Sam glanced at Melanie, who seemed to be memorizing the steamy brew in her cup. "I'll be in touch." He saw her gaze jerk to his, but didn't understand the flash of what could be fear in her eyes. "No more disasters," he murmured. "I promise." He didn't wait for any response from her before he strode out of the room.

A DAY that had begun explosively for Melanie, settled into the mundane and familiar as soon as Dennis had driven up to the winery to get her. He'd been kind and concerned, shocked by what happened with the car, and agreed to not tell her parents anything about it. There was no reason to worry them after the fact, and every reason to keep quiet about it. And it was over with Sam. Done and gone. Thankfully.

It shocked her, after everything that had happened, that she was still in time to open the shop at nine. Working with the holiday crowds all day gave her a diversion, and she had little time to think about what had almost happened. But she couldn't quite forget Sam's parting words about being in touch.

Every time the phone rang, she hesitated, letting Gwen answer it until four o'clock when her helper took her dinner break. Every time the chimes rang warning that someone had come into the shop, Melanie darted a cautious look that way, relieved when, every time, it turned out to be a stranger.

When the phone rang around five o'clock, Melanie excused herself from a customer and crossed to the desk to answer it. "The Place. May I help you?"

"Oh, I think you can," Dennis murmured in her ear.

"Dennis."

"Smart girl," he said softly. "How are you feeling after your ordeal?"

She leaned against the counter and closed her eyes for a moment. "Better, thanks. At least I'll be better when I get my purse back."

"They'll get it to you soon, but what I called for was to ask you if you're up for something special tonight?"

"We're doing the tree at my parents' house. Remember?"

"Oh, the tree," he repeated, and she knew he'd forgotten. "Of course. Right. The tree."

"You don't have to come, if you don't want to."

"No, I want to come, believe me, it's just there's something else I'd like to do tonight. I think we'd have time, actually."

"To do what?"

She heard him take a deep breath. "My parents asked me to drop by this evening, and I thought it was a terrific time for you to meet them."

She wasn't sure "terrific" would be the right adjective, not after Reggie's report when she'd finally met them. "Are you sure about this?"

"Absolutely. We can stop by there, then go to the tree trimming."

She knew she should do it. "Sure, of course we can."

"Great," he said. "I'll come by and get you at seven. That should give us enough time for the visit before the tree trimming."

She didn't want to do this, not now, but she knew she should. "Okay, I'll get Gwen to close for me."

"See you at seven," he said, then hung up.

She slowly replaced the receiver and when the chime for the door rang, she almost jumped out of her skin. She turned to find a young couple coming into the store. Not Sam. He was gone, despite his promise to be in touch. He was gone and she breathed a bit easier.

Chapter Twelve

By seven o'clock Melanie was in Dennis's car driving away from the shop and heading south. She actually felt reasonably calm and confident that things were good with her. Very good. Sam had never shown up or called, and Dennis looked fantastic in a gray cable knit sweater worn with dark slacks. Surprisingly, she found that she was actually a bit eager to meet his parents.

"Very nice," Dennis commented when he stopped for a stop sign and he glanced at her. His eyes flickered over the full-sleeved ivory blouse she was wearing with black velvet slacks and matching jacket.

"Do you think I look okay? I thought I should dress up more, but if we're going to be doing the tree thing afterward, I didn't want to be too fancy."

"Mother and Father will think you're wonderful, and gorgeous, to boot. Absolutely perfect, as usual."

She wasn't even close to perfect. "I'm not—"

"You're wonderful, and you know it." He smiled slightly and reached over to pat her hand resting on her small evening bag in her lap. "Miss Perfect."

Mr. Perfect is with Miss Perfect. The thought was there unbidden, and worse yet, it echoed inside her in Sam's voice. She swallowed hard, trying to ignore the perversity of her own thoughts as she brushed at the front of her jacket. "I really think I should have dressed up more or maybe borrowed one of the good pieces of jewelry from the store to wear with this outfit."

"Stop that." He squeezed her hand with his, then pulled it back as the light changed and he drove off. "Calm down. No matter what happened with Reggie, I can tell you that their bark is much worse than their bite. They'll love you."

She made herself take a breath and smoothed her hands on the black leather of her purse. "What did they say when you told them whose sister I am?"

He was silent for a long moment, then shrugged. "Nothing."

"You didn't tell them, yet, did you?"

He looked a bit taken aback when he glanced at her. Then he suddenly smiled, a smile that reminded her so much of Sam's for a moment, that it made her stomach lurch. "They'll know soon enough," he murmured.

"Oh, Dennis," she said, trying to figure out what was going on with her. Couldn't she look at him without getting things confused and having her feelings get crazy again? "I don't think—"

"Then *don't* think right now. We don't have a lot of time."

"My parents don't care when we get there, as long as we get there," she said.

"But my parents want us there at eight, and we have to stop at the beach house on the way. The agent called and said that she needed another signature from me, and she was in that area, so we agreed to meet there for a few minutes."

It was then she realized that they were on the highway above the beach house. Dennis slowed, then swung onto the narrow road that led down to the house. A large dump truck and a skip loader partially blocked the road. They were scooping up dirt and mud that had fallen onto the road from the drop off below the highway. Nothing like the mudslide from last night, but it still made her neck and shoulders tense.

Dennis managed to get past, and Melanie could see the house. The lights at the gate were on and there was a luxury sedan with tinted windows parked by the stone wall. Dennis drove beyond it, nose into the wall, to park. "Well, she's here. This won't take a minute," he said as he stopped and opened the door. "Do you want to wait out here or—"

"I'll come in," she said, leaving her bag on the car seat as she got out.

She went around the car and walked with Dennis to the open gate and through, into the courtyard. Dennis stood back to let her go ahead, and she stepped into the house, into soft light, the scent of wood smoke in the air. She stopped so abruptly that Dennis bumped into her back.

He gripped her by the shoulders, then looked around her as she stared straight ahead into a face that had the same smile on it that she'd seen on Dennis's just moments ago. Sam was standing by the French doors looking smugly pleased at her obvious shock.

Dennis moved around Melanie and crossed to Sam. They were talking, she knew it, but all she could hear clearly was the pounding of her own heart in her ears. No matter what she'd hoped, the man hadn't gone away. He was bound never to give her room to breathe or to get her bearings.

Just the sight of him scrambled her reason and left her slightly breathless. It didn't help that he never looked bad. Now, in a black band-collared shirt worn with gray slacks, his hair brushed back carelessly from his face, she could barely look at him.

Dennis turned to her right then, smiled, and motioned her over to him with his outstretched hand. "I know Mel feels the same way," he was saying.

She moved across the room, barely feeling the footsteps she took, then her hand was in Dennis's, and she held to him as if he was an anchor in a horrible storm. She looked right at Dennis as the thought that he was, indeed, an anchor settled in her. And the storm was right beside him in the form of Sam Harrison.

"I was just telling Sam that we're very grateful to him for what he did for you last night," he said, squeezing her hand slightly. "We won't forget it."

She swallowed hard. That's just what she was going to do. Forget. Everything. She forced herself to look right at Sam, bracing herself for the contact. "Yes, thank you," she managed to say.

Deep blue eyes narrowed a touch, but the smile that turned up the corners of his mouth seemed genuine. "We were lucky," he murmured as his eyes flickered over her. "I can see that you're none the worse for wear."

Dennis pulled her closer, slipping an arm around her shoulders. "Melanie's perfect."

She cringed at his choice of words, and knew by the slight flicker of a smile in Sam's eyes that he didn't miss the usage, either. "I've heard that no one's perfect, but I'd say she came pretty close. Oh, by the way," he said as he reached to his right, "your purse."

She saw him pick her bag up off a chair by the doors and hold it out to her. Thankfully, Dennis took it from him and smiled at Melanie. "See, I told you they'd find it and get it back to you."

She took the leather bag and gathered it to her middle, pressing it tightly to her. "Thanks," she whispered without looking at Sam.

"No problem," Sam said.

"Problem? Does someone have a problem?"

Angela seemed to burst into the house at that moment, and Melanie turned to see the real estate agent crossing the room toward them. The woman looked almost ethereal in a simple white wool dress that emphasized the fiery color of her hair, which was confined in a single braid.

"No problems here," Dennis said.

"Wonderful. Then we can get this matter settled."

"What did you need another signature for?" Sam asked from somewhere behind Melanie.

"Neither one of you signed the second sheet." She held up two sheets of paper that Melanie hadn't even been aware the woman had in her hand before that moment. "If you'll both sign them, I'll get this settled for you."

Melanie moved to one side, turning to the glass and the night outside. The ocean was wonderfully calm, a distinct contrast to her own feelings at the moment. The storm of last night might never have been, from the look of the world outside this house. But inside her, the storm had left its mark.

"And that's that," she heard Angela say brightly.

"When will we know about the house?" Dennis asked.

"Soon, very soon. Just a few minor things to iron out, and this shall all be settled." Melanie turned and saw Angela shaking hands with Dennis, then she turned and gave a key to Sam. "You mentioned that you needed to check out some things about the house, Mr. Harrison. Just lock up when you leave and put the key in the lock box."

With a wave in her direction, the woman headed for the door. "I have to fly, but I will definitely contact you both tomorrow." And she was gone.

Dennis turned with a smile. "The woman never stops, does she?"

"A human steamroller," Sam murmured.

"More like a whirlwind." Dennis glanced at Melanie. "Now, we need to get going."

She needed out of here, and she didn't fight Dennis at all. She went to him without glancing at Sam, and never looked back when Sam said, "Merry Christmas to both of you."

"Same to you," Dennis said, and led the way out the front door.

Melanie walked quickly behind Dennis, needing to put as much distance between herself and Sam as she possibly could. As she stepped through the gate she was shocked when Dennis exploded. "Dammit all! What on earth?"

She saw him hurry over to where he'd parked, and immediately knew why a man who never got angry was suddenly furious. A huge pile of earth had been dumped right behind his car. It was piled at least four feet high, and totally blocked the car from moving more than an inch or two forward or backward.

Dennis looked up the road, then back at the car. "I can't believe anyone would be stupid enough to do something like this!" he fumed.

Melanie was fascinated that Dennis was showing real anger. She'd always been under the impression that a

Benning never lost their temper. "What kind of idiot would do this?" he demanded as he came back to where Melanie stood by the gate. "Have you got your phone with you?"

"In my bag, in the car," she said.

"Great." He turned and sprinted back to the car.

"I thought you two were gone."

She almost jumped out of her skin when Sam spoke from behind her. With a vague motion of her hand toward the dirt pile, she said, "We were supposed to be gone."

"Oh, shoot," he murmured, and she knew without looking that he was smiling, teasing her, but she wouldn't rise to it. "And who chose to dump that right there?"

"Some construction crew from the city," Dennis said as he strode back to where they stood, the cell phone in his hand. "And they're coming out to clear it."

"That's fast action," Sam murmured.

"Not fast enough. They have to call the crew, who probably aren't even back to their houses yet, then get them back out here with the equipment to remove it. I'd say we'd be lucky if they get here in an hour or more."

"Well, the house is comfortable," Sam said. "And I have the key."

Dennis looked at his watch, which glowed faintly in the night. "Dammit all, it's almost seven-thirty."

"You have to be somewhere?" Sam asked.

"We're due at my parents' place in half an hour."

"Call them and tell them we can't make it." All of her good feelings about this evening were gone, and she didn't want to face the Bennings right now. "We'll go tomorrow evening."

Dennis shook his head. "No, that won't do. Their schedule is full until well past the New Year. Besides, I don't want to put this off."

"Then call a taxi," Melanie said.

"I guess that's the best we can do. We'll be late, but I don't—"

"Where do they live?" Sam asked.

"About fifteen minutes from here, in the Crown Point area."

"I don't have any idea where the Crown Point area is, but if you need a ride, I'm ready to leave and I've got a car that's not blocked by a ton of mud. I can drive you there, if you like?"

Melanie wanted to yell "No!" but before she could even form the single word, Dennis was talking. "Do you mean it?"

"Absolutely," Sam said. "I never say anything I don't mean."

"Then I accept," Dennis said quickly.

"Dennis, we don't have to—"

Dennis interrupted her. "We do. I don't want anything to start this evening off on the wrong foot."

She swallowed hard, cutting off any other words of protest, and simply nodded. "Okay."

"Then let's go," Sam said, motioning to his rental car.

When Sam unlocked the car, Melanie slipped into the back seat of the luxury sedan. Dennis closed her door, then slipped into the front passenger seat as Sam got in behind the wheel.

"Just give me directions," Sam said as he started the engine. "We don't want to get lost."

His words startled her, and when she looked up, he was glancing over his shoulder to back the car up. But she didn't miss the way his gaze met hers, or that perpetual suggestion of an amused smile at the edges of his lips.

Melanie clutched her purse tightly in her lap, and swallowed hard in an attempt to settle her stomach. Tonight was going worse than last night, and there was nothing she could do about it.

As they drove out to the highway and Dennis gave Sam directions, Melanie sat very still and stayed silent. Time was blurring for her, taking on a life of its own. Seconds felt like hours, and the ride to the Benningses' seemed interminable. Just once she looked up from her hands that worried her purse, and saw Dennis and Sam talking together.

The two men seemed easy with each other, talking and visiting as if they'd been friends for years. Suddenly life turned more perverse than it had before. For an instant she saw the two of them, mirror images of each other, the same man blurring together. Closing her eyes quickly, she took deep, even breaths to calm her nerves. She was imagining things, hallucinating, and dreaded having to face the Bennings while she barely had a grip on her own sanity.

Sam, for his part, was having a hard time, too. He'd decided to never see his birth father, now suddenly it had seemed like it was meant for him to see him, and to go to see him with his half brother *and* Melanie. The best laid plans, he thought as they drove north, still a bit surprised that he'd made the offer to take Dennis to the Benning house.

Melanie being there hadn't helped. Just seeing her walk through the door had reminded him how alive he felt when she was around. Then Dennis had been there, the half brother who, despite Sam's determination to dislike him, was actually very likable. If things had been different, he would have enjoyed being around Dennis. But with Melanie there, the tension ate at him, that and the knowledge that he'd do just about anything to make Melanie smile at him the way she did at Dennis.

"Right here," Dennis said as they drove along a quiet street with brick walls on either side. "This drive."

Sam turned onto the drive and stopped at closed wrought-iron gates that blocked the way. "Just a minute," Dennis said as he got out and went around to the security keypad on the driver's side. He punched in a series of numbers, and with a low groan, the gates started to open.

By the time Dennis was back in the car, the gates were fully open and Sam drove onto a cobbled drive that led toward a house with columns and sweeping wings in both direction. A two-story-high portico jutted out over the driveway at the marble-staired entry. Money. Old family. Sam could see the physical evidence of just what the Benning name meant.

As he approached the portico, he tried to think of some reason to go inside to come face-to-face with the man who had fathered him. But when he stopped under the columned structure, he didn't have to come up with any lame excuse at all. The entry door opened and a man came out onto the top step.

"My father has obviously been waiting," Dennis said as he got out of the car, then opened the back door for Melanie. Sam slipped out, closed his door and looked over the parked car at his father in the overhead lights.

Dennis Benning. The man who had fathered him. Yet as the man came down the steps, Sam felt little if anything. He didn't know what he'd expected, but it wasn't to be able to look at the man who'd abandoned his mother and only be aware of the expensive suit he was wearing, and how thick his gray hair was, and how his stiff smile never touched eyes set in a face that held traces of Dennis in the features.

"Father, I'm sorry we're late," Dennis said, "but we had a bit of trouble."

The older Benning stopped at the bottom of the stairs. "Your car broke down?" he asked in a deep, strong voice.

"No, not really," Dennis said. "It's undrivable, but thanks to a very generous offer, we finally made it." He turned to Sam and motioned him to come around the car to where the three people stood. "Sam, come here."

Sam slowly circled the car, getting closer and closer to his father standing with his brother. The older Benning held out a hand to Sam. "Thank you for your help, sir," he said formally.

Sam gripped his hand, but there was no sudden sense of connection. It puzzled him. Wasn't there suppose to be some recognition between blood relatives? "Glad to help," he said as he stepped back.

Mr. Benning glanced at Dennis, then at Melanie, who had hung back a bit behind Dennis. "Dennis, this is…"

"This is Melanie. Melanie, my father."

Melanie took a step forward, and Sam noticed that her chin elevated slightly and her smile came with just a touch of stiffness. He could tell she wasn't enjoying this very much, not any more than the rest of the people at the foot of the stairs seemed to be enjoying it. "Mr. Benning," she murmured.

Mr. Benning glanced back at Sam. "Will you join us for a cup of holiday cheer before you leave?"

Holiday cheer? Glancing at Melanie, he thought she could use some holiday cheer. Perversely, he wanted to extend this meeting, to try to figure out what was going on with him. "Yes, sir, I'd like that."

"Good. Shall we go inside?" his father asked as he turned and started back up the marble stairs.

Dennis took Melanie by the arm, then went after his father with Sam following up the stairs and into the double front entry of the mansion. The foyer was dominated by a sweeping staircase that led up to a balcony on the second level. A huge silver Christmas tree decorated with blue bows and silver bells, stood on the polished floor, creating a scene that would have been right at home in the hotel lobby. Just as perfect, just as cold.

He saw Melanie glance at the tree and before she could hide her reaction, he caught her flashing grimace. *Good girl,* he thought. She felt it, too. The only connection he felt in that house right then was with the woman who was here with his brother. That feeling only deepened as the elder Benning led the way into a sitting area to their left.

Deep burgundy carpeting muffled the sounds of their footsteps, and a fire in a huge rock hearth was just as fake as the tree, made from gas flames and lava logs. Even the books on dark wooden shelves were perfect, and probably never even used. Mr. Benning crossed to an extensive bar on a side wall while Dennis took Melanie to a wing-backed leather couch near the hearth.

Sam crossed to the hearth and stood to one side while the decision to get out of there as soon as he could took form. This was enough, just seeing him. There certainly wasn't anything he wanted from this man or his son.

As soon as he could, he'd make his excuses and leave. There was nothing here for him.

He believed that until he glanced at Melanie. Well, almost nothing, he conceded, and caught her eye. He motioned to the room with a slight nod of his head, and mouthed the word "perfect." But instead of eliciting the smile from her he'd hoped for, he saw her cheeks dot with color and her mouth tighten. She was very nervous.

He almost smiled at the way she worried the cuff of her jacket, and crossed and uncrossed her legs at the ankles. She was beyond nervous. So, she didn't feel as if she fit in here, either. It didn't help that his natural impulse was to grab Melanie and get the hell out of the place.

"Here you go." He glanced to his left to Mr. Benning offering him a drink while Dennis gave one to Melanie.

He took the glass, then took a sip of a spicy drink that had enough alcohol in it to have a kick.

"I'm sorry," Mr. Benning said. "Dennis neglected to introduce—"

"Good evening and happy holidays!"

The voice that made that pronouncement drew all eyes to the entry of the room. An elegantly dressed woman sailed into the room, her precisely made-up face fixed in a politely expansive smile. She paused as she got to the older Benning's side, then glanced at Sam, Melanie and finally at Dennis. "I guess I misunderstood. I thought we were getting together to talk this evening," she said.

Dennis stood when she spoke. "Mother, this is Melanie Clark and—"

She looked sharply at Melanie. "Clark? If I remember correctly, you knew a Clark, but I don't believe it was Melanie.'' She frowned slightly. ''No, Regina. That was it. Regina Clark.''

Melanie stood and Sam watched her face the woman without blinking. ''Reggie's my sister,'' she said evenly.

Mrs. Benning's eyes widened slightly as she whispered a soft, ''Oh,'' obviously regrouping, trying to figure out what was going on without appearing too crass. ''Well, I trust that Regina is well?''

''Reggie's just fine, thank you. She's married, has a child, and is expecting another one in a few weeks.''

''That child at her house—'' Mrs. Benning asked as her gaze flicked to Dennis.

''Mikey,'' Melanie said. ''His name's Mikey and Reggie married his father last year.''

''Oh, my, well, that's…that's interesting,'' the woman murmured, sinking gracefully into one of the high-backed leather chairs. She glanced to Sam. ''I am sorry, I didn't mean to be rude. Dennis didn't mention you, either.''

''I just drove Dennis and Melanie over here.''

She glanced at her husband. ''Could you get me a drink, dear?''

Sam looked at his father and was taken aback to find him watching him intently. Pale blue eyes were unblinking for a long moment, then he silently turned and crossed to the bar.

''You're with Miss Clark?'' Mrs. Benning asked.

''No, I was at the beach house when Melanie and Dennis were there and—''

''You live at the beach?'' she asked, uttering the word ''beach'' in much the same tone she might have uttered ''typhoid.''

"I want to, but no, I don't yet. We were at the house Dennis and I both want to lease, and—"

She didn't let him finish. Her head turned with a snap and she spoke abruptly. "Dennis? Leasing? The beach? What is this gentleman talking about?"

Dennis inhaled deeply as he met his mother's disapproval. "I've been looking for a second place, you know that, and I thought that a place at the beach would be different."

"Where is it?"

He gave her the address, and that brought a disdainful sweep of her hand. "Goodness. What are you thinking of? That will not do at all. If you insist on being at the water, then you have to look at the Lennox area. My dear, I don't know what you or your father would do if it weren't for me making sure—"

"We'd probably do just fine," Dennis said.

His mother sat straighter, then looked at her husband who was just bringing her drink to her. "Dennis, tell your son that we are not amused by his need to do something totally unthinkable. It is ridiculous, like some form of juvenile rebellion."

The elder Benning gave his wife the drink, then turned to Dennis. "You're leasing?"

"For now."

"That's sensible. You can see if you even like it."

Mrs. Benning shot out of her chair, the drink untouched in her hands. "My dear, that is not what I meant."

"I know what you meant," he murmured, and drank from his own drink. "And this is not the time nor place to discuss this. We have guests."

She looked from father to son, then sank back down in her chair and drank almost half of her drink before sighing heavily. "We shall talk about this later," she said, then looked at Melanie with a brittle smile. "So, you and my Dennis are friends?"

"Yes, we are," Melanie said softly.

Dennis reached out and covered Melanie's hand with his. "Mother, Melanie and I are seeing each other."

Sam watched the scene in front of him unfold dispassionately. His only thought, beyond wondering why in the hell Melanie had anything to do with any of the Bennings, was to be grateful that he'd never been part of this family. As much as he resented the old man walking away from his mother without a backward glance, he now almost felt thankful that he had.

He heard the softly uttered, "Oh," that seemed to be part and parcel of Mrs. Benning when she was affronted. Carefully, she finished off the last of her drink before putting the glass on a side table by her chair. "I was under the impression you were bringing a friend."

"Melanie *is* a friend," Dennis said firmly. "And much more." He glanced at Melanie, smiled faintly at her, then back at his mother. "That's why she's here. I want you and Father to get to know her."

Mrs. Benning looked long and hard at Dennis, then flicked her gaze to Melanie. "My dear, tell me, there are...what, a dozen of you?"

Sam was almost sure he saw laughter in Melanie's eyes, but none of it touched her lips or her words. "Nine."

"That's all?"

"Just nine."

Mrs. Benning looked at her husband. "My goodness, that does seem excessive, doesn't it?"

The elder Benning met his wife's gaze, then looked

at Sam. "And you, sir? I'm sorry, I didn't get your name?"

He looked his father in the eye and said, "Sam Harrison."

Chapter Thirteen

There was nothing in the older man's expression, no flicker of recognition. He didn't even know his own son's name. "Mr. Harrison, I'm sorry that our family is discussing personal matters in front of you."

Sam was, too. "I really need to be going, anyway."

Mrs. Benning acted as if Sam hadn't spoken. She was glaring at Dennis. "You aren't suggesting what I think you're suggesting, are you?" she asked with great distaste in her tone.

Sam watched his brother brace himself to face the woman to say the words that Sam was sure he would hate almost as much as he hated the way these people were acting.

"No, I'm not suggesting it. I care very much for Melanie and I plan on having her in my life. We are going to—"

He never got the rest of the statement out because the tiny lady uttered a soft moan as her trembling hand theatrically swept to her forehead. The next thing Sam knew, Mrs. Benning's eyes fluttered and she proceeded to faint dead away.

Melanie was on her feet right away, but neither Dennis nor his father made a move. Neither did Sam. He stood by the mantel, just watching. Dennis, on the other hand, wasn't even looking at his mother. His attention was on his father. Neither said a word. The older man finally shrugged and moved closer to his wife's chair.

"Emily?" he said as he stood over her without touching her. "Emily, my dear?"

"Dennis, call a doctor or something," Melanie whispered, unnerved at how calm the men were about all of this.

Mr. Benning murmured, "Don't fuss," and crossed to the bar. "There's no need to call anyone." He reached for a white towel from a stack by the sink, dampened it, and came back with it neatly folded in his hand. "Emily is quite all right."

Melanie would have argued with the man if Dennis hadn't touched her shoulder. "Melanie, Mother's fine. She just has these spells when she's upset." He shrugged. "Mother is as strong as an ox, but she has difficulty coping with…adversity."

The elder Benning was back at the chair with a damp towel, which he carefully laid on his wife's forehead. She started slightly, then her eyes fluttered and her mouth tightened a bit. So they were right? It was all a well-rehearsed act. Her eyes fluttered again, then she looked up at her husband. "I am so sorry, my dear," she whispered in a pitifully weak voice.

Sam, who had been silent through all of this, suddenly spoke up. "Is there anything I can do?"

Dennis glanced away from his mother to Sam. "Yes, as a matter of fact, there is something you could do, if it's not too much trouble?"

"Anything," Sam murmured, and Melanie could feel his need to escape from this mess. She felt it, too.

As if Dennis had read her mind, he said, "Could you

run Melanie back to the beach house? My car should be cleared by now, and she can drive it to her parents' home.'' His mother moaned softly, but he didn't even look at her. "I have things here that I need to discuss with my parents.''

"Oh, dear,'' Mrs. Benning said, waving a hand weakly in her son's direction. "Please, dear, go. I need to rest. We can talk later when I feel stronger.''

Dennis turned to her. "No, Mother, we'll talk now.'' He reached into his pocket and took out a key ring he handed to Melanie. "Get my car, and go decorate the tree. I'll call you there later.''

When she took the keys, Dennis leaned toward her and kissed her quickly on the lips. "I'm very sorry,'' he breathed. "I'll make it up to you.''

"Dennis, please, just go, we—'' Mrs. Benning began as she finally sat up.

"Emily, please.'' Her husband cut her off this time. "We need to talk, now. The three of us.''

She stared at her husband, looking as stunned as if he'd struck her, and it was obvious that the men in her life just didn't stand up to her...until now.

Dennis exchanged a glance with his father, then looked at Sam and held out his hand. "Thank you for everything.'' Sam shook his hand, then went to stand beside Melanie.

At any other time she would have fought leaving with him. God knew, she certainly didn't want to be in a car with him again. But the alternative of staying here was even less appealing at the moment. She touched Dennis on the arm. "I'll see you later,'' she said, then looked past him at Mr. and Mrs. Benning. "Goodbye.''

The older man looked at her and unexpectedly

smiled, an expression that didn't seem to come easily to him. "I do apologize for all this."

"Yes, sir," she murmured without looking at his wife.

Then Sam had her by her upper arm, murmuring something trite about the holidays, and they were leaving together.

Sam never released her arm until they were at his car and he reached to open the door for her. She scrambled inside, then he swung the door shut and came around the front to get in behind the wheel.

As he closed the door, she braced herself for being so close to him, and for a trip that she wasn't looking forward to at all. But instead of starting the car and getting on with it, he startled her when he hit the top of the steering wheel with the flats of both hands. Then laughed out loud.

She stared at him, at the way his shoulders shook with humor that she didn't understand. "What's so funny?"

He took a deep breath, then sank back in the seat and turned to her. "This…this whole thing," he said. "This family…it's a joke!"

That was when she realized that it wasn't all humor in him. There was an edge to his voice that she didn't understand. Maybe bitterness being smothered by the laughter, but whatever it was, it was off center and wrong. "Not very funny," she muttered.

"Can I ask you something?"

She just wished that he'd start the car and get going, but she nodded. "Sure, why not?"

"How did you keep from hitting her when she said that about nine children?"

That brought a smile to her face, and an easing of

tension that she welcomed. "I thought about it, but she wouldn't change. God, Reggie told me what she was like, but I didn't think anyone could be that snobby and manipulative."

"Fainting like that is straight out of a Victorian novel. Women having the vapors."

"It was, wasn't it?" she murmured. "I thought she…" She took a deep breath. "I mean, it scared me for a minute, until I realized why Dennis and his father weren't the least bit concerned."

He started the car then, and as he slowly drove down the driveway and away from the Bennings, said, "God help them all. They deserve each other."

She wasn't sure of that. "Poor Dennis—"

"Poor Dennis? He's got to be over thirty."

"He's thirty-five."

"Then he doesn't have to be there. He's got the resources to get the hell out."

"Money doesn't have anything to do with it. They're his parents. You don't just cut off parents if they aren't to your liking, any more than you could cut off a child if they aren't to your liking."

"People do. They have," he said tightly.

"Maybe some do, but most don't. Life isn't supposed to work that way, and I respect Dennis for what he's doing."

"I guess you would," he muttered sarcastically.

"What does that mean?"

"Your epiphany. Your moment of clarity. Hang in there no matter what and never wonder about what could have been."

She didn't understand his growing anger at all.

"That moment," he added, "when you decided no

matter what, you were going to deny what you are and be what you think you should be.''

She felt a sudden burning behind her eyes. At any other time, with any other person, she would have gotten angry and told him just what he could do with his opinion. But she found that she couldn't say anything for a moment, and she could feel dampness on her lashes.

When he turned in her direction as they headed south on the highway, she looked away from him into the night. It shocked her when she realized that she was crying, tears slipping silently down her cheeks. She tried so hard, and she'd almost made this work. Until Sam had shown up. ''What do you care?'' she whispered.

Without warning, his hand touched hers, covering her clenched fist on her lap with heat that seeped into her. ''Do you have to ask that?''

She'd done it again. Without even trying. She'd done it again. She knew she should pull away from his touch, that she should tell him to leave her alone, but she couldn't. She closed her eyes tightly, pressing her forehead to the cold glass of the side window and turned her hand over in Sam's so their fingers laced. ''No,'' she whispered flatly. ''No.''

Sam didn't say a thing, just drove, never letting go of her hand, and as they got farther and farther from Dennis and the Bennings, Melanie tried to get control. She eased her hand out of Sam's, and he let her go without a fight. Then she wiped at her damp face, and tried to breathe evenly. As the car slowed, she opened her eyes and saw that they were almost to the beach house. Almost to freedom.

Yet she felt no sense of relief at all. As they went down the narrow road to the house, she knew this was it. She looked ahead of them and saw lights flashing, then saw the skip loader, and the mound of dirt still behind the car. One of the men waved to Sam, motioning him to the same parking spot he'd used earlier, and when they stopped, the man came around to the driver's side.

When Sam opened the door, the man said, "Sorry about this, man, but we'll have it cleared in half an hour. We just got the crew here a few minutes ago."

Half an hour? Melanie felt her stomach sink. Half an hour longer. She sat very still as the construction worker added, "Hey, we wouldn't have dumped it here, but that lady told us to, said that you wouldn't be needing to get the car out tonight."

"The lady?" Sam asked as he got out.

"Yeah, that lady with—" The explanation was cut off when Sam closed his door.

Melanie pressed a hand to her eyes, then jumped when her door was suddenly opened. Sam was there, waiting. "He says it's going to be a while, so why don't we wait inside where it's warmer?"

She grabbed her purse and got out, trying not to make contact with Sam, and headed for the house. He was there, going around her to open the gate and preceding her to the doors. By the time she got there, the doors were open and Sam was already inside.

She stopped at the threshold, something in her knowing that once she went through the door, everything would change. And just the way it had been when Sam had taken her hand in the car, she couldn't fight it any longer. She didn't have anything left in her to do the right thing, to make smart choices. As she entered the house, a single light illuminating the large front room, she saw Sam.

In that moment she was shattered by a very simple fact that had probably been there from the first moment she'd seen Sam. She loved him. Really loved him. And she knew that she'd never loved anyone before. She'd thought she had. She'd been certain she had. But nothing she'd ever felt for anyone in the past could even come close to what she felt for Sam Harrison.

He watched her silently from the middle of the room, then he simply held out one hand to her. "Melanie, come here," he said in a rough, low voice.

And she did. She went to him with a sense of destiny that defied logic. Mistake or not, she knew that her whole life had been preparation for this moment. She put her hand in his, and as soon as the contact was made, her fate was sealed.

The next moment she was in his arms, and they held each other, Sam's arms around her as unsteady as she felt. Then she lifted her face and as Sam breathed, "Oh, love, I know you," she knew he did.

She pressed her forehead to his chest and could feel the hammering of his heart. "Dammit," she whispered.

Sam's rough chuckle vibrated through her. "Oh, girl, you're treading in deep water."

She moved back a bit and looked into his face. Deep water? She was in so far over her head that she couldn't breathe, and she knew that she couldn't tread water anymore. Her hand lifted as of on its own volition and her fingers touched his chin. She felt the slight roughness of a new beard, then trailed her finger to his lips. God help her, she had never wanted a man like she wanted Sam right then. Right or wrong, if it was just for this moment, or forever, she wanted him.

Without a word, Sam pulled her more tightly to him, and for a long moment they just held to each other.

Then she felt Sam press a kiss to her hair and whisper, "This is it."

She didn't understand, and maybe she didn't want to. She lifted her face and when his lips found hers, she stopped thinking. She felt. Pure and simple. She lost herself in the sensations of being kissed by him, of his tongue invading her, his hands on her, one pressed to her hips, the other tangling in her hair.

The explosion of need was overwhelming, white-hot and searing through her, and she couldn't get enough of him. She was close to him, feeling his body against hers, but she couldn't get close enough. She was desperate to be with him, and wished that she could crawl inside him and never come out. That she would exist with only him. And in that moment, that's what she did. Nothing existed but Sam, and nothing would as long as he was right here with her.

When he picked her up, she circled his neck with her arms and buried her face in his throat. She tasted him as he carried her in his arms. She let the taste of him invade her soul, searing into it to never be lost. She felt him tremble when she worked her hand inside his shirt, felt his nipple respond immediately to her touch, and his low groan surround her.

Then she was falling, but falling safe in his arms, into the huge bed in the master bedroom. Somehow he'd tugged the dustcover off, and they were together on the mattress, tangling, the passion so fiery that she knew it could consume them. Time stood still, blurring all around her, centering on Sam over her, on his hands tugging at her jacket, freeing her from its confines, then manipulating the buttons on her blouse.

All the while, his lips trailed fiery paths along her skin, touching the delicate points just below her ear, then at the base of her throat. The silk of her blouse was gone, and his hand was on her bare skin, slipping under the lace of her bra, freeing her breasts, and exposing her to his hands, then his lips. He tasted her, his tongue tracing circles on her nipples, drawing at something so deep inside her that she was shocked at the sensations.

She wanted him against her, with no barriers, and she frantically pulled at his shirt, almost crying with the urgency that filled her. Then Sam moved back and her sense of loss was staggering. She opened her eyes, and he was still over her, but stripping off his shirt. Then he slid off the bed to stand at the side, and he stepped out of his pants. The white of his briefs was stark even in the shadows of the room, then it was gone and she knew that he wanted her every bit as much as she wanted him.

He was over her, hesitating, then she held out her hands to him. "Please," she uttered, "please love me."

He slowly came back to her, and the heat of him was against her, the hard urgency of his need pressed to her. If ever there was a moment of perfect rightness in her life, it was then. Sam slipped her slacks down and off, untangling them from her legs, then his fingers slipped under the elastic of her panties and the sheer cover was gone.

Melanie was very still, unable to breathe as his hand went lower. Then he found her. His hand pressed to her and she gasped, arching toward the contact. His hand moved on her, slowly at first, then faster until she felt she would explode. The mounting sensations were so exquisite, driving her higher and higher, then his touch was gone. She cried out, reaching for him, but the separation was only for a heartbeat.

He was over her, between her legs, and she felt his hard strength against her. As if they'd been lovers for an eternity, she lifted her hips and he entered her, slowly, surely, the trembling in his body matching hers. Then he filled her, wholly and completely, his body over hers, sheltering hers. The first stroke caught her breath, then she moved with him, matching each thrust of his, over and over again.

What had been pleasure before, transformed into ecstasy for her. The sensations growing and growing, centering on this man and shutting out everything but being closer than was humanly possible. Her fingers dug into his back. Her head arched back, and as she felt herself ready to explode, she cried out. Another voice mingled with hers, then the completion came in a burst so all-encompassing that she lost herself in the moment.

Whatever she'd thought before about right and wrong, about what she should be or what she shouldn't be, she knew with a certainty at that moment that she was right where she was meant to be. As she held to Sam, wrapping her legs around his hips to keep him in her for a bit longer, she knew that every moment, every thing she did in her life had been heading toward this encounter and to this man.

The waves beat on the beach below, and Sam held Melanie to him in the shadows of the bedroom. He could feel each soft breath she took, then felt his breathing catch when she turned more toward him and cuddled into his side. His body responded almost immediately to the feel of her against him, and when her hand shifted to rest over his heart, he felt something that didn't make any sense at all.

Regret. Maybe shame that he'd been so selfish and driven by his own needs. There was a sudden feeling of everything being wrong. Moments ago everything had been right, very right. God, he'd never felt like this about anyone in his life. He'd always been able to live through any situation and walk away.

When it was over, it was over, but he knew deep in his soul that that was his past. What he'd found with Melanie would never be over.

And that was the problem. He'd never stop wanting her. He'd never stop needing her. And he'd never stop loving her. That last thought came softly, filtering into him. Loving her was as natural and as needful for him as breathing. And as wrong.

She belonged with Dennis. She belonged with the life she wanted with Dennis. This wasn't reality. This was wishful thinking, a fantasy, and it was his doing and his making. He hadn't played fair, not with Dennis or with Melanie. Especially with Melanie. He should have backed off the minute he knew she was in love with his brother, but instead he'd played on her impetuous nature, on her need to be a bit wild and unconventional.

Melanie stirred, shifting to rest her leg over his thighs, and the heat of her breath brushed his chest. His whole body tightened and despite every truth he knew, he knew one more. That he couldn't let go of her just yet. His response was instantaneous and intense. With the sure knowledge that this was all he'd ever have, he kissed her softly parted lips.

Desperation drove him, passion coming with searing fire and strength, and without a word, he took her again. She matched his urgency, a wild need between them, and when he found a completeness that defied logic and reason, he let himself go. For one moment in his life, he was whole. Then it was gone, and even though Melanie was right beside him, he was alone.

The fulfillment he'd found moments ago fled as if it had never been. None of this was his to take. None. Melanie loved Dennis and Dennis loved her. He'd used every trick he'd known to get her right here with him, playing on her weakness and the attraction that he knew flared between them.

She was his brother's love, his brother's life, and despite the fact that he'd just found that brother, he couldn't destroy him like this. He couldn't destroy everyone's future by his own selfish needs and desires. For the first time in his life, Sam felt a sense of honor for family. A totally foreign concept to him, but one set in stone.

He touched her cheek as she snuggled into his side, and as she whispered, "Thank you," he drew back. For once in his life, he'd walk away, but he wouldn't go unscathed. Not even close. He knew what he had to do, but he just didn't know how he could do it.

Chimes sounded deep in the house, and Sam felt Melanie move. She was propped on one elbow, looking down at him. In the soft shadows she showed no embarrassment at her nakedness, but he couldn't look at it. If he did... No, he couldn't. Rolling away from her was one of the hardest things he'd ever done. But when the bell chimed again, he moved to the side of the bed and, without looking back, stood on the hardwood floor.

He reached for his pants, slipped them on, then without chancing a glance at Melanie, he padded barefoot out into the hallway as the chimes sounded again. As he walked toward the front doors, he knew he was walking away from the only good thing he'd ever find in this life.

Chapter Fourteen

Melanie lay very still in the empty bed as low voices drifted back to the room from the front of the house. She couldn't make out anything that was being said, and as she sank back onto the bare mattress, she just wished that whoever it was would leave. That Sam would come back to her so she could feel him against her again. It seemed odd how she only felt complete when he was with her, how she loved him so completely, yet had only realized it tonight. And it was odd that despite the fact that she'd violated all of her resolutions, that she'd jumped right in with her heart, she didn't feel badly at all.

She stretched on the bed, feeling how sensitive her body was right then. She wanted Sam again, and again, and again. As if a wish had been granted, he was there, silently stopping in the doorway and not coming any farther into the room.

"The car's cleared," he said through the shadows. "It seems the skip loader had problems, and the guy was apologizing for taking so long getting the car cleared."

The car. She'd totally forgotten about it. She'd forgotten about so many things in Sam's arms. "I hope you thanked him for taking so long," she whispered.

"They're gone now," he said in an oddly flat voice. "And we have to get out of here."

She pushed herself up, uncaring that she was naked in front of him. "Can't we stay a bit longer?" she asked, just the shadowy image of the man making her heartbeat rise and an ache start deep inside her.

"No, we can't," he said, then came toward the bed.

She shifted over, waiting for him to come back to her, but he didn't. Instead he sank down on the side of the bed with his back to her, and reached for his shoes.

She scrambled to her knees and went closer to him, reaching out to press the palm of her hand to his bare back. His breath caught, but he didn't turn to her.

"Sam?"

He stilled when she said his name, then he turned, but he didn't touch her. His eyes were shadowed and as unreadable as the first time she'd looked into them when he'd been a stranger. Her stomach lurched when she realized that he was acting as remote as a stranger right then. "Don't," he breathed roughly. "It's over, and we need to get out of here."

"Over?" She repeated the single word, and a cold chill invaded her body, making her recoil. She pressed her hands to her middle as she sank back on her heels. "Over?" She couldn't have heard him right.

"Yes, it's over." He would have turned from her again, but she couldn't bear it. She grabbed at his arm, making him stay where he was, and she could feel his muscles tense in her hold.

Despite touching him, she didn't feel grounded or safe anymore at all. Instead she was starting to feel horribly afraid. "Sam, what's happening? I thought—"

He broke the contact between them when he stood by the bed and looked down at her. Had she ever needed anyone in her life like she needed this man? Or felt so shut out?

"I told you that I'm not good at relationships. I never have been, and right now I'm way out of my league. I'm not even close to what you need."

"You don't know what I need," she whispered, and almost flinched when he leaned toward her. He touched her then, cupping her chin in the heat of his hand.

"You're wrong," he growled, emotions suddenly very close to the surface in him. "Very wrong. I know what you need and what you want, and Dennis is everything you need."

"No," she whispered. "Dennis, he…he…"

"He's right for you. I'm not. Listen to me. I wasn't lying when I told you that I move on, that I get restless and confined and I just leave." His hand trembled slightly, then he pulled back. "Actually, you were right. When I'm around, there's disasters. And I'm getting out of here before this turns into a huge disaster."

She hit at his hand, breaking his touch on her, and wrapped her arms around her middle, fighting against a staggering ache inside her. This couldn't be happening. It couldn't be. Her eyes were painfully dry as she stared at the man over her. God, he was another Robert. He'd lied. Oh, not with stories of what he supposedly was or wasn't, but with his actions. She shivered violently and barely kept from doubling over against the pain in her.

She'd made mistakes in the past, but none of them equalled this. Love had never been involved. This need and this wanting, hadn't even been part of those equations. Thank God, she'd never told Sam how she really felt. At least she had that small part of her dignity preserved.

She'd never told him she loved him, but with a sinking heart, she knew that she'd love him forever. The pain deepened to an excruciating ache.

"Sure, of course," she managed to get out as she awkwardly moved back on the bed to grab at the dustcover caught on the footboard post. She dragged it up to cover herself, and she moved even farther from Sam, until she was on the far edge of the bed. "Yeah, I get it. I finally do."

She slipped off the bed and pulled the cotton cover with her, pulling it almost up to her chin. For a moment she wasn't quite sure that her legs would actually support her. Then she was standing. Standing alone. And she turned her back to Sam. She couldn't look at him, not if she was going to be able to get out of here in one piece.

She heard Sam move behind her, a muffled thud, then silence. Finally she took a deep, painful breath, then turned, reaching for the post at the foot of the bed with her free hand for support. Sam had his shirt on, with the buttons undone, and he raked his fingers through his hair with a harsh sigh.

"So, that's that?" she managed to say in a voice so tight and strange that she barely recognized it as her own.

"I guess so," he muttered as he started buttoning up the front of his shirt.

She gripped the wooden post so tightly that she was certain it would snap as anger came to her. It was a clear, burning emotion that took the edge off of the pain, or maybe it just hid it. She didn't know, but she was thankful for it.

"You damned bastard." His head snapped up. He was staring at her through the shadows of the room. "You make the Roberts of this world look like Prince Charmings!" she hissed.

"I'm not married," he said in a flat voice.

"Of course you're not married! Marriage isn't in your vocabulary, not any more than commitment or staying power, is it? You're scum!"

"I never said that I—"

She couldn't let him use that word. Love had nothing to do with this now. She cut him off. "No, you didn't. You never did, and you never will." She dove into the protection of the anger with her head and her heart. "You had the gall to criticize Dennis and the Bennings. You don't have a clue what a family is, or what ties are, or what makes this life work. So, you wouldn't stick around if you had parents like the Bennings? Well, I've got a bulletin for you, Sam Harrison, you wouldn't stick around if Ozzie and Harriet were your parents."

"Ozzie and Harriet aren't my parents," he muttered.

"And lucky you, neither are the Bennings. Or maybe they're the lucky ones."

Sam stared hard at her, then said something she didn't understand at all. "But they are."

"What?"

"Dennis Benning is my father and I'm still not sticking around."

She had to have heard him wrong. "What are you talking about? Dennis can't be your father. That's crazy."

He tucked his shirt into his pants and spoke without looking at her. "The older one. He's my father."

She went around the bed, dragging the dustcover with

her. "Why would you lie like this, about something that's so ridiculous?"

"I told you, I don't lie."

She stared at him. "You're serious?"

"Very," he murmured.

"The Bennings..."

"No, just the old man." He reached into his pocket and took out his wallet. She didn't understand until he opened the wallet and took out something, then held it in front of her face. Even in the bad light, she could see a picture, the picture of the woman with laughing eyes. "This is my mother."

His mother. "She and Mr. Benning—"

"Oh, yeah. But I didn't know about Benning until my mother got sick about six months ago. She thought I should know for some reason that I failed to understand then, and I still don't understand." He put the picture away and stuffed his wallet into his back pocket. "Who'd want him? I was better off without him or Dennis in my life."

That hit her right in the pit of her stomach. "You and Dennis? Oh, God, he's your brother."

"Good, stable, kind, solid, wonderful Mr. Perfect is my brother." He actually laughed at that, a raw, humorless sound. "Can't say as we have a lot in common, but it's a fact."

Everything fit into place suddenly, even the kiss on the deck. In this shadowy room Sam was a larger, blurred version of his brother, and she knew now why she'd thought she could love Dennis. He'd been a forerunner, a promise of Sam. But the fulfillment of that promise had turned out to be bitter indeed. "You're a Benning, and you knew all the time and you never thought about telling me?"

"I knew all along, but that didn't stop me from going after you. Is that what you mean? I knew, I didn't care. I wanted you. Selfish, unfeeling, whatever you want to call me, it's true. But that was a game. You've got your real life ahead of you, a life with Dennis. Safe, sane, settled. You've got it. And, as hard as this is for me to admit, I think you're probably the best thing that could happen to my brother."

"Dennis doesn't know, does he?" she whispered.

"There's no reason for him to know. Not any more than there is for the old man to know. He was only there long enough to sire me, anyway, then he split. Gone. Finished. Over. He's nothing to me."

"You're just like him. You do what you want to do, then just walk away. You keep going. Gone, finished, over. You split."

"You might have a point there," he conceded.

"Whatever it is, just do me a favor. You owe me."

"What?"

"Get the hell out of here. Do your best imitation of your father and disappear."

He was motionless, then he did what she said. He walked to the door and without looking back, he left. She heard him go through the house, then the front door opened and closed. In the silence, she waited until she heard the sound of a car start up, and knew that Sam was gone.

As the engine sound faded off into the distance, Melanie pressed a hand to her mouth. The cover fell in a tangle around her legs and she collapsed onto the bed. He was gone, just like that. Tears finally came in the form of great, racking sobs that drove her into a fetal position on the mattress. Grief obliterated all of the anger, and she buried her face into the bed to try to muffle the sound of her pain.

ANGELINA CRINGED at the scene she witnessed. It had come from nowhere, stunning her. She'd been so close to perfection on this assignment, and now it was shattered. She allowed Sam to go, backed away from Melanie's sobbing, and retreated to a spot where she could think.

"Angelina?"

She turned and Miss Victoria was there in the quietness of the thinking space. "Yes, ma'am?"

"We came to inform you that the Council has agreed that this error is not correctable. It is very distressing to everyone involved, but it seems that this can not be refashioned after all." Miss Victoria sighed softly. "Now, we need to think of alternatives in this situation. Of course, they have to be acceptable alternatives for one and all."

She had never heard of the Council decreeing retreat on a match, and Angelina herself had never given up on a match before. Especially not when it was so patently right for both people involved. She wouldn't let them give up on Sam and Melanie. "But it's not over, Ma'am. There's still hope for—"

"Ah, yes, hope. Hope springs eternal. Is that not part of the human condition? Hope always, even when the hope is slim? In this case, the hope is nonexistent. The fact is that Mr. Harrison is leaving for Los Angeles as soon as he can. Miss Clark has been hurt again, painfully so, and Mr. Benning…well." She waved one hand. "Mr. Benning…"

"What about Mr. Benning?" Angelina asked. "What's going to happen to him?"

"We do so dislike making any prophetic statements when humans are so unstable, but Mr. Benning will probably manage to convince Miss Clark to marry him. Actually, if that happens, they will be quite comfortable together. Very amiably situated." She wiped her hands back and forth against each other in a dismissing motion. "Now, we need to move on."

"'Comfortable'?" The human word tasted bad even in Angelina's mouth. "Is that acceptable?"

"Oh, it certainly is not our first choice for humans, but yes, many humans are very satisfied to have a marriage that is comfortable."

"But, ma'am, that isn't our goal. We can't quit. Failure is not acceptable, is it?"

"Of course not. But it is not failure to realize when one should quit. The wise and prudent thing—"

Angelina did something then that she'd never done before. She cut off Miss Victoria in the middle of her sentence and actually ignored what she knew had been a decision from the Council. "Ma'am. No, please, we can't let this happen. Let me finish this assignment. I can do it. I know I can. I really feel that it's possible."

"Ah, your record, is that it? We shall make sure that there is an addendum inserted in your files, explaining that this was in no way your fault. There was no lack of trying on your part. Actually, the mouse thing was very creative, and the session with the Bennings, well, we felt that was positively inspired to put Miss Clark through it, to open her eyes, so to speak."

This didn't have a thing to do with her record. Not a thing. "Ma'am, please. Just give me one more day in human time? Just one more day?"

The little woman hesitated and Angelina pressed her advantage. "It would take that long to rearrange the situation down here, anyway, wouldn't it? Let me have that time, ma'am, and if it doesn't work, then 'comfortable' will be the order of the day for these humans.''

The sigh was filled with extended patience, then Miss Victoria did something Angelina had never seen her do before, either. A day for firsts. She backed down and actually agreed. ''Okay, one day in human terms. If this is not settled, then we shall send in the crew to rearrange things so the humans can go on with their lives as if this had never happened.''

''Yes, ma'am, of course,'' Angelina said, hoping against hope that they wouldn't need the crew to wipe out the past two days from the humans' collective memory. ''One more thing?''

''What is it?''

''Do I have your permission to use more extended physical contact with the subjects?''

Miss Victoria frowned slightly. ''All right, but use discretion in the matter. Contact with one's subjects can cause problems.''

''Yes, ma'am, and thank you.''

Miss Victoria came closer, then unexpectedly touched Angelina on the arm, a physical contact that was decidedly unusual from the tiny woman. ''*Bon chance*, my dear,'' she said softly. Then she was gone.

Angelina turned back to the scene below her and tried desperately to think of what she could do to make this right. This couldn't go back to square one. She wouldn't let it. She wouldn't let the past few days go as if they had never been. She wouldn't let Sam Harrison never know there was a Melanie Clark in this world. She wouldn't let Melanie stick herself in a life that she really didn't want. And she wouldn't let Dennis Benning be the victim in all of this. No one should settle for a comfortable match. No one.

She moved quickly and saw that Melanie had gone to her cottage behind the boutique. She was sitting in the darkened living area, not crying now, but looking pale and drawn. Dennis was still with his father, the two men talking, and Angelina didn't have to listen in long to know that the men were really talking for the first time in their relationship. Mrs. Benning was at the house, but had taken to her bed, so upset with her life at that moment that she refused all logic or reason.

And Sam. She found him at the hotel on the phone and it was almost 2:00 a.m. The man was bound and determined to get out of town, one way or another. She wasn't going to let him. No way. He was going to do the right thing no matter what. And Angelina knew exactly what that right thing would be.

"Get me the hell out of the deal," Sam bellowed into the phone he had caught between his shoulder and his ear. With his hands free, he stuffed his clothes into the open suitcase on the bed.

"You woke me in the middle of the night to tell me this? My answer is, no way." His agent, Jerry Watson, didn't sound any happier being awakened in Los Angeles than he was happy about Sam bailing out on this job. "This deal is too sweet. And this company is up and coming. They've got staying power in this business. Believe me."

Sam closed his eyes tightly. Staying power. Yeah, sure. "I don't want a lecture. You work for me, so just do what I'm asking you to do."

"No, you do it," Jerry said. "I don't want be part of you screwing them. You'll never work for them again."

Sam fastened his suitcase shut, then straightened and gripped the phone with one hand. "I can't stay up here."

"Tell me you're doing this because it's life and death and not some stupid whim," he said.

"Okay, it's life and death."

"Why don't I believe you?" he muttered.

"You don't have to believe me, just do this for me. It's important."

"They're set to start the day after Christmas, and if you bail, you'll leave them with a hole in their schedule that will cost a mint—making you liable for breach of contract."

"Okay, okay, I get the idea."

"Finally."

Sam glanced at the clock by the bed. "I can get a flight down and be in your office at four this afternoon to get this settled."

"Sam, no way. Didn't you hear me? You can't do—"

"See you at four sharp," he said and hung up.

Quickly he filled out the express checkout form, then laid the key on it. His wallet was on the desk, and he picked it up, then slipped it into his pocket. Life and death? It felt that way to him. Grabbing his suitcase, he left for the airport to get the first flight out to Los Angeles.

MELANIE STOOD on the porch of Reggie and Ben's house right at eight o'clock the next morning, but hesitated before knocking on the door. The rambling old bungalow was silent, and the only signs of life were the lights strung on every angle of the house, and a wreath on the door. She looked at the signs of love and family and Christmas and in that moment, she felt entirely alone.

She turned and crossed the porch, then dropped down on the top step. Hugging her arms around her legs, she rested her forehead on her knees. She shivered at the chill in the air, her heavy sweater and jeans not much of a barrier to the coldness all around.

After a night of misery, a certain numbness had settled on her. She reasoned that people could only take so much pain, then they shut down out of self-protection. She felt nothing at all—as if a door had closed to hide the mess she'd made of her life. And if she didn't open the door, she didn't have to feel anything.

She wasn't going to open it again. She knew behind that door was an emptiness for her that would be shattering, a world so wrong that nothing could make it right. She needed to make Dennis understand that they should stay friends and not go any further. She still cared about him, but that was as far as it went. Friends. Dear friends.

She'd come here to see her sister. Sensible, level-headed Reggie. She wanted her to look at her, tell her she made a horrible mistake, and knew that Reggie would be there for her when she had to pick up the pieces.

"Mel?" She heard Reggie say from behind her. "What are you doing out here?"

Melanie glanced up as her sister, wrapped in a long white robe, came across the porch and awkwardly lowered herself to a seat beside her. There were still traces of sleep in her eyes. "I'm sorry, I thought you'd be awake by now. Then I got here and there wasn't a sound inside. I thought I'd just wait out here until you were all up.''

"Mom kept Mikey last night so we…" She smiled at Melanie. "Let's just say that Ben and I won't have too much time together when this munchkin makes an appearance." Her smile faltered just a bit. "Okay, now you tell me what brought you here right now? It isn't about last night, is it?''

How could she know? "What?''

"When you didn't show up at the house we all figured that you and Dennis were…" She frowned slightly. "Is this all about Dennis?''

She'd forgotten all about the tree trimming. "I met his parents last night," she said.

That brought a burst of laughter from Reggie. "Good heavens, no wonder you look like you've been through the wars. Is his mother not a work of art? That woman is probably singlehandedly responsible for the existence of the polar ice cap.''

Melanie wanted to smile, to join in the joke, but there was nothing in her to respond to it. "Reggie, I…" She bit her lip. "I need to talk to you. Is Ben—''

"He's still asleep. I just came down to make myself some tea when I saw you out here." She put a hand on Melanie's shoulder and leveraged herself up. "Come on inside where it's warmer and we can talk. I'll even make you some strong coffee.''

Melanie stood and faced her sister. "Maybe some brandy in it wouldn't be a bad idea.''

"It's that bad?" Reggie asked softly, a frown drawing a fine crease between her eyes.

"It's worse than bad," Melanie admitted.

"Oh, sweetie, I knew you liked Dennis, but I had no idea that you loved him.''

"What?"

"The look on your face…" She shook her head, then put her arm around her sister's shoulders as she urged her toward the open door. "You'd have to be in love for it to hurt this badly. Tell me what Dennis did."

"He didn't do anything." They stepped through the open door into a house that was warm and secure, and everything that Melanie didn't have in her life. "This is all my fault. It's my mistakes, my stupid impulsiveness."

Reggie hugged her as they slowly walked past the living room to the kitchen beyond the stairway to the upper story. "Everyone makes mistakes, sweetie, but they usually aren't fatal. I certainly made my share."

"But look what you've got."

Reggie let her go as they stepped into the cavernous kitchen, and patted her swollen stomach. "Yes, just look what I've got. But if you think I've got all of this— Mikey, Ben, the new baby, and this life—because I'm so smart about doing the right thing, you're way off the mark." She crossed to the stove and picked up a tea kettle, then turned back to Melanie in the doorway. "It's all dumb, stupid luck that worked out for me."

Melanie could hear Sam's voice. "Dumb, stupid luck." And that's exactly what it all was, but this time the luck had backfired on her. "Well, some of us are lucky and some aren't," she murmured as she crossed to the table and sank down onto a chair.

"Reggie?" Ben's muffled voice carried down from the upper story. "Reggie?"

"Down here, Ben. Melanie dropped by, and we're going to have some tea."

"Hey, Mel!" Ben called. "Why aren't you at that

store of yours getting ready for the Christmas Eve rush?''

Christmas Eve. She'd even forgotten about that. "I'll be going soon, then you can have Reggie all to yourself.''

"Thanks," he called back to her. "Merry Christmas!''

Melanie looked over at Reggie. "That's some dumb, stupid luck.''

Reggie put the kettle on the stove, turned it on, then came to the table. She gripped the back of the chair across from Melanie. "Okay, come on. Tell me everything.''

Melanie took an unsteady breath. "Okay, but it's a long, horrible story.''

"I've got time. Start at the beginning, where you met Dennis and knew that he was Mr. Right. Then what happened?''

"I met Mr. Wrong…again," Melanie said softly.

Reggie frowned at her. "What?''

"Mr. Wrong. I was going to meet Dennis at that beach house he was looking at. You remember I told you about him deciding to—''

Reggie's eyes widened, then she said softly, "Oh, my God.''

"I told you Dennis wanted a change," she said, not certain why Reggie was so taken aback by the idea. "Reggie, you know what I—''

"Oh, wow," she breathed.

"Reggie, for Pete's sake, you can't be surprised—''

Reggie cut her off. "Mel, call Ben." She grimaced. "My water just broke. And I'm having contractions.''

"Ben!" Melanie screamed as she stood so abruptly that her chair crashed over backward. "Ben, the baby's coming!"

Chapter Fifteen

Sam stared at the girl at the ticket desk in the airport terminal, her bright coppery hair a distinct contrast to the navy blue and white uniform.

"I've been here since before dawn, and it's now—" He checked the large clock right above the ticket counter, then looked back at the attendant. "It's almost three o'clock. I've had to cancel a very important meeting, and now you're telling me that there are still no openings on any flights to Los Angeles?"

"Sir, I told you before that if a seat becomes available, you'll be paged. You're on our list."

"How about San Diego?"

"We have checked San Diego, Palm Springs, Ontario, Orange County. There is nothing. As I said before, it's the holidays. This is Christmas Eve. Everyone wants to get home to their families. We understand that, but we are also at capacity on all of our flights. Maybe a charter?"

"There's none available."

"Perhaps a car rental might work for you? Los Angeles is only a three hour drive and—"

"There's nothing available there, either."

"Then might I suggest that you get a bite to eat,

relax, and I promise you will be paged the moment something opens up."

Sam felt as if he was beating his head against a brick wall. If he hadn't turned in his rental, he'd have a car at least. But right now he was at the mercy of the airlines and the holiday crush. What sleep he'd managed had been sitting in a chair, and his head was beginning to ache.

"Thanks a lot," he muttered, then picked up his bag and headed across the way to a coffee shop.

He'd barely made it to the door of the restaurant when he heard his name over the loudspeaker. "Sam Harrison. Mr. Sam Harrison. Please pick up a white courtesy phone."

He looked around, spotted a phone station and crossed to pick it up. "Sam Harrison. You had me paged?"

"Yes, sir. Please go to the Skyway Lounge across from gate ten."

He had little patience left. "What for?" he asked more abruptly than he intended.

"I wouldn't know, sir. Just tell the attendant at the lounge entry who you are and that you were paged."

Sam hung up, then spotted gate ten halfway down the busy concourse. He made his way through the press of the holiday crowds, and finally made it to a very discreet set of gold doors marked Skyway Lounge, Members Only. As soon as he neared the door, a uniformed attendant approached him. "Can I be of assistance, sir?" the lady asked.

"I'm Sam Harrison. I was asked to come down here."

"Yes, sir," the woman said with a jarringly bright smile. "Come with me." She opened the gold doors and led the way into a denlike sitting area. As soon as the door closed behind them, all the noise and bustle from the terminal was shut out and quiet elegance was shut in.

Sam glanced around the space with its leather chairs, wooden touches, and the hint of expensive cigar smoke in the air, and saw a man by the windows overlooking the runway.

"Dennis?" Sam said.

His brother turned to him, his face grim. "The hotel told me you went to the airport, that you were leaving, and I came over on the off chance that you'd still be here."

As the attendant discretely withdrew, Sam shrugged. "I'm not exactly taking off anytime soon. The holiday rush has every flight loaded, so I'm on standby."

"Lucky for me," Dennis murmured.

Sam went across the plush carpeting to where Dennis stood. "Your luck is my curse," he quipped. "So, if you're here about the house, it's yours. You're welcome to it."

There was an unsettling tightness in his brother's eyes and around his mouth. "The house?" he repeated, then said, "No, I'm not here for that."

"Then why are you here?"

"I almost didn't come. I was pretty shaken last night, and it took me a while to sort things out."

Sam knew it was too simple for him to get out of there without something else happening. But the last thing he wanted was for Dennis to have found out about Melanie and him. "What are you talking about?"

"I know everything," Dennis said, and Sam felt his heart sink.

For the first time in his life Sam experienced a pain

from his actions. He hadn't meant to hurt anyone or ruin anyone's life, but he knew he might have ruined everyone he'd touched in the past two days. It felt a hell of a lot like guilt and disgust with himself.

"I can explain," he said quickly, but knew the magnitude of that lie.

He couldn't explain something to Dennis when he didn't understand it himself. But that didn't stop him from trying. "Know one thing for certain, that I didn't want this to happen, and it's all my fault."

"Like hell it is," Dennis snapped angrily.

"Hey, if you want to be mad at anyone, be mad at me."

Dennis shook his head. "Mad? I'm not mad. I'm still in shock and trying to figure it all out. That's why I came here." He raked his fingers through his hair and exhaled harshly. "For God's sake, I find out that I have a brother, that my father's been lying to me all of my life. I'm having a hell of a time trying to make sense out of all of it, but I'm not mad at you. No way."

Relief came in a flood, then Sam saw the pain in Dennis's eyes, and his relief was short-lived. "He told you?" He couldn't use the word father right then.

"Yes, after you both left, and Mother took to her sickbed after having a snit about Melanie and her family." He was grim as he continued. "Father told me that he loved your mother, but when it came right down to it, he couldn't get past what was expected of him as a Benning. God, it makes me sick to be so tied to a name that you lose yourself."

"Yeah, sick," Sam muttered.

Dennis eyed Sam for a long moment. "Dammit, a brother." His chuckle was rough and had very little humor in it. "Actually, I always wanted one. I had this fantasy about having a brother, growing up together, and maybe even fighting over things, sibling rivalry and all of that. I sure as hell didn't expect the stork to drop you full-grown into my life.''

Sam held up a hand. "Hey, I'm not in your life. I never intended to be. I just came here to—"

"What do you mean, you aren't in my life? You're my brother. I've spent hours trying to figure this out, and the one thing I know is, I don't want you to just fade away." He looked uncertain. "But maybe that's just a fantasy on my part. After what Father's done to you, and after what happened last night, I wouldn't blame you for running like hell.''

He didn't deserve this acceptance by his brother, not after the way he'd betrayed him. It wasn't a fantasy, but more like a nightmare. It was better for him to leave and hopefully shake free of the nightmare. "You've got your life here," Sam said. "In fact, you've got a great life, and I'm not a part of that life at all.''

"But you can be," someone said from behind Sam.

He turned to face Dennis Benning Senior. The older man looked strained and pale, but stood ramrod straight in a deep navy suit. Sam could tell whatever had gone on between him, his wife and Dennis hadn't been pleasant. It had left its mark on him, and at one time Sam would have thought that was what the man deserved. But now, he hated to see it. "You never let on you knew who I was last night. How did you know?"

"How wouldn't I know?" he asked softly as he came closer. "Your mother sent me pictures all the time, telling me about what you were doing with your life." His expression tightened with each word he uttered. "But I had no idea that she'd told you about me. She always insisted that you shouldn't know. I abided by that, and when I saw you, I couldn't say a thing. I'd made my life, and you and she had made yours."

"Yes, we made ours, but for some reason she told me about you just before she died."

"You wanted to meet me?"

"Just to see you, then get out of there," he admitted.

His father paled a bit more. "I know that this sounds selfish, but I'd like to get to know you. I can't make up for what's been done, but I don't want you to disappear on us." He motioned with one hand. "It's up to you. I'm willing to abide by whatever you decide."

Sam turned away from the man to stare out the windows. The lights on the runway glowed with a blue hue, and he remembered what Melanie had said about her brother's blue year. She had eight brothers and sisters, and he really didn't have one. "I have to get back to Los Angeles."

"I understood that you have a job up here?"

"I do, but I don't think I'll be taking it after all." He touched his hand to the cool glass. "It's time for me to leave."

"If you could make the time in the future, I'd like us to talk," his father said. "And I'd like you and Dennis to get to know each other. I regret so much of what's gone on."

Sam stared at a jet that was taxiing along the runway. Everyone did things they regretted in this life, he knew that all too well. Maybe what Melanie had said was more than true, that he and his father were a lot alike. "Maybe, sometime. Right now I need to find a way to get to Los Angeles."

"I thought you were flying down," Dennis said.

"I've been on standby all day, and so far, nothing."

He turned to his brother. "There's not even a rental car to be had, or I'd just drive down."

"Take mine."

"What?"

"Take my car. I can fly down in a few days and pick it up." He reached into his pocket and took out a key chain that he held out to Sam. "It'll give me an excuse to see you again, and maybe we can figure out what sort of relationship we can have...if any."

"You got your car back?" Sam asked, his last sight of the Jeep by the beach house when he left Melanie.

"Early this morning."

He knew he shouldn't ask, but he couldn't stop himself. "Melanie isn't here is she?"

"No, her assistant gave me the keys. Her sister Reggie's in labor and Melanie's at the hospital." He shook his head. "Those Clarks, they might give my mother fits, but they're something else again. Every one of them's at the hospital waiting for that baby to be born."

"I guess you'd better get used to it," Sam murmured. "I don't think Melanie comes without the rest of them."

"No, she doesn't," Dennis said softly, and the tension was back. "That's probably partly why I love her."

Sam felt his gut clench, and he backed away emotionally from the words. "I'm sure it is," he said.

Dennis was still holding the key. "Take the car. Just give me an address or phone number where I can reach you after the holidays."

Sam reached into his pocket for his wallet, took out a business card and handed it to Dennis. "My agent's number is there. He'll know where I am and how to reach me.'' He took the keys from Dennis. ''How are you going to get home?''

''I'm not going home. I'm going to the hospital. I need to see Melanie and to check on Reggie.''

Sam clenched his hand so hard on the key that the ridges bit into his palm. ''Thanks for the loan.'' He turned and looked at Mr. Benning, who hadn't moved. ''We'll talk sometime.''

''Thank you,'' he said in a low voice. ''We'll talk.''

Sam crossed to where he'd left his case, picked it up, then turned back to the two men. ''Thanks for coming,'' he said.

His father nodded, and Dennis said, ''The car's in the front lot, aisle fifteen. It's a black Jeep, and—''

''Sure, I remember,'' he said, then left the lounge and headed directly for the exit. He couldn't see the last of Santa Barbara and these past two days soon enough to suit him.

MELANIE HAD KNOWN that the numbness wouldn't last, and it hadn't. It had begun fading during the eight-hour labor, and was gone completely by the time the baby was born. When Ben had put the little girl into Reggie's arms, the feelings were back full-force, and barely endurable.

She felt a loneliness that defied explanation with all of her family around. Yet she felt as if she'd been set adrift with nothing to anchor her. One by one the others left, until she was the only one there and she knew it was time for her to go. She went to the bed in the birthing room and looked down at her niece. ''She's beautiful,'' she whispered, gazing at the tiny face, which seemed almost serene, huge eyes so dark they looked black, studying her.

Reggie, her face free of all makeup and her hair still damp from the labor, cradled the baby gently to her. "You were hard work," she said, "but well worth it."

Ben brushed at Reggie's hair and Melanie could see the slight trembling in his touch. It hadn't been easy for him to see Reggie in so much pain. "Thank God it's over, and…" He looked down at his daughter, and Melanie could see his relief finally settling in that everyone was okay. He bent to kiss the baby lightly before he looked at Reggie, then whispered, "I love you."

Melanie stood back, almost embarrassed to see so much love between two people. "Mom took Mikey back to their place," she said. "And I need to get going."

Reggie looked at her sister. "We never got our talk in, did we?"

"That's okay. Some things aren't helped by talking," she said.

Reggie eyed her for a moment. "We'll talk soon, okay?"

"Yes, sure, and now I have to go."

"Aren't you going to say goodbye to your niece?" she asked.

"If I knew her name, I'd say goodbye."

"Then meet Angelina Joy."

"I thought it would be something like Sarah or Emily."

"We both thought of Angelina." Reggie looked down at the baby. "Angel. It fits her, don't you think?"

"Yes, it does," Melanie said, then turned and reached for her jacket she'd discarded on a side chair hours ago. "Now, I'll leave so you can all rest up. Mikey's waiting for the homecoming, and you're going to need a lot of stamina to get through that."

"Thanks for being there for me," Reggie said.

"I wouldn't have missed this for the world." Melanie crossed to the door, opened it, then glanced back just before she stepped out. Ben was sitting on the bed with Reggie, his arm around his wife and his child. And the isolation in Melanie grew.

She slipped on her jacket, then headed down the corridor to the elevator and down to the entrance by the parking lot. The air was chillingly cold as she walked through the lot toward her car, and she tugged her jacket more tightly around her. She didn't know where she was going, but she knew that she wasn't going back to the shop. Melanie knew that she had to keep moving.

She didn't want to stop, because if she did, she knew that she'd start remembering and she couldn't deal with memories yet. Maybe one day, memories wouldn't hurt, but right now they were dangerous for her. She looked ahead of her, then stopped in her tracks. If memories hurt, the sight of Sam striding toward her was excruciating.

She took half a step back, hoping against hope that he hadn't seen her, then he lifted a hand toward her in a partial wave and called out her name. It was too late to run, and too late to protect herself. Then as he came closer, she knew that once she'd thought Sam was Dennis. Now she thought Dennis was Sam.

"Melanie, I was hoping I'd find you," he said with a smile, his hands held out to her.

Then she was in his arms, being pulled to his chest, and for one moment she let herself lean against him. Whatever perverse joke of Fate had made Dennis so much like his brother that she could mistake them for each other? But nothing could make her feel as if Sam was holding her when it was Dennis. Sane, sensible, gentle Dennis.

She held to him tightly, burying her face in the softness of his corduroy jacket. But no matter how hard she tried, she couldn't pretend he was Sam. Tears came then, and she pressed her face harder against his chest while she balled the soft corduroy in her hands.

"Mel, what's wrong? Is it Reggie or the baby?"

"No, no," she breathed, her voice muffled against his chest. "She's fine. They're fine. Everyone's fine, but me. I need to talk to you."

He pulled back and framed her face with his hands. "Strange, that's why I'm here. I need to talk to you, too." He brushed at the moisture on her cheeks with his thumbs. "Life is so crazy. Just when we think we've gotten it figured out, the rules change and everything's different."

He knew about Sam being his brother. She knew that without asking. "And we change."

"Yes, we change." He shifted to put his arm around her shoulders, then pull her to his side to lead the way back to where she'd parked. "Let's go. We could both use a strong cup of coffee and a good talk. I think we both have things we need to say to each other."

"Yes," she said as she went with him and knew that this phase of her life was over.

SAM DROVE SOUTH on a four-lane highway trying to find a way to get on the freeway to Los Angeles. He glanced at the dash clock in the Jeep. Almost six. As the sun slipped lower and lower in the winter sky, he flipped on his headlights and he started wondering just how confusing Santa Barbara could be.

In the past few hours he'd gone in circles, been

caught in holiday traffic where he sat for an interminable amount of time without going anywhere, been detoured by construction, taken the wrong turn more than once, and now he was stuck behind a truck that was going all of ten miles an hour.

It was like something out of *Alice In Wonderland*. He was falling down the rabbit hole. The huge semi lumbered along ahead of him and a line of cars as far as he could see followed behind him. Cars came in a steady stream from the other direction and it looked as if everyone in the area was on the road on Christmas Eve.

Sam could feel his nerves aching in his neck and shoulders and it got worse when he saw that the truck was from Sanbourn Vineyards. He barely kept himself from hitting the horn to get the truck out of his way, but he knew that was useless. It's never going to end, he thought with an invasive weariness, and imagined that he was beginning to feel like a soldier who fights battle after battle but loses the war to the enemy. The logo screamed down at him in blue flowing script on the white trailer.

When he spotted a side road, he turned onto it, not even caring where it went as long as he got out of sight of the truck and was moving with some degree of speed. But a simple turn didn't block the flood of memories springing to life...finding the shed in the vineyard...holding Melanie.

Maybe that was when he'd started to love her. No, he knew that wasn't true. He'd started to love her the moment he turned and kissed her. It had all begun with that kiss. He could almost taste her, even now. He rubbed his hand roughly across his mouth, then muttered to Fate or whatever was taunting him. "You can stop now. The joke's over. I'm leaving. I'm out of here, as soon as I can find the way.''

MELANIE HADN'T PAID much attention to where she was going after she kissed Dennis goodbye, gotten in her car and driven off. She simply drove without any destination in mind, not even paying attention, until she passed a truck on the highway and saw a huge blue logo on its side—Sanbourn Vineyards.

She almost flinched at the sight, then pressed the accelerator to get past the truck. She'd felt tight in her chest since her talk with Dennis, and knowing that she'd never be able to look at Dennis and not think of Sam. And even though he'd understood everything, nothing felt right. There was no relief in her.

For a fleeting second she had such a sense of Sam being close to her, that she almost hit the brakes and stopped. But she was afraid if she did, she'd find him, that she'd see him coming toward her. She slowed as her heart pounded, and she knew it was all her imagination, something born out of her own desperation. He wasn't here, not even close.

She was alone. She shivered as that thought settled in to become a reality for her. No matter who she was with, or how many people were there, she'd always be alone. Sam wouldn't be there. That conjured up thoughts that literally made her heart hurt. And for a minute she thought that the people who said you couldn't die from a broken heart were liars. But she was still breathing, still alive. There was no hiding from the pain at all.

When a car ahead of her slowed suddenly, she was startled when something fell into her lap. She looked down and saw a key was there, resting on her thigh, a key with a paper tag on it. The key to the beach house. She could have sworn she'd put it in the lock box when she left there last night, but she must have tucked it behind the sun visor. It certainly hadn't fallen out of nowhere.

She picked it up and closed her hand around it, the metal biting into her skin, and suddenly she knew where she was going. What she had to do. She had to go back to the beach house and say goodbye to a part of her life that was over before it began. Maybe she could figure out what to do with the rest of her life after she said goodbye to Sam.

Chapter Sixteen

Flashing lights came out of nowhere ahead of Sam, and
as he approached them, he realized that three police cars
were blocking the intersection in both directions. He
stopped behind a line of cars, then saw a uniformed
officer walking alongside the car coming in his direction, a police woman.

She approached his car, stopped and tapped on his
window. When he rolled down the window, the woman
bent down to look in at him. She was tall and slender,
with bright red hair confined under her service cap.
"We're very sorry for this delay, but you can't go
through here. It's closed off ahead and will be for the
next half hour."

Sam ran a hand over his face and exhaled harshly.
"Great, just great."

"Is there a problem, sir?"

He glanced at the name on her badge, but all he could
make out was her first name, Annette. "I just need to
get going. I'm trying to get to Los Angeles tonight."

She frowned at him. "Well, a lot of people are needing to be somewhere tonight, to get home to family and
loved ones. I'm sure you're no different than they are."

But he was very different. There was no one waiting

for him, and his apartment would be totally empty. As empty as he felt since he left Melanie at the beach house. "I just need to get there." Yet there was an odd feeling in him, that someone *was* waiting for him, somewhere. No, that wasn't true at all. It was just another cruel trick his own mind was playing on him.

"It's important?"

"Yes, it is."

She looked back at the group of police cars with their lights flashing into the night, then back at Sam. "Okay, tell me, is it a matter of life and death?"

His agent's words echoed between them, and Sam stared at her. "What?"

"Just tell me it's a matter of life and death," she said. "And make me believe it."

He didn't understand any of this, but one thing he knew, it was a matter of life and death for him to put as much distance as he could between himself and Melanie. If he was close to her again, he wouldn't leave. He couldn't. And he wouldn't do that to her or Dennis. "It's a matter of life and death," he repeated to her.

"Why didn't you say so to begin with?" Annette asked with a smile. "I'll get you out of here. Go back a block, turn right, then go about a mile to an intersection that has stop lights. Turn left there and keep going."

"Thanks," Sam said.

"Hey, I'm just doing my job making sure that people get where they belong." Then she was gone.

Where he belonged? It didn't matter what road he took, he'd never find that place. Because he didn't have any idea where it was or if it even existed.

He turned around, headed back, followed her directions and found himself pulling out onto the Coastal

Highway. He turned and with the ocean on his right, he drove south. He'd barely gone a mile before he knew where he was, and despite every atom of his being willing him to go faster, he actually found himself slowing. The turnoff was there, and as if the car had a mind of its own, he turned off the highway and onto the narrow road that ran parallel to the road above.

Maybe it was masochism, or maybe it was insanity, he didn't know. He didn't understand any of it, but he drove down the road toward the lights that framed the gates at the beach house. As he got nearer, he saw a car, and he slowed even more when he realized it was an old car, a car he'd seen before. Melanie's car. It was parked by the rock fence near the gates, and despite the fact he knew he should turn and get the hell out of there, he didn't.

He pulled in beside the car and turned off the engine, but he didn't get out. If there had been any sanity left in his world, he'd be driving south, putting real distance between himself and everything that had to do with Melanie Clark. But sanity was in short supply right then.

He stared out at the house, remembering that feeling he'd experienced the first time he was inside it. The peace and sense of freedom. Then Melanie had exploded into his world, and there hadn't been any peace since then, and as for freedom, he had never felt more confined in his life.

Maybe if he saw her again, if he looked at her, found out she was happy with Dennis now, he could walk away without this knot in his stomach. And he could be in this world without always feeling she was close by. Maybe he could find some peace again.

Slowly he got out of the car, then started for the gate.

He went through into the courtyard area, over to the front doors and rapped on the damp wood. Nothing happened. He knocked again, and when there was no response, he reached for the knob and turned it. The door clicked, then swung back and Sam stepped into the house.

The minute he got inside, he knew it was empty. He could feel it. If Melanie had been there, he knew he would have sensed her. But then again, he'd thought he felt her at the traffic jam. If there was one certainty in this, he knew he couldn't trust anything he thought was true. He couldn't trust anything.

He stood in the silent room, then noticed that the door at the back was slightly ajar. Crossing to it, he pushed it open and stepped out onto the deck. But Melanie wasn't there. He went to the rail, gripped the damp wood, and looked out into the night. It was full circle. Him on the deck at this house. But everything was changed.

He looked out at the darkness of the ocean, the sky with deep clouds partially blocking the rising moon, then he looked below at the sands of the beach. Full circle. But Melanie wasn't coming up behind him, putting her arms around him, kissing him. He almost turned to leave, to stop this before it began, but movement on the beach below caught his eye.

He leaned over the rail, then he saw her. A lone figure at the water's edge, standing facing the horizon. Melanie. Full circle, he thought and turned to go to the end of the deck to steps that led down the bluff to the beach. He went down the stairs, stepped onto the beach and felt his feet sink into the sand. Slowly, he crossed toward the water and Melanie.

As he got closer, he slowed his steps, then stopped.

He simply looked at her. And in that moment he felt as if he'd come home. He was at a place that had been waiting for him all the time. The idea shook him to the core, going against everything he'd believed about himself.

He went closer, taking in the way the light wind ruffled her hair, the way she looked so slender, even in the bulky sweater, and the way she hugged her arms around her middle. She rubbed a hand over her face, and her deep sigh was brought to him on the night breeze. He took another step toward her, swallowing sudden fear that she'd see him and run. Or that Dennis would show up at any minute.

All he wanted was a few minutes. A few minutes of honesty, then whatever happened, happened. He'd deal with it. But he couldn't walk away this time. He couldn't leave without telling her that he loved her.

"Melanie?" he said.

MELANIE STARED out at the ocean, letting that sense of limitless space ease her pain. She'd been right to come here. She'd needed the closure. It didn't stop the pain, but it made it something she knew she could eventually deal with. She was getting past what could have been, past regrets, and past the grief.

She thought she'd heard her name being spoken, as if it had drifted out of her soul and into reality. Sam.

She didn't move, she couldn't. Then she heard it again. Slowly she turned, and saw a ghost. Sam, on the beach, looking deceptively real. If she blinked just right, she knew he'd be gone, the image would vanish, and she'd be alone again. But she couldn't blink. She didn't want him gone yet. Not just yet.

Then she saw him move, slowly coming toward her,

and she knew how wrong she'd been again. With each step he took, reality solidified, and she knew he was really here.

"You," she whispered.

"Yes, me," he said, his voice running riot over nerves that were so painfully close to the surface.

She turned away from him, unable to bear the sight of him. She stared out at the ocean, but couldn't block out the man behind her. "Go away," she said.

"No." The single word was spoken right behind her, startling her, and she barely covered her shock. "I'm not going anywhere just yet."

"Then I am," she muttered, and turned to leave, but barely taking a step before Sam caught her by the arm.

She spun on him, jerking free, horrified at the idea of him touching her again. "Don't!" she snapped. "I told you not to touch me."

They were separated by barely two feet of space, facing each other on the beach, and she could hear his rough breathing. He held up both hands, palms out toward her.

"Okay, okay, I won't. Just don't leave."

"Oh, I'm leaving," she muttered.

"Stay. You owe me."

"Owe you?" she breathed, the idea making her feel physically sick.

"I saved your life."

He said the words so calmly, so rationally, she could almost believe they were rational. "You what?"

"In the car, before it went over the side. You're alive, aren't you? Pay me back with five minutes of your life."

Thank God for the dimness of the light. She couldn't see his eyes, and he couldn't see hers. She wouldn't have wanted him to see the pain in them produced by his words. She was alive, but she wasn't at all sure she wanted to be. Five minutes with him would be more like an eternity of regret and pain. She wasn't sure she could give him five minutes. "Okay, just say what you want to say."

"Just listen, then do whatever you want to do. I won't stop you."

She hugged herself tightly. "Do I thank you for that?"

"I don't want your thanks, just those five minutes."

She bit her lip hard, then said, "What do you want?"

He hesitated, then moved toward the water's edge and the foaming tide as it came up to the beach. "I was on my way to L.A., but never made it. I meant to go. I was in the car, on the road, heading south, then saw the turn for this place and saw your car out in front. I almost drove off and left."

"You should have," she said softly, avoiding looking at him. She kept her eyes on the house built on the bluff and the low lights from the main room.

"Maybe I should have, but I couldn't. You remember when you told me about Dennis and you, about your mutual turning points?"

"Oh, God, don't start talking about—"

"Hey, it's my turn," he said, and she knew he was looking at her. But she didn't look at him. "This is my story."

"I've heard it before." Her eyes ached from the need to cry, but no tears would come. "I've heard it from the Roberts in this world, from the other Mr. Wrongs I've managed to dig up in my life. I don't want to hear it from you."

"I'm not Robert, and I hope to hell I'm not Mr.

Wrong," he said softly, and she knew he was closer to her.

"Don't be too sure about that," she muttered.

"Melanie, I'm no Dennis, I never claimed to be."

"At least you're right about that. Dennis knows when to give up."

"What does that mean?"

She exhaled, not at all sure why she would tell him any more. But the words came before she could stop them. "Dennis and I...we aren't seeing each other anymore. We both knew this was wrong. Actually, we're terrific at being friends, but anything else...well, he's got all this new stuff going on in his life, like a brother who came out of the blue. And I've got..."

"Does he know about what happened?"

"Good heavens, no. I don't want him to ever know what I did. I've made mistakes, but that was..." She trembled at the memory. "Just do one thing for me and don't ever tell him. Don't ever give in to some need to confess your transgressions to him."

"You and Dennis broke up?"

"I just told you—"

"Why?"

"I told you, we're friends, real friends. I love him, but I'm not in love with him, and he's not in love with me." She actually heard herself laugh softly, but there wasn't much humor in the sound. "I think he's in love with my family. He's never been around anything like it, and it fascinates him. He's been alone most of his life."

"Not hardly, but I can see why your family intrigues him." He was so close now that she could have sworn she felt the heat of his breath on her neck.

She took a step forward to build some space between

them and try to ignore all the feelings this man could draw from her just by being here. Things she never wanted to feel again. "Your five minutes is almost up," she said.

"Okay, I'll make this short. That turning point, I had it. I mean, I thought I'd had a few in the past couple of days, but they were little steps, minor changes that seemed like more than they were at the time. But this change, this moment of clarity, just came to me five minutes ago."

He was quiet, and Melanie found that she was holding her breath, waiting for him to finish. But he didn't. Finally, when she couldn't take the silence any longer, she turned and he was right there. "Do you want me to guess?" Her voice was shaky and she couldn't bear him being so close, yet knowing she would never touch him again.

"No, there's no room for guessing here," he said in a low, rough voice. "I came down those stairs and the craziest thing happened. I came home." His shoulders hunched slightly, yet his eyes never left her face. "I mean, really home. I've never felt like that before, so I hope that's the right way to say it, but I was home."

"I know you like this house," she whispered, aching inside at the way he shifted from foot to foot, the way his voice grew lower and lower.

"It's not the house," he said, then stood a bit straighter, his feet shifting farther apart, as if he was bracing himself for something. "I don't know how to say this. It took me all this time to find that place where I want to be forever, where I want to stay. I want what everyone else seems to find so easily in this life."

Melanie was terrified. She was making this up, putting words in his mouth, a hallucination borne out of her own needs and pain. But when he touched her, she knew how real it was. His hand touched her cheek, just the tips of his fingers, and they were shaking. "I don't...I..." She touched her tongue to her cold lips. "I don't understand."

He framed her face with his hands, and the heat radiated into her. "I'm not good at this. I've never really said this before and understood any of it." He took a sharp breath. "I love you."

The words were there between them, but Melanie couldn't believe them. Love? He'd told her that he didn't do any of this well. And she couldn't say the words to him. She couldn't expose herself that way, then find out that this was all a lie. "You don't love me," she said flatly. "You can't."

"Oh, but I do."

"No," she said, shaking her head and breaking the contact with him. She took a step back. "Don't do this. Sam, just go away. You don't even know what love is."

"I know what it is. I love you." He hesitated, then said, "Okay, I'll go if you can look at me and tell me that you don't care about me at all."

"I'm not playing games like that. You aren't going to make me say things."

"Just say it. Just say, 'Sam, I don't love you, I don't care about you, now get the hell out of here,' and I'll leave."

"And I'm not going to swear, either," she muttered.

"Oh, 'bastard' doesn't count?" he asked, and although she couldn't see him clearly, she had the sinking feeling that the smile was there.

"You deserved it."

"I did. You're right. And I'll tell you something else, I don't lie. I told you that and I wasn't lying."

"Okay, you *think* you love me," she argued around a tightness in her throat.

"Let me prove to you that I love you," he said.

"Why are you doing this?"

"I'll tell you, but not down here. Up at the house."

"Oh, no, no way. I'm not going back up there with you."

"Yes, you are," he said. The next thing she knew, he was picking her up. With one quick movement he lifted her and put her over his shoulder. "Oh, yes, you are," he said, making his way across the beach.

"Put me down! Now. Put me down!"

She might just as well have saved her breath. He kept moving toward the stairs up to the deck, and he started up.

"Sam, stop it! Let me go. Now."

"Calm down," he said in a slightly breathless voice from the climb. "And hold still. This isn't easy climbing these stairs and it's downright hard with a madwoman on my shoulders."

"Then let me go," she said tightly.

"I will, in a minute. This will all be over and you'll see that I mean what I say."

She gave up fighting him as he stepped onto the deck. He kept going into the house, but didn't stop there. He headed for the arched doorway.

"Oh, no, you don't," she said. "Not in there."

He stopped at the doorway, then unexpectedly turned and eased her down onto her feet. One minute she was over his shoulder, the next he was facing her in the softly lit room. "Truth time," he said, and she stared in horror as he started to unbutton his shirt.

"What are you doing?"

He undid the last button. "Proving I love you," he said, then pulled his shirt out of his jeans and opened it, exposing his naked chest. "There. Living proof that I love you, Melanie Clark."

Her mouth went dry at the sight of him, and she just stared.

He tugged his shirt off completely and tossed it over his shoulder for it to land somewhere near a dustcover-shrouded chair. "See." He turned around, arms out at his sides, then looked at her with that suggestion of a smile. "No hives. Not one. Nowhere, no place, no how. A clean bill of health, and I can even say the C-word, as in 'commitment,' without going into some sort of medical seizure."

That slight smile was gone as quickly as it had come, and for a fleeting moment Melanie saw fear in Sam's eyes. "I don't want to be alone any longer, and I want a home. I want you. I love you, Melanie, and I want you to marry me."

"Oh, Sam," she whispered, and reached out, touching her hands to his naked chest. She could feel his heart pounding against her palms. "You do?"

"Oh, yes, I do," he breathed.

Joy exploded in her, and she threw herself into his arms.

He held her to him, her reality all tied up in this man as he whispered, "It took me a long time, but I know exactly where I'm going and what I want."

She pressed her lips to the silky heat of his skin. "No more hot-wiring?" she whispered.

"Now that I'm not promising," he said on a rough chuckle. Then he tipped her head back and looked down into her eyes. "But I will promise to spend as much time as it takes to make sure you never, ever, think of me as Mr. Wrong.''

Her smile came so easily and felt so right. ''How long do you think that might take?''

''I'm hoping for forever.''

Epilogue

One week later.

Exactly one hour before the stroke of midnight, the exclusive New Year's Eve gathering at the Benning mansion ended abruptly. It happened right after Mr. Benning introduced Sam as his son to the elegantly attired party-goers and toasted Sam's marriage to Melanie. Mrs. Benning collapsed, and the guests, after offering their wishes for her recovery, all left.

"So, are you sorry we had to leave?" Sam asked Melanie half an hour later in the bed, in the shadows, at the beach house.

"Do you have to ask?" She rested her thigh over his and relished the feeling of his naked body against hers. "If we were still there, we'd still be dressed, hovering around Mrs. Benning, waiting for her to come out of her swoon, and...we...we wouldn't be here." Her words faltered when Sam skimmed his hand up over the curve of her hip, to her stomach and up to her breast. "Do you think I'm sorry?" she asked in an unsteady whisper.

"I'll do my best to make sure you aren't," he said in a rough whisper as he teased her nipple.

Every resolve of hers to go into the kitchen before midnight to make bacon, lettuce and tomato sandwiches, slid away. She pressed her lips to the sleek heat of his shoulder. "You're doing just fine," she whispered. "Although, I am a bit sorry my family didn't get to have the big wedding they wanted. But a big wedding would have taken so long to put together, and I couldn't have waited that long."

"Amen to that." His hand spanned her diaphragm, then shifted lower and sensations exploded in her. She arched toward the exquisite pleasure of his touch on her body.

"Oh, my," she breathed, and lifted her hips to press against his palm. She trembled at the explosion of pure passion in her, and cried out when Sam let go of her. "No," she gasped and twisted toward him, but he wasn't leaving her. His hands spanned her waist and pulled her up and over him until she was straddling him and he was entering her with exquisite slowness. "Oh, Sam," she gasped.

"Oh, yes," he said through clenched teeth as she leaned forward toward him, bracing her hands on the linen by his shoulders.

She shuddered as she settled with him deeply inside her. "Oh, no, the television," she gasped when he started to move. "And...and the sandwiches... midnight...we have to..."

"We'll start our own traditions," he rasped when she started to move with him.

As their rhythm built with each thrust, every thought of the outside world was pushed aside. It was just them, together, flying into a place where nothing mattered but the moment when every feeling in her centered on the world she made with Sam. A place where she trusted him with her soul.

When the world shattered into a million shimmering pieces of completion, her cries mingled with Sam's. Then she was floating slowly back to earth. "Oh, damn," she whispered as she collapsed onto Sam's chest. "Damn, damn, damn."

She felt the vibration of his chuckle against her breasts and his breath ruffled her hair. "I've heard that using profanity shows a limited vocabulary."

She sighed deeply. "Sometimes there just aren't words."

"How about 'I love you'? Simple, straightforward, and nice to hear."

As she and Sam moved as one onto their sides to face each other, he never left her. She looked at him in the softness of the night, while the echo of the ocean below the cliffs sounded faintly in the background. That smile was there, the smile she loved. "Okay, I love you, and after this movie is done, I'll go to France with you, or to Spain or to Hollywood, or wherever you go." She spread her hand on his chest over his heart. "Forever and ever."

"*Finally.*"

"Finally, what?" Sam asked.

"I didn't say 'finally.' You did."

"No, I don't think I did," he said. "But then again, I was just thinking how lucky I was to finally get up here and meet you. I could have gone to a job in New York, or one in Mexico, but I took this one."

She touched his chin with the tips of her fingers, relishing the slight feeling of a new beard. "Dumb, stupid luck?"

"Oh, no. Fate, planning, something way beyond

dumb, stupid luck.'' He shifted to catch her more closely to his chest and she snuggled against him, wishing she could melt right into him and hide there forever. ''Maybe magic, but whatever made this happen, it turned out perfectly.''

''It was very well done.''

.Sam brushed the hair back from her face, his touch light as it skimmed over her skin. ''Exactly,'' he whispered.

''Exactly, what?''

''Very well done,''' he murmured as he tasted the sensitive area by her ear. ''I'm just agreeing.''

Melanie frowned. ''I never said—''

His lips stopped her words and any thoughts of what had or hadn't been said, were gone. Her love for Sam was overwhelming, and needs that she thought had just been satisfied, were there again. One more thing she'd been wrong about in this life. She'd never have enough of this man.

As Sam drew back to look down at her, she heard the sound of horns off in the distance. ''Happy New Year.''

''Happy forever after,'' she breathed.

''Amen.''

''Amen,'' Sam said and gathered Melanie to his chest.

''AMEN AND AMEN,'' Angelina echoed as she and Miss Victoria withdrew from the scene.

''Very well done, indeed,'' Miss Victoria said in the quiet place. ''We are very pleased. And to have that dear child named after you, Angelina Joy, well, we approve very much indeed.''

Angelina still couldn't get over the thrill of hearing

the name of Reggie and Ben's daughter. Even the middle name was right. "So do I," she said.

"We agree that you did a...wonderfully inventive job this time."

"I don't mind saying that truck driver was hard to get to take the truck on the highway, and then the police barricade, well..." She shook her head. "It was a lot of work."

"The Council gave their approval for you to have a nice break before your next assignment."

Her next assignment. She knew what it was going to be and didn't want any part of it. Someone else, maybe Grace, could take over the Dennis Benning, Francine Clark pairing. "I'm not sure I should be involved in—"

"Hush," Miss Victoria said abruptly. "We shall talk about this at a later date. For now, you need to rest."

"Yes, ma'am," she said, and would have left if Miss Victoria hadn't spoken again.

"Angelina, you must stop thinking of humans as inferior. Perhaps you need to be reminded that humans look for love with no insights, no extra powers or outside knowledge. Until one is human, one will never know just how difficult a process finding love could be. One should understand what humans have to contend with in their search for love. How easy it is for them to find a Mr. Wrong."

Angelina couldn't believe she was hearing what she thought she was hearing. "I need my...rest," she said as she turned to leave. The Council would never believe that becoming a human would be a viable learning tool for one of her kind. Never.

"Never say never," Miss Victoria called after her.

COMING NEXT MONTH

#701 IN PAPA BEAR'S BED by Judy Christenberry

Once Upon a Kiss

In a cabin in the woods, runaway Jessica Barnes rested in a chair that was too big, ate leftovers that were too small, and slept in a bed that was just right. When Rob Berenson and his kids returned home, one look at the naked blonde between his sheets and as much as he had his own secrets to hide, Rob didn't want this Goldilocks to run away!

#702 A DARK & STORMY NIGHT by Anne Stuart

More Than Men

Katie Flynn sought shelter from a storm but on a windswept cliff she found a moody recluse named O'Neal. Trapped, she fought his sensuality, but she suspected that something haunted the man...something that only O'Neal himself could reveal....

#703 OVERNIGHT WIFE by Mollie Molay

Ditching her Christmas Eve wedding, Arden Crandall fled to the airport in time to take the honeymoon by herself, but she ran smack into a snowstorm and the mysterious Luke McCauley. The man was trouble, but she thought she could resist him—and then came the announcement that the airport would be closed all night....

#704 MISTER CHRISTMAS by Linda Cajio

The Holiday Heart

Holly had to help Raymond Holiday find his heart by December 25th or he'd lose it for good. He'd dodged love for years, from his family, friends, women—though he had a way with the latter, and with female elves like herself. She only hoped he found his heart before she lost hers....

AVAILABLE THIS MONTH:

Look us up on-line at: http://www.romance.net

Take 4 bestselling love stories FREE

Plus get a FREE surprise gift!

Special Limited-time Offer

Mail to Harlequin Reader Service®

3010 Walden Avenue
P.O. Box 1867
Buffalo, N.Y. 14240-1867

YES! Please send me 4 free Harlequin American Romance® novels and my free surprise gift. Then send me 4 brand-new novels every month, which I will receive months before they appear in bookstores. Bill me at the low price of $3.12 each plus 25¢ delivery and applicable sales tax, if any.* That's the complete price and a savings of over 10% off the cover prices—quite a bargain! I understand that accepting the books and gift places me under no obligation ever to buy any books. I can always return a shipment and cancel at any time. Even if I never buy another book from Harlequin, the 4 free books and the surprise gift are mine to keep forever.

154 BPA A3UM

Name	(PLEASE PRINT)	
Address	Apt. No.	
City	State	Zip

This offer is limited to one order per household and not valid to present Harlequin American Romance® subscribers. *Terms and prices are subject to change without notice. Sales tax applicable in N.Y.

UAM-696　　　　　　　　　　　　　　　©1990 Harlequin Enterprises Limited

It's a stampede...to the altar!

by Cathy Gillen Thacker

You loved Montana maven Max McKendrick who gave his nephews and niece forty-eight hours to marry the spouses of his choice—in the first three Wild West Weddings books.

Now that wily ol' coot is back—and at the triple wedding ceremony he's given his family attorney, "Cisco" Kidd, an ultimatum: not only marry Ms. Gillian Taylor, but *stay* married to her for a week!

Don't miss the grand finale to the wacky, wonderful Wild West Weddings:

SPUR-OF-THE-MOMENT MARRIAGE (#697)

Available October 1997 wherever Harlequin books are sold.

The West was never this much fun!

Free Gift Offer

As Seen on TV!

With a Free Gift proof-of-purchase
from any Harlequin® book, you can receive
a beautiful cubic zirconia pendant.

This stunning marquise-shaped stone is a genuine cubic
zirconia—accented by an 18" gold tone necklace.
(Approximate retail value $19.95)

Send for yours today...
compliments of ◈HARLEQUIN®

To receive your free gift, a cubic zirconia pendant, send us one original proof-of-purchase, photocopies not accepted, from the back of any Harlequin Romance®, Harlequin Presents®, Harlequin Temptation®, Harlequin Superromance®, Harlequin Intrigue®, Harlequin American Romance®, or Harlequin Historicals® title available at your favorite retail outlet, together with the Free Gift Certificate, plus a check or money order for $1.65 U.S./$2.15 CAN. (do not send cash) to cover postage and handling, payable to Harlequin Free Gift Offer. We will send you the specified gift. Allow 6 to 8 weeks for delivery. Offer good until December 31, 1997, or while quantities last. Offer valid in the U.S. and Canada only.

Free Gift Certificate

Name: _____

Address: _____

City: _____ State/Province: _____ Zip/Postal Code: _____

Mail this certificate, one proof-of-purchase and a check or money order for postage and handling to: HARLEQUIN FREE GIFT OFFER 1997. In the U.S.: 3010 Walden Avenue, P.O. Box 9071, Buffalo NY 14269-9057. In Canada: P.O. Box 604, Fort Erie, Ontario L2Z 5X3.

FREE GIFT OFFER   084-KEZ

ONE PROOF-OF-PURCHASE
To collect your fabulous FREE GIFT, a cubic zirconia pendant, you must include this original proof-of-purchase for each gift with the properly completed Free Gift Certificate.

084-KEZR

We're thrilled to bring you another special edition of the popular MORE THAN MEN series—and thrilled to bring you another unique book by the inimitable, RITA Award-winning author Anne Stuart.

Like those who have come before him, O'Neal is more than tall, dark and handsome. All of these men have extraordinary powers that make them "more than men." But whether they're able to grant you three wishes, or live forever, make no mistake—their greatest, most extraordinary power is that of seduction.

So make a date with O'Neal in...

#702 A DARK & STORMY NIGHT
by Anne Stuart
November 1997

**Don't miss these Harlequin favorites
by some of our bestselling authors! Act now and
receive a discount by ordering two or more titles!**

HT#25720	A NIGHT TO REMEMBER	$3.50 U.S.	☐
	by Gina Wilkins	$3.99 CAN.	
HT#25722	CHANGE OF HEART	$3.50 U.S.	☐
	by Janice Kaiser	$3.99 CAN.	
HP#11797	A WOMAN OF PASSION	$3.50 U.S.	☐
	by Anne Mather	$3.99 CAN.	
HP#11863	ONE-MAN WOMAN	$3.50 U.S.	☐
	by Carole Mortimer	$3.99 CAN.	
HR#03356	BACHELOR'S FAMILY	$2.99 U.S.	☐
	by Jessica Steele	$3.50 CAN.	
HR#03441	RUNAWAY HONEYMOON	$3.25 U.S.	☐
	by Ruth Jean Dale	$3.75 CAN.	
HS#70715	BAREFOOT IN THE GRASS	$3.99 U.S.	☐
	by Judith Arnold	$4.50 CAN.	
HS#70729	ANOTHER MAN'S CHILD	$3.99 U.S.	☐
	by Tara Taylor Quinn	$4.50 CAN.	
HI#22361	LUCKY DEVIL	$3.75 U.S.	☐
	by Patricia Rosemoor	$4.25 CAN.	
HI#22379	PASSION IN THE FIRST DEGREE	$3.75 U.S.	☐
	by Carla Cassidy	$4.25 CAN.	
HAR#16638	LIKE FATHER, LIKE SON	$3.75 U.S.	☐
	by Mollie Molay	$4.25 CAN.	
HAR#16663	ADAM'S KISS	$3.75 U.S.	☐
	by Mindy Neff	$4.25 CAN.	
HH#28937	GABRIEL'S LADY	$4.99 U.S.	☐
	by Ana Seymour	$5.99 CAN.	
HH#28941	GIFT OF THE HEART	$4.99 U.S.	☐
	by Miranda Jarrett	$5.99 CAN.	

(limited quantities available on certain titles)

TOTAL AMOUNT	$	_____
DEDUCT: 10% DISCOUNT FOR 2+ BOOKS	$	_____
POSTAGE & HANDLING	$	_____
($1.00 for one book, 50¢ for each additional)		
APPLICABLE TAXES*	$	_____
TOTAL PAYABLE	$	_____

(check or money order—please do not send cash)

To order, complete this form and send it, along with a check or money order for the total above, payable to Harlequin Books, to: **In the U.S.:** 3010 Walden Avenue, P.O. Box 9047, Buffalo, NY 14269-9047; **In Canada:** P.O. Box 613, Fort Erie, Ontario, L2A 5X3.

Name: _____

Address: _____ City: _____

State/Prov.: _____ Zip/Postal Code: _____

*New York residents remit applicable sales taxes.
Canadian residents remit applicable GST and provincial taxes.